CONSPIRACY!

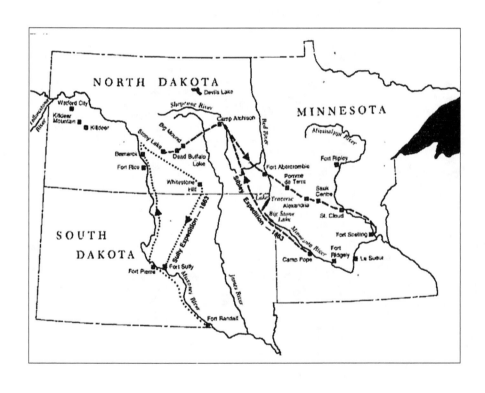

Conspiracy!

Who Really Killed Lincoln?

Dean Urdahl

NORTH STAR PRESS OF ST. CLOUD, INC.
St. Cloud, Minnesota

First Edition: July 2012

Printed in the United States of America

Published by
North Star Press of St. Cloud, Inc.
P.O. Box 451
St. Cloud, Minnesota 56302

www.northstarpress.com

Dedication

I dedicate this story to the memory of those who struggled
and died for their land and what they believed was right,
be they Union or Confederate, Dakota or settler.
I also dedicate this to my wife, Karen,
who once again has proved invaluable
to helping me tell my story.

❧ Foreword ❧

VER SINCE A LITTLE BALL OF LEAD became embedded in the head of President Abraham Lincoln, controversy has swirled around that history-changing moment.

In some ways Booth had failed. The government was not sent into chaos, the Confederacy did not continue, and the South did not rise to support him.

In another way he did change history. Reconstruction was much different than it would have been had Lincoln lived, and southern states found a way to bring back a form of slavery with the Black Codes. The Civil Rights struggle that peaked in the 1960s bore the legacy of Lincoln's death.

This is the story of what did happen and what might have happened to President Abraham Lincoln. I have woven various conspiracy theories into one story. I have used actual statements and events wherever possible. Jesse Buchanen and Nathan Cates are fictional. But nearly all the other names used in the story are those of real people and much of what is ascribed to them is what they really said and did. Obviously, dialogue is, for the most part, conjecture.

This is a work of historical fiction, and I can't say with absolute conviction that all is true. I will say that some people believe some or all of these conjectures to be true. It's likely that the Confederate government was intimately involved in the plan to first kidnap and then to assassinate Lincoln and to blow up the White House.

Did Booth escape? It's an intriguing possibility, but ultimately unlikely.

Catholics and Irish immigrants for the most part viewed Lincoln as an adversary. In my story, Catholics are not the perpetrators, but the scapegoats, for the crime. Albert Pike was a high-degree Mason and the head of the Illuminati in America. But I do not assert that Masons were involved either. Speculation is that Pike created a level beyond the highest order of Masons. These men used Mason connections but not the order as they contrived to commit murder.

My story includes the conclusion of the pursuit of Indians into the Dakota Territory by Sully's army. This mission was ordered by President Lincoln. I rely heavily on primary-source material and the words of Alfred Sully. The course of the expedition is as it happened in 1864.

We will never really know what happened or how it happened regarding the events leading to Lincoln's death. This is one story of what could have happened to the greatest man ever to lead our nation.

Dean Urdahl

1

APRIL 14, 1865

IT WAS GOOD FRIDAY, not usually a good day for attendance at theatrical events. But this evening during the Civil War was different. Lee had just surrendered to Grant at Appomatox Court House and, with a national sigh of relief, many in Washington had chosen to celebrate this night by going to Ford's Theatre in Washington City.

Another reason encouraged nearly a thousand to attend the performance of *Our American Cousin*. Word was that President Abraham Lincoln and General Ulysses Grant were going to attend. Many wished to see and salute the heroic victors.

As the third act opened, a trim, athletic-looking man, just under six feet tall and wearing a dark suit with a matching slouch hat, coolly walked up the stage to the dress circle and advanced along the narrow aisle between the wall and the seated patrons. He paused near the door leading to the president's box.

The man was the famous actor John Wilkes Booth. At age twenty-six, he had glossy dark hair, a trim mustache that drooped down at the edges and dark eyes that burned intently like hot coals. His admirers considered him the most handsome man in America.

Booth was not concerned with his acting career this night. A single-shot derringer pistol, loaded and ready, rested in his suit pocket. A ten-inch knife, hidden by the coat, hung from a scabbard at his belt.

The actor burned with passion and hatred. He had decided to end his acting career with one final grand performance, and he would do it onstage at Ford's Theatre, where he had performed many times before.

An army captain was sitting in the aisle in front of the box door. Booth asked him to move so he could pass. He then stepped a few feet forward, looked over the house with an easy manner, and took a pack of visiting cards from his pocket.

Removing one, Booth returned the others to his pocket, watched the play for a few seconds and then turned to a man seated on an aisle seat before the door—Charles Forbes, the president's footman. Booth showed the card to Forbes. "I'm Wilkes Booth," he whispered. "I'd like to see the president."

Forbes smiled and waved him toward the entrance. With a nod the actor turned and opened the door. He entered a short passageway. Two doors were on the darkened wall before him. They led to box seats held by Lincoln and his party.

A chair sat strategically located before the first door. Designated especially for the president's guard, John Parker, it was vacant. Parker was nowhere in sight. Booth picked up a wooden brace and wedged it between the door and the passage wall to prevent access to anyone else. Then he peered through a small hole drilled into the box door.

He could see four occupants seated as he expected, two men and two women. One of the men was President Lincoln. "Aha! My target is here!" he whispered.

Like the practiced actor he was, Booth waited for his cue, a laugh line with one actor remaining onstage. He listened. A woman's voice lofted up to him. "I am aware, Mr. Trenchard, that you are not used to the manners of good society, and that alone will excuse the impertinence of which you are guilty!"

Two actresses exited the stage, leaving one lone actor, Harry Hawk. From his position at rear center stage, Hawk delivered the cue line. "Don't know the manners of good society, eh! I'll turn you inside out, old gal, you sockdologizing old man trap."

President Lincoln joined in as the crowd erupted in laughter. Peals of merriment drowned the noises of the box door creaking open and the

2

several quick, furtive footsteps that carried the attacker to his prey. Booth placed the pistol behind the president's right ear and pulled the trigger.

A young officer was sitting to Lincoln's rear and off to the right. Paralyzed for a moment in shocked disbelief, he rushed at the assailant. Booth dropped his pistol, drew his knife and lunged at the soldier.

The young man raised an arm to deflect the blow. Booth sliced it from shoulder to elbow. Blood gushed from the wound.

The attacker pivoted toward the stage and firmly fixed a hand atop the box railing. Beneath him lay the stage he knew so well. He swung his feet over the railing to drop to the platform below, feeling a bit smug at his unorthodox stage entrance.

The railing and outside of the box were festooned with flags and bunting. They snagged the assassin's spur, and he thumped awkwardly onto the stage before a shocked Harry Hawk. The audience gaped in stunned bewilderment and horror as Booth twisted and stomped on a United States flag that entangled his spur.

Booth regained his balance and raised the bloody knife above his head. As Hawk fled the stage in terror, Booth reveled in his last theatric moment and triumphantly delivered his final line from a stage. "Sic Semper Tyrannis!" (Thus always to tyrants!)

For a moment time seemed frozen as dazed and confused onlookers wondered what to do. Then the plaintive cries of Mary Lincoln turned the spell to rage, as her wails echoed from the balcony. "They've killed the president! They've killed the president!"

A question hung unanswered in the air. Who were "they?"

❧ 2 ☙

WINTER 1854

TICK, TOCK, TICK, TOCK. The grandfather clock in the corner advanced its hands in a steady march toward 11:00, the appointed hour for the morning meeting. Father Charles Chiniquy sat in a stiff wooden chair, trying to ease his jitters while awaiting his first encounter with the new bishop of Chicago.

Slight and small in stature, the forty-four-year-old priest smoothed back his thinning hair and tugged at a bushy, white-streaked beard that sprouted below his chin and smooth-shaven cheeks.

He sighed, his mind meandering back to his years as a priest in Canada. So much had transpired since he had joined the priesthood as a young man of twenty-four back in 1833. For eighteen years he had toiled in his native Quebec. The temperance movement had become his passion, and some claimed that 200,000 had turned away from alcohol because of the work of Father Chiniquy.

Charles reached into the pocket of his black robe and removed a folded piece of paper. He had brought documents in case they were needed to buttress arguments. He re-read the final paragraph from the letter given him by his last parish in Quebec:

> We console ourselves by the assurance that, wherever you go, you will raise the glorious banners of temperance among those of our countrymen who are scattered in the land of exile. May these brethren put upon your forehead the crown of immortality, which you have so well deserved for your noble work in our midst.

4

A small smile played at Chiniquy's lips. The task given him by the preceding bishop far surpassed promoting temperance. At his first meeting with then-Bishop Vandeveld, groundwork was laid for Charles to establish a settlement for Roman Catholic immigrants on such a grand scale that they would someday rule the government of the state of Illinois.

He had traveled three days south to Bourbonnais to meet the priest there, Father Courjeault. Initially, all had been pleasant and Courjeault had welcomed the newcomer, supposing that he was sent by the bishop to help expand the small congregation. Father Lebel in Chicago had made the same assumption regarding his parish.

Both were surprised and keenly envious to learn otherwise. No sooner had Courjeault warmly shaken Charles's hand than the new priest announced, "I am sent here to found, in the very heart of Illinois, settlements of a large scale. I am to go farther south and start my own parish."

Courjeault had paled before responding. "It was my supposition that you would encourage immigrants to join established parishes such as mine. What sense does it make to start anew elsewhere? Let us build on what we have begun here."

Charles politely disagreed. "It is my belief that God wants a new settlement devoted to immigrants. The bishop concurs."

"Well, Father Lebel concurs with me," Courjeault had bristled.

But Charles had remained undeterred. "Let us work together in harmony. It's already November and I want to start up the new settlement before the heavy snows begin. I welcome your assistance."

"I won't assist you in undermining my authority in this part of Illinois."

In the bishop's ante room Charles ruefully shook his head at the recollection. If he had known what pitfalls faced him, he would never have left Canada for Illinois. However, in spite of his rough start with Courjeault and Lebel, the new colony had a grand beginning. South of Bourbonnais on one of the highest points of the Illinois prairie, Chiniquy founded St. Anne Parish near the little settlement of Kankakee. Six of the most respected citizens of Bourbonnais joined him immediately. Within ten days, fifty families from Canada erected their tents around Charles's.

The colony expanded with amazing speed. In a short time it contained forty buildings and more than 200 people. In January construction was started on a church and, thanks to a mild winter, it was finished in April of 1852. By that time St. Anne was populated by one hundred families, including 500 adults. Nearly all were French-Canadian immigrants.

Charles's heart was overjoyed that his church was gaining great expanses of prize land. Bishop Vandeveld was a visionary who saw beyond the religious influence of the church, one who was convinced that Catholics could play a vital role in the formation and governance of the United States.

Vendeveld had formulated a plan with other priests to expand Catholic influence in America by gaining control of state governments from the Gulf of Mexico to the headwaters of the Mississippi. That was why Charles had been brought to Illinois. He was to lead the effort to bring Catholic immigrants from Canada, Belgium and France.

The plan was well on its way. But events had taken a turn, painfully reminding Charles of the old adage, "The best laid plans of mice and men oft times go astray."

Charles was dismayed that his mission had been sidetracked and led astray by the two jealous priests, Courjeault and Lebel. They and other Jesuits were fighting Vandeveld, asserting that, under his plan, the forces of Catholicism would be scattered and the power of the church dissipated.

Father Lebel had been vehement before Charles left Chicago. "We must concentrate in the cities and the larger towns and fill these up as rapidly as possible with immigrants. In this way the Roman Catholic vote can be directed by bishops and priests to tip the balance of power between the political parties in those areas."

This position was subsequently endorsed by a Catholic leadership conference in Buffalo, New York. The Vandeveld plan was condemned, and all progress toward it began to unravel. Charles vividly recalled one of the breaking points.

He glanced up at the clock—10:45. Fifteen more minutes to fill with recollections.

It had been a joyous spring day. His church at St. Anne was completed. The settlement and congregation seemed to grow each day, and Bishop Veldeveld had come to bless the chapel.

After the blessing, Vandeveld had asked Charles, "Will you accompany me to Bourbonnais? I have to confer with you and the Reverend Mr. Courjeault on important matters."

In two hours they had reached the parsonage of Courjeault. After a sumptuous dinner with town dignitaries, the three churchmen had settled down alone to the business at hand.

The bishop had removed a bundle of weekly newspapers from his satchel, all from Montreal, and asked, "There are several letters in these newspapers. Did you write them?"

Charles had scanned them quickly. Each of the letters insulted and personally attacked the bishop. Chiniquy had glanced up during his reading, first at Vandeveld and then at Courjeault. The priest's expression had changed ever so slightly, with just a hint of guilt slipping over his face, and Charles had deciphered the situation in a flash. Courjeault's attempts to undermine his work at St. Anne were no secret. But Charles had not comprehended the depths that his rival priest would stoop to until now.

Charles had gazed forthrightly at his bishop. "My lord, I have no words to express my surprise and indignation when I read those letters. I assure you that I am not the author of those malicious writings. I would rather have my right hand cut off, than allow it to pen such false and perfidious things against you or anyone else."

"Then, can you tell me who did write them?" the bishop had pressed.

Charles had looked at Courjeault, who was visibly squirming as he stared at the floor. Then he'd responded, "Put that question to the

Reverend Mr. Courjeault. I think that he is better equipped than anyone to answer your question."

The truth had become obvious to the bishop as well. The priest from Bourbonnais had turned sickly looking. Sweat had become beaded on his forehead, his face pasty, and his knees had begun to tremble.

It was enough for Bishop Vandeveld, who had indignantly proclaimed, "Mr. Courjeault, you are the writer of these slanderous letters! Three times you have written, and twice you told me, verbally, that they were coming from Mr. Chiniquy! I do not need to ask you if you are the author of these slanders against me. I see it written on your face. Your malice against Mr. Chiniquy is really diabolical. You wanted to ruin him in my estimation as well as in that of his countrymen.

"To succeed the better in that plot, you published the most egregious falsehoods against me in the Canadian press, to induce me to denounce Mr. Chiniquy as an impostor. How is it possible that a priest can so completely give himself to the devil?

"Mr. Chiniquy, I beg your forgiveness for having believed this. Mr. Courjeault, the least punishment I can give you is to turn you out of my diocese, and write to all the bishops of America that you are the vilest priest I ever saw and that they should never give you any position on this continent."

An emotional scene had followed. Courjeault had fallen to his knees, sobbing and begging forgiveness from both Charles and the bishop, and both men had been affected. Vandeveld had turned to Charles and asked, "What do you advise me to do? Must I forgive him?"

Charles had wiped tears from his own eyes before responding, "Yes, my lord, please forgive and forget the errors of that dear brother. He has already done so much good for my countrymen of Bourbonnais. I pledge myself that he will hereafter be one of your best priests."

Bishop Vandeveld had placed his hand on the kneeling Courjeault's head and answered his pleas. "You are forgiven. But we can have no more of this. There must be no more intrigue or subterfuge."

While it had seemed that all problems in Bourbonnais had been put to rest, the détente had lasted all of about two hours. Around 3:00 in the afternoon, the priests had separated to say vespers and to pray. Then Charles had spotted Courjeault stumbling down a path toward him.

Strange, Charles had thought, *this man does not drink and yet he appears half-drunk. A mixture of terror and sadness stains his face.*

Courjeault had mumbled something that Charles couldn't understand. Then he'd covered his face to drown out tears and sobs. Charles had sat on a bench and motioned for the other priest to join him.

"Forget your past actions against me, I said that you were forgiven. Do not think more of the past. You may look upon me as your most devoted friend."

Courjeault had plopped next to Charles and mumbled softly, "Dear Mr. Chiniquy, I have to reveal to you another dark mystery of my miserable life. For more than a year I have lived with a parish officer's daughter as if she were my wife. She just told me that she is to become a mother and that if I don't give her 500 dollars she will denounce me publicly to the bishop and the people if I do not support her and the child. What should I do? I've considered concealing my shame by going back to France and my family. I've even been tempted to throw myself in the river. Could the bishop forgive this new crime? Is there a place for me in the diocese? What can I do?"

Many thoughts had flooded over Charles, with scandal, deception and hypocrisy at the forefront. He'd advised the priest, "Your misfortune is really great. If the bishop were not here, I might, perhaps, tell you my mind about what I think. But in fact the bishop is here. He is the only man to whom you have to go to know how to come out of the bottomless abyss into which you have fallen. He is your proper counselor. Go and tell him everything, with total honesty, and follow his advice."

In less than an hour, Bishop Vandeveld had sought out Chiniquy. Obviously distraught, his face pale, his eyes reddened with tears, he had exclaimed, "Father Chiniquy, what an awful scandal! What a disgrace!

Until today I thought that Mr. Courjeault was one of my best priests. Now I find him to be an incarnate devil."

"What will you do?" Charles had wondered.

Shaking his head as if trying to clear it, Vandeveld had replied, "I'm told by Courjeault that no one suspects his transgressions. We will pay the girl and send her to a house in Canada. She will be out of the way and beyond suspicion.

"Mr. Courjeault is most penitent. I pray that hereafter we have nothing to fear from him and that he can remain here as a good priest. If I remove him, suspicion will follow and the church will suffer."

Charles had returned to St. Anne praying that the scandal had been nipped in the bud. But it had not. Five days later a delegation from Bourbonnais had knocked on his door to make a request that Charles had hoped would never come.

Their spokesman had asked, "Would you please come to Bourbonnais with us and go to our unfortunate priest to tell him that his criminal conduct is known by the whole people? Tell him that we cannot decently keep him a day longer as our Christian teacher. He has rendered great service to us in the past, but he must leave us now."

Three hours later Charles and the parish delegation had stood before Courjeault. When Charles had delivered the wishes of the Bourbonnais parish, the accused priest had received the words as if they were his death warrant. He had hastily settled his affairs, packed, and left for Chicago at midnight.

In the absence of a priest, Charles had agreed to fill in and conduct some evening services. A week later he was just concluding a service when he heard whispers sweeping through the congregation. Turning around to face the worshipers, he had joined in their amazement. A smiling Father Courjeault was sauntering down the center aisle, grinning at his former parishioners, saluting others, and shaking hands with a few.

He had laughed as he'd approached Charles. "Oh, oh! Our dear little Father Chiniquy here? How do you do?"

"I'm quite unwell, since I see that you are so miserably destroying yourself."

"I do not want to destroy myself," Courjeault had replied. "It is you who want to turn me out of my beautiful parish of Bourbonnais, to take my place. I see you now before my congregation. With the four blockheads who accompanied you, the other day, you frightened and persuaded me that my misfortune with Mary was known by all the people. But our good bishop understood that this was a trick of yours, and that it was one of your lying stories. I came back to take possession of my parish and turn you out."

Charles had looked sadly perplexed before he responded, "Father Courjeault, if the bishop sent you back here to send me back to my own dear colony, then so much the better. He knows more than anyone that I came to America for a great purpose. I cannot do what I came to do if I must remain here to take care of Bourbonnais. I will go at once. I leave you with your parsonage and your parish. But I pity you. I see a dark cloud hanging above you. Goodbye."

"You are the only dark cloud that hangs above me. When you have left, I will be at peace as I was before you ever set foot in Illinois. Now leave here and never come back unless you are invited."

Shuddering at the recollection, Charles pulled himself back into the present. His eyes turned once again toward the clock. Still several minutes to eleven. What would he say to the bishop? Thoughts and more memories raced through his mind.

It was May 9, 1852, when Charles had returned to St. Anne from Bourbonnais. Sunday services had gone on as always. But then word came from Bourbonnais that all had not gone well for Courjeault.

That bright, beautiful Sunday, with the church filled to overflowing, Courjeault had beamed in the joyous belief that his parishioners had come in great numbers to welcome him back.

Hymns and liturgy had gone smoothly as planned. Then the priest had taken to the pulpit to deliver his sermon. Just as he'd begun, all the congregants rose from their pews and hurried from the church as if it were on fire.

Courjeault had stood alone, dumbfounded, finally face to face with himself. He had raced to the church entrance and called after his parishioners as they departed.

"Please, please listen to me! I beg of you, let me have my say!" Tears had run down the priest's cheeks as he stifled a sob, struggling to compose himself. Most of the congregants had turned to face him.

"I see that the hand of God is upon me and I deserve it. I have sinned and made a mistake by coming back to you. You do not want me anymore to be your pastor. I cannot complain of that. This is your right, you will be satisfied. I will leave this place forever tonight. I only ask you to forgive my past errors and pray for me."

There were no answering calls of affirmation or condemnation. Just a deadly silence hung over the people. A distant bird chirped from a tree branch as some dabbed tears from their eyes. The people had gone back to their homes and were never to see their fallen priest again.

Charles's eyes were tugged in the direction of the grandfather clock once again. It had nearly marched its way to 11:00. He would be meeting the new bishop shortly. He nervously unfolded another piece of paper from his satchel. It was a letter from Bishop Vandeveld dated May 20, 1852.

The bishop had apologized in his letter for his handling of the Courjeault affair. He had explained how the priest admitted his complete failure and that the bishop had advised him to return to France. The 500 dollars was regretfully paid to the girl to prevent Courjeault from going to court and likely jail.

Then the bishop had penned another warning. "The malice of that priest against you has received its just reward. But my fear is that you have another implacable enemy here in Mr. Lebel, whose power to do evil is greater than Mr. Courjeault's.

"Before you began your great work of directing the flood of Roman Catholic immigration toward this country to secure it to our holy church, he was in favor of that glorious scheme. But his jealousy against you has suddenly changed his mind. He sent a letter to the press in Canada that is filled with lies. The Bishop of Montreal, as you know, opposes our plan here. He was more than willing to publish Lebel's letter in his journal. If we weren't in such great need of a French-speaking priest in Chicago, I would send him away. I did warn him that any more lies from him would result in punishment."

Unfortunately, both Chiniquy and Vandeveld had misjudged their opposition. The St. Anne parish had continued to mushroom in size. Charles had received threats while ministering to St. Anne and continuing to fill in at Bourbonnais.

In January of 1853 the threats had turned real. His church of St. Anne had burned to the ground. As Charles had stood before the smoldering, still hot ashes, the town constable had approached.

"Father, it looks like somebody started this. There was no lightning or anything like that. Looks like nobody was in the church."

"Correct, all lamps and candles had been extinguished. What makes you think it was set?"

"LeCroy, he lives nearby. He is convinced that he saw two men running from the church just before the flames started."

Charles had sadly poked into the ashes with a stick. "I'm not surprised."

Within a week Bishop Vandeveld had come to Kankakee and to St. Anne's. At first Charles was encouraged as the bishop discussed plans to rebuild the church.

Then Vandeveld had added, "All the facts we gathered point in the same direction. I believe that those who started this fire were emissaries of Lebel and Courjeault."

"I feared as such," Charles had replied. "Will you expose them? Can you help us?"

Unexpectedly, the bishop had burst into tears. "My dear Mr. Chiniquy, I must tell you something I have not revealed to anyone. I cannot remain any longer bishop of Illinois. It is beyond my power to fulfill my duties."

"Why?" Charles had wondered in astonishment. "What is the reason?"

"If I were to follow the regulations of the canon, I would have to remove almost all of my priests. Courjeault is but one. The depth of corruption and moral turpitude is astounding. My predecessor here tried to combat wayward priests. He was poisoned and died. Now I fear for my life.

"I cannot punish one of them and leave the others free in their abominable doings when they are almost equally guilty. The moment I punish anyone they will raise a lying, poisonous finger against me. It is bad for the church. If by leaving I can salvage our mission, I will do so."

Tears had streamed down the bishop's face as Charles asked, "What will you do?"

"I will go to Rome. I will renounce, at the feet of the pope, the bishopric of Chicago. If I am given another diocese with a better set of priests, then so be it. If not, I will take a small congregation and not have on my head the awful responsibilities that are killing me here. I simply cannot do this anymore."

Delays had followed before Bishop Vandeveld's resignation was accepted and he was appointed Bishop of Natchez in Louisiana. Another delay had occurred before Bishop O'Regan was named successor to the bishopric of Chicago. Then O'Regan had sued Vandeveld, claiming that the previous bishop had taken 100,000 dollars from Chicago to Natchez. Scandal and lawsuits had reigned until the pope put an end to the squabble and divided the money between the two diocese.

Charles had been in no hurry to meet the new bishop. But the day had finally arrived. *Bong!* The clock struck. *Bong, bong,* eight more would follow as Charles Chiniquy rose to meet his new bishop. He cleared his mind of what had brought him to this moment and steeled his resolve for what may lie ahead.

ॐ 3 ॐ

ST. ANNE'S PARISH, ILLINOIS

HARLES WALKED INTO A NEAT, well-furnished room. A man of medium height, dressed in the robe of a bishop, rose from a desk and strode toward his visitor. He extended his hand as Charles fell to his knees before him and kissed his ring.

This hand, Chiniquy silently reflected, *is as cold as ice, like a corpse*. He stood up and gazed into the one of the ugliest faces he had ever seen. A large nose was thrust between two chubby cheeks and below narrow eyes. His head looked like a piece of clay plopped down on shoulders with no neck.

"So you are Father Chiniquy," Bishop O'Regan proclaimed. "I am glad to see you. But you took your time asking for an interview. It is December of 1854. I have been here near a year."

"I have been most busy, my lord. Just yesterday fifty more new immigrants came to St. Anne."

The bishop gestured to a chair as he replied, "Please sit down. I want to hear from you about a certain very strange document, I have just read today."

O'Regan held up a legal document. Charles recognized it at once.

"Do you know this paper?" the bishop queried.

"Yes, my lord, I know it. It is the deed to the eleven acres of land which I bought and on which I built the chapel of St. Anne."

O'Regan's head bobbed in agitation. "You must know that the title is a fraud. You ought never to have signed."

"I don't know legal ramifications other than your venerable and worthy predecessor has accepted it," Charles rejoined. "What might have been technically incorrect was made valid, by his acceptation."

15

"I do not care a straw about what my predecessor has done," O'Regan dismissed. "He is not here to defend himself, and neither are we here to discuss his merits or demerits. We have not to deal with my lord Vande-veld, but with a document which is a deception, which must be thrown into the fire. You must give me title to that property!"

O'Regan angrily balled up the deed in his fists and flung it to the floor.

Charles bent down and picked up the paper. "I exceedingly regret, my lord, that such an unpleasant act should be the object of our first meeting. I pray that the good will that God must have placed into our hearts is not destroyed.

"I am the last and least of your priests. I see that you are very busy. I will not take any more of your valuable time. I will take this rejected document with me and try to make another one which will be more agreeable to your views."

With those words Father Chiniquy departed. A storm was brewing, and he knew it. He left Chicago with a heavy heart. This new bishop would be hard to deal with indeed.

Charles also determined that he should concentrate on his parish of St. Anne and not try to continue to minister to Bourbonnais. When he arrived home he sent his resignation to the bishop. He reasoned that St. Anne's had needs enough without the added charge of Bourbonnais. With Courjeault gone, there was great opportunity for a new priest there.

But hope and expectations were dashed when O'Regan announced the new priest at Bourbonnais. It was to be the infamous Father Lebel, and Charles recognized that this was no friend. Lebel had been turned out of Chicago after rumors of an affair with his own niece. Charles's concerns were well founded. By September of 1855, Lebel was called back from Bourbonnais because of an episode of public drunkenness that even O'Regan could not ignore.

Next in line to minister to the parish was Father Carthuval. Charles had hopes for his success until four men from Bourbonnais appeared at his door.

A tall man, Pierre Boudalou, spoke for the others. "Father Chiniquy, you must come back to us."

"I must be sent by the bishop. I can't go on my own. What is the problem? Father Carthuval seems to be a fine priest."

"We thought so at first. But sometimes truth takes longer to get here than a fast horse."

Chiniquy was puzzled. "What do you mean?"

Pierre unfolded a piece of paper and gave it to the priest. "This is from a friend in Chicago who knew Father Carthuval. It says that the father was a native of Belgium. He was expelled for wrong dealings there and came to Chicago. He changed his name and made a fortune keeping a house of prostitution there. Then he tired of that occupation and offered money to Bishop O'Regan to accept him as a priest. In need of money, the bishop sent him to Kankakee and us."

"You have more proof? Are you sure of this?" Charles was incredulous.

"It has been verified by others that we contacted. Will you help us?"

"There is little I can do without the sanction of Bishop O'Regan. Yet, as a strange irony, fathers Lebel and Carthuval are to be dinner guests here tomorrow night."

"Why?" Pierre's voice was just above a whisper.

"Sometimes I try to accommodate the bishop. I know he wants me to get along with my brother priests, and by doing so maybe I can keep them from doing damage or mischief. Rest assured that I remain steadfast in my conviction that Lebel was involved in the burning of my church. But I have no proof. I will do what I can to help you and to find the truth."

The dinner with Lebel and Carthuval started badly and ended even worse. Both men were half drunk when they showed up at Charles's door. After eating, the two guests went off on a prairie chicken hunt and returned barefooted, having lost their shoes in a slough, and fully intoxicated.

Charles had to half carry both men to a carriage. The next day he wrote a letter to them forbidding them ever to set foot in his house again. Shortly thereafter a letter arrived from Bishop O'Regan.

The prelate wrote, "I am sorry to hear that you refuse to live on good terms with your two neighboring brother priests. This ought not to be, and I hope to hear soon, that you have reconciled yourself with them, in a friendly way, as you ought to have done long ago."

Charles's reply to O'Regan infuriated the bishop. "It is my interest, as well as my duty, to obey my bishop. I understand that. But as long as my bishop gives me for neighboring priests men such as these—one of whom has lived publicly with his own niece as his wife, and the other who has kept a house of prostitution in Chicago—I respectfully ask my bishop to be excused for not visiting them."

O'Regan tore up Charles's letter and slammed his fist onto his desktop. "Mr. Ryan," he turned to his administrative assistant, "I would give anything to the one who would help me to get rid of that unmanageable Chiniquy!"

Only weeks later, on June 11th, Bishop O'Regan traveled to St. Anne to administer the sacrament of confirmation. He brought fathers Lebel and Carthuval with him. Charles was deeply distressed that the two wayward priests had accompanied the bishop.

Following the confirmation service he obtained a private moment with O'Regan. Charles vehemently protested the presence of the antagonist priests in his parish. O'Regan just as forcefully answered, "Mr. Chiniquy, you forget that I am the bishop of Illinois and that you are a simple priest, whom I can interdict and remove from here when I like. I do not come here to receive your lessons, but to intimate to you my orders. You seem to forget that charity is above all others the virtue which must adorn the soul of a good priest.

"Your great zeal is nothing before God, and it is less than nothing before me so long as you have not charity. It is my business, and not yours, to know what priests I must employ, or reject. Your business is to respect them, and forget their past errors, the very day that I see fit to receive them among my priests."

Chiniquy considered briefly and replied, "Your lordship may ignore the vices of his priests and may give them your support and confidence.

But nothing will destroy the faith of our French Canadian people as surely as seeing such men in your company. Especially when you are here to administer the sacrament of confirmation. I tell you this in respect for you and concern for your success."

O'Regan's face flushed red as spittle formed at the corners of his mouth. He hotly countered Charles. "I see, now, the truthfulness of what people say about you. It is to the Gospel you constantly appeal on everything. The Gospel! The Gospel is surely a holy book. But remember that it is the church which must guide you. Christ has said, 'Hear my Church.' I am here the interpreter, the ambassador and the representative of the church. When you disobey me, it is the church you disobey!"

"My lord, I said what I felt bound by honor to say. I promise that through my respect for you I will treat these two priests as if they are worthy of the honorable position you have given them. They will be welcome in my house."

"All right," O'Regan replied, "then let's eat."

At dinner Carthuval seemed unwell and begged off, saying that he needed to lie down. Later a housekeeper informed Charles that Carthuval had helped himself to a bottle of communion wine, which took him five minutes to consume in her presence.

After dinner the bishop turned to Charles. "Come. Walk with me," he commanded. The two strode out upon the church grounds.

"Father Chiniquy, you have chosen a beautiful site for your village and chapel."

"Thank you, my lord, it was chosen by God."

"And Charles, God made it even more lovely with such a fine sunlit day. See how even the greenery shimmers in the bright light."

They walked in silence until they reached a partially finished stone house.

"Whose house is this?" O'Regan asked.

"Mine, my lord."

"Yours? And to whom does that lovely garden belong?"

"Also mine, my lord."

"Costly, is it not? Where did you get the money to purchase such a fine piece of land and to build such a house?"

"The same way all hardworking, honest men do, by the sweat of my brow."

"Well," the bishop exclaimed, "I want that house and that piece of land!"

"So do I," Charles rejoined.

The bishop colored slightly and then continued. "You must give me that house, with the land on which it is built."

"I will not . . . not as long as I need them."

O'Regan reddened more and swelled like an over-ripe tomato. "I have often been told you are a bad priest. Now you confirm it by disobeying your bishop."

"How am I a bad priest to keep what God has given me?"

"Are you ignorant of the fact that you have no right to possess any property?"

Charles sighed and then responded in a firm voice, "Yes! My lord, I am indeed ignorant of any law in our holy church that deprives me of such rights. If, however, your lordship can show me such law, I will give you the title of my property immediately."

The bishop angrily stomped his foot on the green grass. "If there is not such a law, I will get one passed."

As bile rose from Charles's stomach, he resolved to be respectful, yet steadfast. "You are a great bishop," he praised. "You have great power in the church. But even you have insufficient power to get such a law passed in our holy church."

Anger erupted like a broken dam as the bishop cried, "You are an insolent priest. I will make you repent your insolence!"

O'Regan wheeled around without waiting for a reply. "Prepare my carriage immediately!" he shouted to a stable boy. In fifteen minutes Lebel, Carthuval and the bishop were gone.

$\wp$ 4 ∞

CHICAGO

SLENDER MAN FURTIVELY SLIPPED into the doorway of Bishop O'Regan's residence in Chicago. He looked over his shoulder before disappearing inside. In moments he was in front of the bishop.

The man bowed respectfully as he stood before the seated prelate. He was nearly cadaverous in build. His dark eyes shone from a face that looked as though it permanently sucked a lemon.

"You are Peter Spink?" O'Regan asked.

"I am, your lordship. I've admired your service for . . ."

"To the point, please," the bishop interrupted.

"You and I have a common enemy."

"And who is that?"

"Charles Chiniquy."

O'Regan leaned forward with interest. His eyes bore into Spink. "What is your dissatisfaction with the good priest?"

"First, I don't believe he's such a good priest. Yes, he drew fame in Canada because of his fight for temperance. But there are stories, I believe true, that he propositioned a young lady in a confessional."

"I've heard them," the bishop answered. "She later recanted."

Spink rubbed the fingers of his right hand together. "Money can buy whatever words you need."

"Even if that were true, what you speak of was in Canada. How have you come to enmity with Chiniquy?"

"I'm a land speculator at St. Anne's. During one of his sermons, Chiniquy accused me of advising clients to enter public lands on which

French Canadians had cut timber. The priest told his parishioners that my plan was to make the French Canadians pay for the wood. It was a false and malicious accusation. But it hurt my business. My clients began to lose confidence in me. He slandered and perjured me."

"How do I enter into this?"

"My lord, I know you've had difficulties with Chiniquy. There have been reports in the newspapers. As a dealer in land, I know you have a land dispute with him."

"Yes, Mr. Spink, it is not a parish priest's right to claim property as his own. All belongs to the church. What is your remedy for our shared problem?"

"A lawsuit for slander. I'll file it in Kankakee County."

"What do you expect from the church?"

"Nothing except that you won't help Chiniquy."

The bishop laughed and shook his head. "You have no fear from me on that count. Do you think your charges will hold? You have witnesses who will come forward?"

"There are witnesses. I'm one of them. I'm also one of Chiniquy's parishioners. There are also possible charges of immorality. But for now, I think slander's enough."

O'Regan rubbed his forehead and replied evenly. "I hope so. It becomes tiring to defend alcoholic or immoral priests. I have my own problems with slander and libel. It seems that nearly every day there are accusations in the papers."

Spink smiled. "But in this case you won't have to defend."

"Try to keep it to slander. It's bad, but easier on the priesthood than other charges."

"But if I have to?"

"Do what is needed. But I hope that Chinquy will soon see the error of his ways and that this will not be necessary. I'll be meeting with him. I hope it will be more agreeable."

ANY HOPE FOR RAPPROCHEMENT soon evaporated when Charles made a trip to Chicago at the pleading of the French Canadians of Chicago.

"Remember the fine vestments we bought for our church?" a church elder asked Chiniquy. "The bishop took them for his own. The Germans claim he swindled them out of a fine lot upon which they were going to build a church. They say he sold it for $40,000 and kept the money for his own use."

"Let us bring him to court!" another churchman cried.

"No," Charles answered thoughtfully, "insulting his lordship publicly or making legal charges against him will do no good for the church or you. I'll speak with him."

"When?"

"Tomorrow."

The next morning, with reluctance sucking at his feet with every step, Charles made his way up the walkway to Bishop O'Regan's residence. He raised the heavy knocker on the panel and twice struck the entrance with it. O'Regan himself stood in the doorway as the door swung open.

The bishop smiled and waved Charles into his house. "Enter and sit, Chiniquy. We got off on the wrong foot when we met last. I trust this meeting will be more pleasant."

"It is my hope that we can find accommodations on the issues that confront us."

As both took seats upon fabric-covered chairs, O'Regan turned apprehensive. "To what issues do you refer?"

"First my lord, the true Catholics of Illinois are filled with sorrow by the articles they find, every day, in the press against their bishop."

"The church is accused of plots to take control of the Mississippi River basin. How absurd!" the bishop exclaimed. "Our bishops at the Buffalo Conference rejected this nonsense. The hatred and bias being fanned by the Know Nothing Party against Catholics and all immigrants is inexcusable."

Charles hesitated, wondering if he should tell O'Regan that his predecessor had brought him to Illinois for the very reasons the Know

Nothings complained about, political domination. He thought better and tried a different approach.

"They make vile accusations and hide in secrecy. When asked, they claim to 'know nothing.' What cowards they are."

O'Regan was abrupt. "The good Catholics must be sad indeed to read such disgusting attacks against their superior. But it's not just Know Nothings, I notice that some of the attacks are made by French Canadians. Can you not prevent your insolent countrymen from writing libel?"

"My lord, I came to Chicago today to try to put an end to these scandals."

"Good, Father Chiniquy, you have great influence over your people. Put an end to this rebellious conduct and I will know you are a good priest."

"By doing two things, you can help ensure my success in helping you."

O'Regan's face twisted into a quizzical expression. He asked apprehensively, "And what are they?"

Chiniquy steeled his resolve and answered, "The French Canadian congregation in Chicago worked diligently to raise money for fine church vestments for their priest. I, myself, contributed to their effort. My lord, you took the vestments. Also, I ask you, your lordship, to cease selling the sand of burying ground that covers the tombs of the dead."

Puffing up like a blowfish, the bishop slammed his fist upon a small table. Without speaking, he rose to his feet and strode across the room. Then he turned and stormed back to Charles, his face burning with rage.

He jammed a forefinger into the priest's face. "Mr. Spink was right. You are not only my greatest enemy, you are the head of all my enemies. You have taken sides against your bishop! The vestments are mine and I will never give them back. They are mine just as the French Canadian church is mine. It was a disgrace I was covered in rags while the priest in a miserable little church in Chicago was robed in finery. It was my duty to preserve the dignity of the church that I should be clothed in rich and splendid vestments.

"If my office means anything to you, you will go to your countrymen and tell them I took what was rightfully mine from a church that is mine and brought them to a cathedral that is altogether mine. Tell them to hold their tongues and show respect for their bishop."

"My lord," Chiniquy answered directly, "this is a human law. I found nothing in the Gospel that gives you such power. What you claim is an abusive, human authority, not divine power. The vestments do not belong to you."

O'Regan stood thunderstruck, as if a bolt from the sky had left him immobile. Then he cried out. "The Gospel! The Gospel! You hold up the Gospel to defame the laws and regulations of our holy church! Do not frighten me with your pronouncements about the holy word. I tell you, you must obey the church, and the church rules you through your bishop. I warn you, Father Chiniquy, the road you take has many pitfalls. You are making a great mistake and it will cost you."

"My lord," Charles countered, "of course I want to obey the church. But the church I follow must be founded on the Gospel. It must respect and follow the Gospel."

O'Regan pointed to the door. "Get out of my sight. I have no more time for insane babblings. You have made your intent clear and you will hear from me again. Now, LEAVE!"

ঙ 5 ଔ

KANKAKEE, ILLINOIS

CHARLES CHINIQUY WAS NOT SURPRISED when a 10,000-dollar lawsuit for slander was filed against him in the Kankakee Court. He surmised that O'Regan and Spink were in it together and that the bishop would use a guilty verdict to remove him as a priest.

Charles hired two lawyers, Osgood and Paddock, and was brought to trial in the Criminal Court of Kankakee. A mistrial was declared when the child of a juror died and the man returned to his home.

A new jury was selected and the trial resumed. Charges and counter-charges were hurled between Spink and Chiniquy and their lawyers. Finally, the second trial ended in a hung jury after failing to reach an agreement.

Charles treated it as a victory and was happily thanking God in prayer when his lawyers found him sitting amidst greenery on a park bench.

"Father," Osgood cautioned, "Mr. Spink has just taken an oath that he has no confidence in the Kankakee Court. He has asked that the case be retried in Urbana, in Champaign County. His request was granted."

"It's not over?" Chiniquy's shoulders sagged.

"No," Paddock confirmed, "and this time your friends and acquaintances will not be on the jury. Spink recognized that a guilty verdict could not be had in Kankakee because you live here and are well known. Urbana is another matter."

"When?"

"Next term," Osgood replied, "May 19, 1856."

Chiniquy bowed his head in frustration and said quietly, "Leave me, please. I must pray. My heart is heavy."

A short time later he felt a hand on his shoulder and heard, "Father Chiniquy, I'd like to talk with you."

The priest looked up at a nondescript, middle-aged man. The man's face was kind and he spoke softly. "I have followed your case from the beginning. I think that the problems facing you are greater than you think.

"I believe that Spink and your bishop are hand-in-hand in this. In fact, I think that Bishop O'Regan is the real land shark in all this. The private and public scandals that surround him are destroying our church. Because you stand against him, he's determined to get rid of you."

"He's failed so far," Charles proclaimed.

"This is just the beginning. When you fight one bishop, you must expect other bishops to join their brother. You'll face new charges, falsehoods, and perjuries. Urbana won't be the sanctuary for you that Kankakee was."

Alarm flashed across Charles's face as if he had heard a fire bell. "What can I do?"

"Your lawyers were good. Now you need the best. There's a man in Springfield. His name's Abraham Lincoln. If he defends you, you'll win."

Charles looked up with questioning eyes. "Lincoln? Who's this Lincoln? I've never heard of him."

"He's the best lawyer and most honest man we have in Illinois. Retain him and good luck to you."

As the man turned to leave, Charles called, "Thank you for your sympathy and advice. But, who are you?"

"Just another Catholic who, like you, doesn't like bad things happening to his church. That's all you need to know about me." He then turned and walked away, leaving Charles alone on the bench.

After a few minutes of contemplation the priest rose and walked to the Kankakee Telegraph Office. The message he sent was simple: "Mr. Abraham Lincoln Esq., although I am a stranger to you, would you defend my honor and my life at the next May term of the court of Urbana?"

Charles waited only twenty minutes before the clattering of telegraph keys signaled a reply. He eagerly snatched the message from the operator.

The answer came in one sentence: "Yes, I will defend your honor and your life at the next May term at Urbana." It was signed, "Abraham Lincoln."

The months crawled by with agonizing slowness as Charles performed his priestly duties and awaited the spring court term. Each day, thoughts of the impending trial hung over his head like a heavy cloud. It was with great relief that he reported to the sheriff of Kankakee to be transported to Urbana.

"It's time to get this over with," he said as they boarded the northbound train. "May God see that right prevails."

Charles arrived in Urbana one week before his scheduled trial. As the date of the trial neared, a circus-like atmosphere swept the town. Partisans on both sides overran the community. With hotels full, some people camped out in the open. Musicians, parrots, pet dogs, and con artists were in great supply.

One of his attorneys, Joseph Osgood, summoned Charles to meet in a courthouse office regarding his case. He entered the small room where Osgood and another man were seated at a small round table.

The stranger rose to greet Charles. He was tall and gangly with unruly dark hair. The man extended a large, powerful hand that swallowed Charles's hand.

"Father Chiniquy, I'm Abraham Lincoln."

The priest was taken aback by Lincoln's size and by his face. *Some might think him homely*, Charles pondered silently, *but never in my life have I met a man who looked to be so kind and direct.*

Aloud, the priest answered, "It is my pleasure to meet you, sir. I am honored you have agreed to help me, even though I'm a stranger to you."

"Father," Lincoln chuckled, "you're mistaken that you're unknown to me. I know you by reputation. Your lawyers and others have told me of your opposition to your bishop and your defense of French Canadians in Illinois. It appears that the good bishop is trying to get rid of you. This will not be an easy task, but I will try to protect you against his machinations."

"Thank you, Mr. Lincoln. I was told you were the best and most honest lawyer in the state."

Lincoln's face creased as he laughed aloud. "Were you also told that I'm the ugliest lawyer in Illinois?"

"Certainly not, sir."

Lincoln smiled. "Then we won't worry about my appearance. But we can worry about your case. Let's sit down and talk about it."

The two men joined Osgood and began to discuss the lawsuit.

"Father, I've been going over things with Joseph here. Seems that you've got a bobcat by the tail. Spink insists that you've slandered him, told lies about him from the pulpit no less. Is this true?"

"I told the truth. Mr. Spink was tricking people into moving on public land where wood had been cut by French Canadians and then making French Canadians pay for the wood they had cut. It was dishonest."

"Is there anything else I should know?"

"Like what?"

"Anything in your past, any skeletons that might be brought up?"

"They may lie. Lebel and Carthuval are my sworn enemies, and I'm sure they are working with Spink."

Lincoln's kind hazel eyes hardened as he looked directly at Chiniquy. "I must not be surprised. There are reports from Canada that you had a liaison with a woman there, and I've heard reports that you embezzled church money."

"None of that can be proven. There is no basis for it."

"Then, Father Chiniquy, you have nothing to fear. For I'll defend you and I won't lose if right is on my side. If you omitted anything, let me know immediately. For now, please leave us. I need to confer with Mr. Osgood."

"Thank you, Mr. Lincoln. This means my life to me."

Charles stood, shook Lincoln's hand and left the room.

Lincoln turned to Osgood. "Is the good priest to be believed?"

"I believe he's been above reproach in Kankakee," the lawyer answered. "There were stories that followed him from Canada about a young woman and his relationship with her. I also believe that Chiniquy tends to exaggerate his claims a little."

"Then you'll have to help filter his claims to me. He won't be the first man I've defended who had questions raised about his character. But I've had my own problems with the bishop and his church. It's one reason why I'm inclined to help Chiniquy. I think he's being smeared and mostly is in the right."

Lincoln gazed out the window into the sunlit town square. It was filled with people singing, hawking wares, praying and holding banners.

"I just don't like surprises," he said just under his breath, and more to himself than to Osgood.

∞ 6 ∞

MAY 1856, URBANA, ILLINOIS

THE COURTHOUSE AT URBANA was filled to overflowing when the trial began. Benches were set up on the green, and messengers were poised to deliver periodic reports to those unable to gain entrance.

After the bailiff called the court room to order, Judge David Davis took his place at the bench. He wore a black robe that draped over his portly body. His hair was beginning to thin and gray. Davis's glasses perched uneasily on his nose as the judge sternly peered over them at the assemblage.

"There will be no outbursts in this court," he admonished. "You will maintain proper respect and decorum at all times. Read the charges, please."

The bailiff stood and intoned, "Father Charles Chiniquy of St. Anne's Parish is charged with slander."

"The prosecution may proceed." Davis nodded to the prosecution lawyer, Robert Williams.

The short, slender attorney had the look of an elf in stature. But from his diminutive body sounded a deep voice. "Your honor, I call the Right Reverend James Lebel to the stand."

With a smug expression glued to his face, Lebel sat in the witness box.

"Father Lebel," Williams began, "how long have you known Father Chiniquy?"

"Directly? Two years. But I've known *of* him for years before."

"What did you know of him?"

"That he was an advocate for temperance while a priest in Canada and that he came to Illinois to further French Canadian migration here."

"Did you come to form a personal opinion as to his character?"

A trace of a smirk flashed over Lebel's face as he stared at Charles. "Chiniquy is one of the vilest men I ever met. Bad rumors were constantly circulating against him. Why, his previous bishop in Canada even warned him in a letter to avoid close attachments with women."

Lincoln, sitting at the defendant's table with Charles, sprang to his feet. "I object, your honor! What proof is there of this? How do we know this is founded on truth? Is there a copy of the letter?"

Judge Davis looked down at Williams. "Do you have a copy of the letter, Mr. Williams?"

"No, I do not. But let me continue. You'll soon see that I don't need written proof. I have an eyewitness to Chiniquy's misdeeds."

Davis paused in thought and then replied, "Objection is denied. I want to hear more."

Williams stood before Lebel and continued, "Father Lebel, you in fact have more intimate knowledge of Father Chiniquy's misdeeds than almost anyone, do you not? Does this not affect your own family?"

Lebel hesitantly looked down and then to either side. In a reluctant voice he responded, "I only tell what I know with deep regret. It pains me to have to speak today against the honor of Father Chiniquy. But his actions involve the good name of my dear sister, and it must be told."

"And from where does this knowledge come?"

"My sister, sir. My sister, Madame Bossey. Father Chiniquy attempted to do infamous things with her. She herself told me the whole story under oath."

As a low gasp spread like a wave over the room, Williams asked, "Where is your sister?"

"She is at home, in Chicago, forced to silence by illness or she would be here to unmask this wickedness."

Lincoln whispered to Charles, "How much of that is true?"

His client answered, "Every word is a lie. I met Madame Bossey but once and only for a few minutes. Lebel seemed so sincere. In each bushel of perjury someone might find a kernel of truth. I'm shocked by his wickedness."

Once again Lincoln unwound his long body and stood to object. "Your honor, there are no facts here. Just hearsay and stories."

Davis replied, "You will have your chance to rebut this. Continue, Mr. Williams."

"What more can you tell us about Father Chiniquy? Was he a good priest?"

Lebel sadly shook his head. "He stole land from his bishop, and from the pulpit he slandered the good name of his own parishioner, Mr. Spink."

"And that is what this trial is all about, isn't it?" Williams stared directly at the jury. "Can a priest act with impunity and say whatever he wishes before the altar of the Lord?

"That's all for now, Father Lebel. Your witness, Mr. Lincoln."

Lincoln looked up from scribbling on a notepad. "Nothing now, later."

Next Peter Spink himself took the stand. He recalled the charges that Charles had leveled at him for dishonest land dealings and the selling of wood cut by French Canadians on the land he owned.

"I acted honestly," Spink proclaimed. "The accusations of Father Chiniquy cost me dearly in my business, to the tune of 10,000 dollars, at least."

The testimony was sketchy but damning against Charles Chiniquy as Abraham Lincoln began his defense.

Lincoln called Lebel to the stand as his first witness. He stood before the witness stand and asked Lebel, "How well do you know Bishop Regan?"

"He is my bishop."

"Is he your friend?"

"He is my superior. He is my bishop."

"He is your good friend and confidant, isn't he?"

Lebel paused and looked down, then said, "We are on friendly terms."

"Have you confided the details of this case with him?"

Lebel hesitated, then replied, "He knew I had had difficulties with Father Chiniquy. But I never discussed this case with him."

Lincoln turned his back on the witness and looked at the jury as he spoke. "Well, this isn't getting us anywhere. How about I try something else?"

He turned to face Lebel again. "It seems convenient that the prime accuser of my client can't get here to make her charges in person. Could your sister be here tomorrow?"

33

Lebel shifted uneasily and replied, "I'm afraid not, sir. She's quite ill. I don't think she ever fully recovered from the episode with Chiniquy."

"When was that episode?"

Lebel put his fist to his forehead as if trying to push a date into his mind. "I can't tell you. Some time in the last two years."

"Some time in the last two years?" Lincoln repeated as his voice rose incredulously. "That's the best you can do? You've made charges that could ruin a good man's life and you can't fix a date? Not even to the year?"

"Sorry, I can't."

"Reminds me of the time I got on a mule and it started to buck. I tried to hold on for a bit and then slid off. I said, 'I've had enough of you,' to the mule. I've had enough of you, too, Mr. Lebel."

Lincoln then launched into his attempt to destroy Lebel's testimony by calling a series of twelve witnesses to the stand. The theme set by the first gentlemen was similar to all that followed.

"Mr. Coulliard, what do you know of Father Lebel?"

"That he was a drunken priest at Bourbonnais."

"How did you come to know him?"

"He was my priest."

"Did he speak of Father Chiniquy?"

"Often, sir. He was vicious in his remarks. He became a very public enemy of Father Chiniquy."

"Was he believed?"

"I would not believe a word Father Lebel said. Even if he swore an oath to our Heavenly Father."

Through a long afternoon and into the evening, Abraham Lincoln meticulously questioned each witness. Finally court was adjourned at 10:00 p.m. Lincoln stretched his fatigued limbs and addressed his client and the two other defense attorneys.

"We have things we need to go over. I'd like you all to come to my hotel room now. We made progress today, but like I said, I don't like surprises and the story about Lebel's sister was a big surprise. He left us with a millstone around our necks and we're dragging it uphill."

7

URBANA, ILLINOIS

In his small hotel room, Lincoln lit an oil lamp. He stood as Chiniquy perched on the only chair and Osgood and Paddock sat upon the rumpled blankets of a short cot. Lincoln looked down at the priest with concern and compassion.

"My dear Mr. Chiniquy, tomorrow I hope to destroy the testimony of Mr. Lebel against you. But I must concede that I see great dangers ahead. I have no doubt that every word he has said is a sworn lie. Yet, I fear that the jury may think differently."

"Why?" Paddock wondered. "It's all hearsay. The jury will see through this ruse."

"Gentlemen, I'm a pretty good judge of juries. I've been riding the circuit and dealing with them for over twenty years. I believe our jury thinks that Father Chiniquy is guilty."

Osgood shook his head with disgust. "Then, what's your plan?"

"The only way to perfectly destroy the power of a false witness is by another direct testimony against what he said, or by showing from his very lips that he perjured himself. I tried to do that tonight but I failed. Now, we've hurt their case a tad. But, Charles, I need your help. Do you have an alibi? Is there any witness who was there when you met Madame Bossey who could contradict what has been said?"

"Mr. Lincoln," Charles replied, "it's hard to do that when they won't even fix a time when this supposedly happened."

Lincoln sighed. "Correct. Without fixing a precise date, we can't raise questions about a time. They've used diabolical skill to concoct your destruction. I tried to get Lebel to admit that he was on friendly terms with the bishop of Chicago to link the accusers together. Our jury's Protestant, and I think it's helpful to imply that you're fighting the Catholic Church, even though you are Catholic yourself.

"I must be blunt, Father. I fear for your chances. The surprise I anticipated was delivered us in the specter of Madame Bossey. She may be here tomorrow after her brother created a favorable impression of her for the jury."

"She's sick," Osgood reminded.

"A feint. She's no sicker than any of us," Lincoln replied. "But if they continue the ruse, the court will send someone to Chicago to get her sworn statement. That will be even harder to rebut than her verbal declarations in court."

"Mr. Lincoln," Charles pleaded, "what can we do?"

"Pray. It'd make things much easier if the Almighty were to take your part and reveal your innocence. I'll prepare as best I can. Go to your room and pray."

Charles left as instructed and Osgood commented to Lincoln, "Getting kind of desperate, aren't you? All we have to cling to is a prayer?"

Lincoln smiled and surveyed his two assistants. "Gentlemen, I do have other fish on the line, but I thought it best to encourage Father Chiniquy to do what he does best. Besides, a little divine help never hurts."

It was eleven o' clock when the anguished priest closed the door to his room. Almost immediately he fell to his knees at the side of his bed. Resting his arms and head on the lumpy straw mattress, he fervently prayed aloud.

"My God, deliver me from the hands of my enemies. Do not forsake me. I ask for your infinite mercy."

For the next four hours Charles prayed. Doubt mingled with hope, and tears struggled with confidence. Through the agony of the night he hoped against hope for mercy.

At three in the morning three knocks rapped sharply on the priest's door. Charles instantly flung it open to find Abraham Lincoln beaming down at him. Lincoln noticed the red eyes and tracks of tears on the priest's face.

Clapping his client on the back, Lincoln exclaimed, "Cheer up, Mr. Chiniquy! We have the lying priests in our hands."

"How? What happened?"

Lincoln shut the door as he stepped into the room. "A Chicago newspaperman telegraphed back to his paper that things looked bad for you. The little Irish boys, with a bent toward sensationalism, sold their papers by crying out, 'Chiniquy guilty! Chiniquy to be Hung!'

"Now a certain young woman, Miss Philomene Moffat, heard the cries and read the paper's account. She came here to help you because she knows the truth. She and another woman have direct knowledge of what happened, and Miss Moffat is prepared to testify with the assistance of Narcisse Terrian, the other woman's husband."

Charles's face lit up with a smile. "I know Narcisse Terrian. He's a friend of mine."

"Father Chiniquy, as of today he's the best friend you have in the world."

"I prayed for a miracle."

"Your prayer was answered."

∞ 8 ∞

URBANA, ILLINOIS

THE NEXT MORNING THE COURTROOM in Urbana was again filled to overflowing. Judge Davis looked sternly at the assemblage and then spoke, "Mr. Lincoln. Do you have a witness or do you rest your case?"

"Your honor, I have one more witness, Miss Philomene Moffat."

Peter Spink turned and looked questioningly at Lebel.

A petite young woman with curly blonde hair strode resolutely to the witness stand. After being sworn in by the bailiff, she took her seat.

Lincoln smiled down on her and asked, "Where's home, Miss Moffat?"

"Chicago."

"Do you know the principles in this case, fathers Chiniquy and Lebel?"

"I know of Father Chiniquy. I know Father Lebel."

"How did you come to know Father Lebel?"

Philomene glanced quickly at Lebel and continued, "I'm a friend of his sister, Eugenia Bossey."

"What brings you to this court? Do you have evidence pertaining to Father Chiniquy and the charges against him?"

"Yes, I do."

Lincoln paused and looked at the jury. The spectators leaned forward as if to hear every word better.

"Tell us what you know, Madame Moffat."

"I was in Father Lebel's parsonage on Clark Street. Sara Terrian, another friend of mine and Madame Bossey's, was visiting, too."

"When was this, Miss Moffat?"

38

"May of 1854."

"Just over two years ago. Continue please. What happened in the parsonage?"

"The two of us were in the sitting room visiting with Madame Bossey when Father Lebel called her into an adjoining room. She left and shut the door between us. But it didn't close completely. It was left open a crack."

"Could you hear conversation in the other room?"

"Quite plainly."

"What did you hear?"

"I heard Father Lebel's voice, he said that Father Chiniquy was a dangerous man and an enemy, that he had caused many of Father Lebel's congregation to leave him and settle in Father Chiniquy's colony. Then he said, and I remember it like it was just yesterday, 'You must help me to put him down by accusing him of having tried to do a criminal action with you.'"

"What did Madame Bossey say?"

"She said that she wouldn't say something so completely false."

Lincoln turned to look at Father Lebel. The priest's face turned red as a ripe strawberry as he squirmed in his chair.

The attorney turned back to Philomene. "What did you hear Father Lebel say to that? What did he say to his sister?"

"He said, 'If you don't do what I say, I'll see that you are cut out of the family inheritance.' He told her that he had 160 acres he was going to give her and if she didn't do as he asked, she would live and die poor.

"But Eugenia, she stood up to him and cried, 'I don't care if I never have that land. I'd rather live and die poor than lie to please you.'

"Then Father Lebel, he said things about how she didn't care about him and their family. She was sobbing and crying when she told him again and again, 'I won't damn my soul by lying, even if I never get an inch of land.'"

"But," Lincoln countered, "she's sworn a lie."

"Father Lebel wouldn't give up. He told his sister that Father Chiniquy would destroy the Catholic Church if he wasn't destroyed first.

Then he told her that if she thought what he asked Eugenia to do was a sin, he would pardon her when she came to confession.

"Eugenia asked directly, 'Do you have the power to forgive a false oath?' Father Lebel answered that he did and that the power came from Christ. At that she gave in. Eugenia said that since he promised that the lie would be forgiven and if he gave the promised 160 acres, she would do as he asked.

"Father Lebel said, 'All right.' Then I heard a noise and the door was pushed tight and nothing further could be heard. A few minutes later Eugenia rejoined us as if nothing had happened. I heard nothing more about this until I read yesterday's newspaper."

"Miss Moffat," Lincoln slowly raised his voice, "remember that you have sworn before God that this is true."

"Every word is as I heard it. I swear."

"What about Mrs. Terrian?"

"She's home sick in Chicago. But she asked me to come here and set things right."

Spink, pale and shaken, looked at his attorney and then stood up. "Your honor," he began hesitantly, "allow me to withdraw my prosecution against Mr. Chiniquy. I am now persuaded that he is not guilty of the faults brought against him before this court."

Davis abruptly rapped his gavel. "Case dismissed. Father Chiniquy, you are free to go."

The courtroom erupted into a mixed reaction of cheers and boos. All stood as Davis left the bench. Lincoln turned to Charles and warmly shook his hand.

"You've won, Chiniquy. It's a great day for truth!"

To Lincoln's surprise, the priest's eyes welled with tears. Both men watched as a dozen black-robed men rose from a couple of benches and somberly walked out.

"What's wrong?" the lawyer asked.

"It is a great relief. You have saved me. But I fear for you. Those men in black are Jesuits from St. Louis and Chicago. They came here to support

Bishop O'Regan and to see me punished. In their minds, you have exposed the church and them as infamous and diabolical. They will not forget this, Mr. Lincoln. The day will come when they will come after you for revenge. My church does not lose easily. Your life is not safe."

Lincoln laughed. "I don't see a death warrant anywhere." Then his face grew serious, and he continued, "I know that Jesuits never forget nor forsake. But man must not care how and where he dies, provided he dies at the post of honor and duty." Then he clapped Chiniquy on the back and said, "What will you do now? I don't expect your bishop will welcome you back with open arms."

"There's no place for me in the Catholic Church. Bishop O'Regan has accused me of being half Protestant. I guess I'll go the rest of the way."

Lincoln's giant hand swallowed the priest's once again. "Take care of yourself, Chiniquy. Our paths may cross again."

$\mathfrak{so}\,9\,\mathfrak{cs}$

SUMMER 1859, LITTLE ROCK, ARKANSAS

LBERT PIKE EAGERLY SNATCHED a much-anticipated packet from the postmaster in the Little Rock post office. Then the huge fifty-year-old rushed down the street to his nearby office as hastily as his bulk and age would permit. En route he flagged down a young boy on the walkway, scribbled a quick note, gave it to the lad and flipped him a coin.

"Take this to the address on the note. Be quick about it."

The boy's face brightened at this unexpected good fortune. He carefully tucked away the coin, then scurried on his errand. Pike trundled to his office building and huffed with effort up the stairs leading to his office space. He unlocked the door, entered his room and immediately relocked the entrance.

To help ensure his privacy, he pulled the curtains nearly closed, leaving just a sliver of light for him to read. His wooden chair creaked as Pike breathlessly settled his six-foot-four-inch, 300-plus-pound frame into it.

Pike had many interests in his life. A native of Boston, he had been a teacher, hunter and trapper in New Mexico, a newspaperman in Arkansas, and then became a lawyer in Little Rock and a thirty-third-degree Mason. He had just been elected Sovereign Grand Commander of the Scottish Rite's Southern Jurisdiction.

But politics and intrigue were Pike's true passions. He was formerly a member of the Whig Party but now favored the anti-immigrant Know Nothing Party. His great intellect and skills had been fueled by revolutionaries in Europe. Among them was Giuseppe Mazzini of Italy.

Mazzini had introduced Pike to a secret, most powerful organization that sought world domination. He had named Albert Pike to lead America's branch of the Illuminati. Pike knew that the small packet contained instructions from his mentor. His full, dark beard quivered with excitement as he ripped the envelope open.

"My dear friend," Mazzini wrote, "we must have a respectable forum for our secret activities. We must allow all the federations to continue just as they are, with their systems, their central authorities, and their diverse modes of correspondence between high grades of the same rite, organized as they are at the present, but we must create a supreme rite to which we will call certain Masons of high degrees whom we shall select.

"With regard to our brothers in Masonry, these men must be pledged to the strictest secrecy. Through this supreme rite, we will govern all Freemasonry, which will become the one international center, the more powerful because its direction will be unknown."

"A new order!" Excitement and a sense of heightened power surged through Pike as he reread the missive. "A new order, above and beyond the others. Oh, the power! We shall recruit the most powerful in the world. We shall have our One World Order!"

Startled by a sharp rap at the door, Pike shoved the letter into his inner vest pocket.

"Did you hear?" a voice on the other side demanded.

Pike relaxed as he recognized his good friend and assistant.

A slender man with thinning, graying hair thrust himself into the room as Pike unlocked it. "Did you hear from Mazzini?" he asked. "Is it time?"

"Sit down, Phileas." Pike was in control again. "We must discuss this."

Pike handed him Mazzini's letter. Phileas Walder read with fervent interest, growing eager. "It is time! Things are in place. All the signs are there."

Pike agreed. "John Brown has incited insurrection in Virginia. The black Republican Lincoln is running for president, rumors of Southern secession abound, and the Knights of the Golden Circle is growing. Out of this chaos a new order will rise."

Walder demurred, "But the Knights are not Masons."

"No, but they spawned from Freemasonry. One must adapt as events change," Pike responded. "At one time the Knights existed to expand our country into territory suitable for slavery, like Mexico and Cuba. More slave states would expand the power of the South.

"I don't think that dream's viable now. But as the North strangles our economy and our culture, we must find means to save our way of life."

Walder considered thoughtfully, "They have impressive goals, a half million men, primarily in the lower Midwest with the stated purpose of fermenting revolution and the expulsion or death of the abolitionists and free negroes."

"I hope their numbers and goals aren't exaggerated," Pike responded.

"Albert, Mazzini wants a new rite. How can we separate them from the others?"

"We use the Knights, for one thing. Many are at the thirty-third degree of passage. Some of them will become members of the supreme rite, if they are found worthy."

"So," Walder suggested, "most Masons below the thirty-third degree are good, hardworking folks that the enlightened ones use as a disguise."

"And those who rise above do so by participating in the 'Killing of the King' ritual. Lower levels will do their part and never realize their role in the ritual," Pike declared. "We will not involve Freemasonry as such. It must remain pure. But we will use our contacts within the order to create a force beyond that of regular Masons. It's not exactly what Mazzini has in mind, yet it will serve our ends here."

"It's too bad that some kings really have to die," Walder commented.

Pike shrugged. "President Taylor got in the way. He stood against Southern rights and our needs."

"The verdict of his death was indigestion."

"Yes, Phileas, our doctors did their work well."

"What are our immediate plans?"

"Expand the network. We have sympathizers in the North, in Congress and all walks of life. There are many high-degree Masons who share our vision. And we have the Knights of the Golden Circle, an army of 500,000 spread into every state. The only thing lacking is enough money to finance our needs. We'll find the means as it becomes necessary."

Walder's eyes glowed. "Albert, we'll rebuild the world by starting here."

"And," Pike added, "may God, or Satan, help any who get in our way."

"Will war come?"

"It will, and it will be our war."

᎓ 10 Ꮿ

JULY 1863, NEW YORK CITY

he Confederate government began an intelligence-gathering network in the early stages of the war. The Signal Corps, using flags to convey messages, communicated between Washington and Richmond. The corps soon evolved into couriers and a sophisticated spy web.

By late 1861, the Confederacy had set up a clandestine base in Canada, with Halifax becoming a key to their use of British Territory in North America. Blockade runners trying to supply Confederate states used Halifax as a base of operations. The need to track ships putting into Halifax on their way to the South and to watch travelers made an network there essential.

In August of 1862, a significant boost in Canadian operations came with the arrival of George Sanders of Kentucky. For the rest of the war Sanders would travel between Canada and Europe, carrying dispatches and seeking help by offering trade incentives to England and France.

In early July 1863 he met with renegade Congressman Vallandigham of Ohio at Sanders's home near Niagara Falls. Sanders had approached President Jefferson Davis with a scheme to use Canada as a base and to work with Southern-sympathizing Democrats of the North, known also as the Peace Party or Copperheads, to disrupt the Union from beyond its northern border.

Davis shelved the idea, but Sanders moved on it anyway. Vallandigham was a key to the plan. The falls roared in the distance as Sanders took the banished congressman into his home.

Sanders was of medium height, his hair dark with a chin beard and mustache. "I've wanted to meet you for over a year," he told Vallandigham.

"And I, you. Your fame precedes you."

"Fame," Sanders shrugged. "Hardly. I'm best left unknown."

"But you are known. Consul to London during the revolutions of 1848, a friend and confidant of the great revolutionaries, Marx, Hugo, Garibaldi, Mazzini, and many others. You nearly forced an annexation of Cuba. Like me, your activities caused you to fall out of favor with the powers that be."

"I was right to urge that the people of France overthrow Louis Napoleon. I believe that the murder of tyrants is justified."

"That was nine years ago. I hope that France has forgotten."

"Different time and different leaders," Sanders answered. "To the matter at hand. How many Peace Party stalwarts are there?"

"About half a million."

"Who leads them now that you're banished to the Confederacy?"

Vallandigham smiled. "I still make regular undercover visits. We do have a secret echelon involved."

"The Knights of the Golden Circle."

"Yes, I am one."

"I've been following your activities with my good friend Albert Pike," Sanders acknowledged. "I believe the Knights can be very useful in our plans."

"How?"

"The draft's going into effect for Union soldiers. The first drawing of conscripts is on July 11th, the second on July 13th. Riots in New York City would create chaos and throw the Yankees into turmoil. Can you arrange it?"

Vallandigham grinned. "Easy. The Irish already hate the Republican government. Hell, they hate negroes, too. They don't want to fight in this war, but the draft will fall heavily on them. It won't take much more than a match or two to get this flame started."

"What about the Irish who do fight for the Union? At Fredericksburg it was Union Irish charging into a stonewall backed by Confederate Irish."

"Mr. Sanders, I admit that some Irish are on the wrong side, but most are with us. We can inflame New York."

Sanders looked pleased. "Good, Congressman. Go home and do it."

In two days Vallandigham was in New York City. There he met with two knights of the Golden Circle, Patrick O'Riley and Richard Hennessey.

"The eleventh was uneventful," Vallandigham commented, "but tomorrow when they draw numbers again it must be different. Meet people on the street corners. Inflame them as to the injustice that Lincoln is heaping upon them. It won't take much. We need them to turn this town upside down."

The next morning, July 13, O'Riley stood on a street corner as men, mostly immigrants and Irish, began to file by to register for the draft. O'Riley raised his arms above his head shouted. "Hold on there, lads! Where are you off to? This isn't your war. It's a poor man's war that rich folks profit from. They don't even have to fight. For 300 dollars they buy replacements. But you, Irish lads, you fight and die! For what? For black-lovin' Republicans like Abraham Lincoln. For the nigras that come north, work for less and take your jobs. Do you want to free more of 'em so more can come to New York and take the food out of our children's mouths? Do you want that! Do you?"

"NO!" answered a chorus of shouts.

"Look!" someone yelled, "there be the police superintendent."

John Kennedy had come to check on the situation. He was not in uniform and was unarmed. The mob recognized him and attacked with a frenzy. They left him lying bruised and bloodied in a heap.

Within minutes the mob grew. They attacked the provost marshal's office where the draft was taking place, throwing paving stones through the windows, smashing doors and setting the building ablaze.

The riot spread. Public buildings were burned. Then the mob moved on the *New York Tribune*, a leading Republican newspaper. They were turned away by newspaper staff operating Gatling guns, the new machine guns.

Blacks became targets as Irish vented their anger about losing their jobs. Any who fell into their clutches were beaten, tortured and/or killed. One man was attacked by 400, beaten to a pulp, then hanged from a tree and set afire.

It took three more days to restore order. Vallandigham met with his compatriots. "See!" he exclaimed, waving a newspaper before them. "This is what we can do! One hundred twenty Yankees dead, eleven Nigras hanged and God knows how many other dead, over 2,000 injured and fifty buildings burned to the ground.

"Do you know what this is? This is the equivalent of a Confederate victory, and you have done it! This is just the beginning. There are plans for much more!"

෨ 11 ଔ

AUGUST 1863

HE LONE RIDER SEARCHING in the inky blackness paid little heed to the wretchedly hot, humid night, the kind of Maryland night in which a man could work up a sweat standing still. He briefly rubbed a soggy handkerchief across his face as he peered for a glimmer of light that would lead him to Surratt's Tavern and a glass of whiskey.

John Wilkes Booth was on a mission. He would meet a man at the tavern and deliver a package to him.

"There!" he exclaimed to no one. "I see the light. The tavern's near." He spurred his mare into a trot and within minutes reached the tiny village of Surrattsville.

He dismounted before the tavern. Banjo music and boisterous voices greeted Booth as he strode toward the porch entrance. Then a voice stopped him. "Mr. Booth, I'm Ben Stringfellow. I believe you have something for me."

A tall, slender man stepped out from the shadows. Booth reached for the packet on his saddlebag and handed it to the man.

"Quinine," he said, "not a lot, but all I could get. There'll be more later."

"It's much needed, Mr. Booth, and your deliveries of so many needed medical supplies are most appreciated."

"I wish I could do more, Lieutenant. I was at Harper's Ferry, you know. I was a member of the Richmond Grays. We oversaw the hanging of that madman, John Brown."

"You're in a better position to help the Confederacy than if you were fighting with a rifle. Your standing in society gives us avenues we would not otherwise have, this quinine, for instance."

48

"I performed before the devil just last night. He and his wife sat in their box at Ford's Theater. He wanted to see me later, but I slipped out early. What a glorious opportunity there is for a man to immortalize himself by killing Lincoln."

Stringfellow grimly nodded at Booth. "That's not in our plans just now. You may be of assistance in other endeavors that are planned."

"Sir, you're the greatest spy the Confederacy has. I have only an arm to give. My brains are worth twenty men, my money worth a hundred. I have free pass everywhere. My profession, my name is my passport," Booth boasted. "My knowledge of drugs is valuable, my beloved precious money is the means, one of the means, by which I serve the South. I'm at your service. Just tell me what you want."

"For now, continue to act as a courier," Stringfellow replied. "Bring drugs and other contraband. The blockade is tightening and we can't get the supplies we need without people like you."

"Through my schooling and my theatrical training I'm well-trained in shooting, riding and fencing."

"Mr. Booth, fencing is a lost and unnecessary art. Folks seem to do a lot of shooting nowadays without dueling with swords. But someday your knowledge of guns might come in handy. I'm leaving now," he nodded and then mounted a nearby horse. "Until next time."

In moments the Confederate spy disappeared into the protective blanket of night.

Booth glanced at his horse and then at the beckoning lights of the tavern. He strode to the door and walked in. The tavern was half full with men crowded around the bar. A few working girls stopped all activity and gaped as Booth walked in. He was the most handsome man they had ever seen.

Dressed in a black suit with knee-high boots, he moved gracefully with a strong physique, black wavy hair and glowing dark eyes. His face seemed slightly pale, but that enhanced his mystique.

"Mr. Lloyd," he addressed the barkeep, "a whiskey, if you please."

49

As the drink was poured, a pretty young girl approached. "You're John Wilkes Booth, ain't cha. The most famous actor in the United States."

Booth chuckled and with his handkerchief wiped some rouge from the girl's cheek. "I am he," he proclaimed, "although my brother Edwin might suggest his fame is greater. I do know something about makeup, however, and yours is a bit too thick."

The girl swooned at the attention of a man idolized by women across the North and the South. "It's late and such a dark night. What brings you out to Surratsville?"

"Nothing but business, my dear. But it's concluded."

"You don't intend to go back to Washington tonight, do you?"

"Are there rooms available in the tavern tonight? I won't share a room with any of them." He gestured to the men.

"Mr. Booth, I'm sure I can find you a room that's much less crowded."

Booth smiled knowingly and took the girl's hand in his.

❧ 12 ❧

SUMMER 1864, ST. PAUL, MINNESOTA

ESSE BUCHANEN TRUDGED SLOWLY UP the pathway to a stately house on Summit Avenue in St. Paul. His shoulders slumped and each step felt like his boots were filled with lead. All of his memories here were joyous. But they all contained thoughts of JoAnna, and now JoAnna was gone forever. There was no more joy in this house. He didn't want to see her father, not yet.

At the door Jesse paused and smoothed his blue uniform. He straightened his shoulders, ran his hand over his short blonde hair and finally rapped the iron door knocker.

The door opened slowly, as if objecting to the impending reunion. But once it opened, Stephen Miller, governor of Minnesota, stood in the doorway. Miller struggled to smile but the sadness in his eyes betrayed his feelings.

"Jesse, thank you for coming. I need to talk to you."

As Jesse entered the large house, his host gestured to the sitting room. Melancholy engulfed Jesse the instant he spotted the love seat.

"Sir, could we sit somewhere else?" The words tumbled out as Jesse fought back vivid memories.

"Certainly. I was thoughtless. That was a favorite place for you and JoAnna to sit together, wasn't it?"

"Yes, sir, it was."

Miller presented a contrast to Jesse. The governor was short, somewhat stocky and dark. Jesse, tall, slender and blonde. Both had fought against the Dakota Indians in Minnesota and Dakota Territory. Now Stephen Miller was the third governor of the new thirty-fourth state.

Miller led the way into a spacious living room, where each took a seat across a long wooden table.

"Jesse," the governor spoke softly, "I miss her, too."

"We shouldn't have let her go west. The Crow Creek Reservation was no place for her."

Miller searched for words of consolation. "You know as well as I do that JoAnna had a mind of her own and usually found a way to pursue what she wanted. Her determination helped her become the strong, independent woman she was. JoAnna loved being a nurse and saving lives of Indian people on that forlorn piece of ground. She felt needed and was doing what she wanted to do.

"But I have regrets, too," he admitted. "JoAnna would have been safe here."

Jesse contemplated that perspective for several moments. Then the realization took root that neither he nor JoAnna's father could have kept her confined in a safe, sterile environment. That would have been unbearably stifling and unfair to her.

"Well, smallpox could have struck her here as well," Jesse said. "There was illness at Fort Snelling among the Sioux before they were sent to the territory. She worked as a nurse at Crow Creek."

"God decides, Jesse."

But the emotional wrestling demons who were haunting the young man would not release their hold. "We were to be married." Jesse choked on the words.

"I know, but God had other plans." Miller hesitated. Perhaps redirecting their conversation at this point would help Jesse. "That leads me to another reason why I asked you here today. We have plans for you, too."

"What plans?"

"There's to be another expedition to the west. I want you to be part of it."

"I'd prefer to go east. I've already ready missed three years of the fighting there."

"That will come too, Jesse. But first, this. There's a bigger job for you. Sully and Sibley met with General Pope to plan the summer campaign. Sully is hell bent to track down every Sioux in the territory. Sibley's losing his stomach for it. He wants to concentrate on Minnesota and is very willing to let Sully have the western campaign to himself.

"Pope sees it differently. Sully will be sent on an all-out assault on the Indians west of the Missouri. But Sibley doesn't get to just stay in Minnesota. Pope wants a line of forts over the plains to protect miners and settlers traveling through. Sibley's to build a fort on the James River. He's also to send a brigade of Minnesota troops to join Sully. Colonel Thomas is to lead them, and I want you with him."

"Another summer in hell." Jesse sighed.

"I need someone I trust out there. Sully will be leading Minnesota boys. You'll be my eyes, ears and, if need be, my mouth on the expedition. By fall you should be back. Then I have a curious request from the office of the president himself. I think you might be interested."

"What does the president want, Governor?"

"You might know that a secret service has been established to protect the president. But it's new, flawed and already infiltrated with spies. They want an outsider, someone not known in Washington, to work outside of the secret service and provide protection to Lincoln.

"They particularly asked for someone from the west, from Minnesota. You possess the traits they're looking for: courage, dedication and resourcefulness. Plus, your legal training should be helpful. You'll report to one man only, Ward Lamon, one of President Lincoln's most trusted friends."

"If I'm needed and they fear for the president, why wait until fall?"

"Lincoln's up for re-election in November. They think they have a handle on things now. But afterward, assuming he wins, and that's by no means certain, other challenges will arise. Right now the focus of his enemies is to end Lincoln's presidency by beating him at the polls. If he wins, then we expect other attempts will be made to end his presidency by different means."

"You mean assassination."

"Yes, and it'll be your task to help stop it."

"Hold on, Governor. That's way more responsibility than I care to assume!"

Miller laughed. "Maybe I was being a little too melodramatic. But I hope you're interested. I told Lamon that I had a good prospect for him. Come September, no matter what's going on in the Dakotas, I want you back here."

"This is not what I had in mind. I expected to fight rebels in the East, not become some type of secret agent. But," Jesse reflected, "this would be an amazing assignment. Helping to save this one life might do more to save the Union than I could hope to do by helping to kill any number of rebels. I'll do it."

Miller rose and clapped Jesse on the back. "I know you'll make me proud." Then the governor's voice softened. "JoAnna would be proud, too. I'll see you in September."

∞ 13 ∞

MINNESOTA PRAIRIE

I N MAY OF 1864 ALFRED SULLY was poised to move up the Missouri River from Sioux City, Iowa. Sully's First Brigade was to rendezvous at Fort Sully on the Missouri with Colonel Minor Thomas and the Second Brigade, which had been ordered from Fort Ridgely, Minnesota.

General Henry Hastings Sibley accompanied the army from Fort Snelling to Fort Ridgely. At Ridgely the general held an officers' call. Jesse Buchanen, attached to Thomas, was among them.

The fort, situated on bluffs overlooking the Minnesota River, had been the site of a pivotal two-day battle with Dakota warriors in August of 1862. Outnumbered by four-to-one odds, the soldiers had held on and maintained their hold on the river valley.

Sibley assembled the officers in the large stone commissary building as he had done two years earlier. Lean and of medium height, with a dark mustache and retreating hairline, Sibley slapped dust from his tailored blue uniform and addressed the soldiers seated before him.

"Gentlemen, things are much different from the last time I held officers' call in this room. We put down an uprising of the Sioux and drove them from our state. We pursued the Indians over the Missouri River in Dakota Territory, executed or imprisoned war criminals and, through President Lincoln's signing of the Indian Removal Act, we have sent a couple thousand to be confined at the Crow Creek Reservation in the territory.

"So while much has been accomplished, more duties remain ahead for us. General Sully and I met a few months ago with General Pope to formulate our plans for the summer.

"General Sully has a threefold task: to travel into the Dakota Territory to subdue and punish the Sioux for the outrages of 1862 in Minnesota, to drive the Sioux from the overland routes to the gold fields of Idaho and Montana, and to establish a line of forts to keep settlers and immigrant trains from being harassed.

"I'm to build a fort on the James River in Dakota Territory and send Minnesota troops to join Sully at Fort Sully on the Missouri. To that end, Colonel Thomas," Sibley nodded at a solidly built, full-bearded officer, "will proceed up the Minnesota into the territory and then to the Missouri.

"The Eighth Regiment of the Minnesota Infantry, eight companies of the Second Cavalry, Brackett's Battalion, and Jones's Artillery Battery will form Thomas's Second Brigade and will join Sully's First Brigade."

From near the back of the room, Jesse called out a question for Sibley. "General, last summer you chased the Sioux over the Missouri. Then Sully finished them off when they re-crossed. Are they still a threat?"

"General Sully expressed the opinion that we were driving the Dakota people into poverty and that poverty would bring traditional enemies together. He claims we can expect the Sioux, Cheyenne, Blackfeet, Arapahos and others to join against us.

"But more directly, even though Sully killed hundreds and captured hundreds more at Whitestone Hill, thousands of Sioux are still on the loose. It's our charge to destroy them and see that they never threaten Minnesota again. Gentlemen, good luck to you. This should all be wrapped up by fall."

Jesse walked across the fort's parade ground to his bivouac area. As he approached his tent, Jesse spied two familiar figures perched on camp stools and sipping coffee. One was older, muscular and clean shaven. He wore a wide-brimmed black hat. The other was younger and slender with a bushy black beard. They were Solomon Foot and Jim Atkinson, scouts from the 1863 expedition.

A wide grin broke out across Jesse's tanned face. "Old man, Jim, you two are a sight for sore eyes! I'd hoped you'd join us."

"It took some convincin'. Ady and the little Foots wanted me to stay in Sauk Centre. But I said, 'One more time.'"

"It kinda gets in yer blood," Atkinson added. "One more scout for me, too."

Foot rose to warmly shake Jesse's hand. "How's Cates, our one-armed friend, doin'?"

"Last I heard, Nathan's fine. He's still teaching and working with the Sioux at Crow Creek."

"Emily still there too?" Atkinson wondered.

"And JoAnna." Jesse's voice was barely audible.

Foot placed a big hand on his shoulder. "It'll take time. It's not even a year. She was a fine young lady and deserves to be remembered."

"I know." Wanting to change subjects, Jesse asked, "Are you assigned to Thomas or Sibley?"

"Thomas," Foot answered. "Both of us. If it was Sibley, I'd've stayed put in Sauk Centre. If I'm doin' this, I wanna see some action, not build forts. How 'bout you?"

"Looks like it's together again. I've requested to be with the scouts. I assume you are as well."

"Yep, under Captain Stuift."

"We leave tomorrow," nodded Atkinson.

On June 6, 1864, nearly 2,000 Minnesotans under Colonel Minor Thomas moved up the Minnesota River from Fort Ridgely. It was hot, and a strong wind from the west blew dust into their faces. The scouts rode a mile ahead of the army.

Jesse, Foot and Atkinson looked back at the following train of troops.

"Jim, you didn't leave here with us last year. We had twice as many men with Sibley. The procession was near four miles long. It was quite a sight," Jesse recalled.

Atkinson tugged his beard. "Still looks impressive to me." He looked westward. "It all looks impressive. By God, this is beautiful country. Green prairie grass tall as a horse. Purple flowers blowin' in the breeze. The prairie looks like a big lake."

"This is Minnesota," Jesse rejoined, "you've been to Dakota. You know what we have to look forward to there."

"Brown grass, alkaline lakes, and a blast furnace fer heat. I know."

"Well," Solomon drawled, "let's enjoy good grass and water while we've got it."

June 9th found the Second Brigade camped on Wood Lake, scene of the final battle of the conflict in 1862. It was the site of Little Crow's last battle and final defeat in Minnesota.

The army hit the trail early in the morning, in the saddle by 5:00 a.m., but they often called a halt by mid-afternoon to allow their horses to rest and feed. The three scouts huddled together trying to heat coffee over a fire that was still in its infancy.

Solomon pointed to high ground alongside the lake. "See there, Jim, that's where Jesse and Nathan Cates saved Captain Welch from gettin' shot up worse than he was. They dragged him back to camp over here just as the battle was turning. Sibley finally woke up to what was happenin'. The battle started by accident. A few wagons with soldiers were headed up there to the abandoned agency to look for garden vegetables. They near rolled over Indians hiding in the ground to ambush us.

"That started the whole thing. The Third Minnesota rushed in to fight. Sibley tried to call 'em back, he didn't want a battle there. But the fight seem to have a mind of its own. When the general realized that the tide was turning our way, he sent in more troops and the battle was ours.

"I was shot up myself and couldn't fight that day. But Jesse and Nathan did and when they brought a wounded officer back, I met Jesse for the first time."

"What's that?" Jesse pointed at an approaching dust cloud.

Solomon peered intently into the distance. "Don't know, looks like it could be wagons, and it seems they're headed this way. We'll know for sure soon enough."

An hour later a wagon train rolled alongside the camp at Wood Lake. Colonel Thomas, his red hair and a full red beard disheveled after a hard day, watched as the wagons circled and camp was set up. Shortly, a few riders came from the wagon camp to the soldiers.

A tall, slender man slid off his horse and approached Thomas. The man wore several days' growth of graying beard stubble that covered pockmarked cheeks. He greeted the colonel. "Name's Thomas Holmes. We got some settlers and some miners on the way to Idaho gold country. Thought we'd tag along with you fellas."

"What!" Thomas exclaimed. "The hell you are! I'm not babysitting a slew of miners. This is a tough enough journey the way it is."

Holmes spat a stream of brown tobacco, then wiped the spittle from his face with the back of his hand. "Well, sir, I figgured that ya might say that. Lookey here." He reached into his pocket and removed a wrinkled brown envelope, and handed it to the officer.

Thomas took it and removed a letter. He read quickly, then shook his head. "This is crazy." Thomas turned to officers who had gathered nearby. "This fella has a letter from General Pope. The general ordered us to safely escort these people through the Dakota Territory. I don't understand . . ."

Thomas stared at the growing camp of wagons. "How many of you are there?"

"'Bout 250," Holmes answered.

"Wagons?"

"Around 150," said Holmes.

"And I've got over 2,000 men, along with mules and horses. I can't feed you."

"Don't worry none 'bout us, Colonel. We jest need ya around in case trouble comes up. You know, the kind that shoots arrows and such."

Exasperated, Thomas threw up his hands. "I guarantee nothing! I can't stop you from traveling with us, but stay out of my way! Now get back to your wagons. I don't want to see you unless you've got something urgent to tell me."

For the next month the Second Brigade and the civilian wagons rolled across the prairie, trying to cover twenty miles a day in sometimes stifling heat.

Grass and water were abundant through Minnesota and into the rolling hills in the couteau region of eastern Dakota. Occasional buffalo were sighted, and the scouts happily hunted them to enrich the soldiers' food supply.

Wood for campfires, however, became increasingly scarce, and buffalo chips comprised the main source of fuel for the expedition. Each day soldiers scoured the nearby prairie, collecting the dried manure to burn.

Signs of Indians were evident. Solomon came upon an abandoned Indian camp of twelve tipis. Farther down the trail he spied tracks of horses along with telltale grooves sliced into the earth by travois, the long poles that were pulled by ponies and held bundles of Indian belongings. But no actual Indians were sighted.

After the army settled into camp near the James River on June 21, Jesse, Solomon, and Jim were called to Colonel Thomas's tent. Their commander met them outside, mopping sweat from his forehead as they drew near.

"Another hot one," he complained, "too hot to meet inside my tent. This will be short, anyway." He handed Atkinson an envelope.

"Take this dispatch to General Sully. He should be on the Missouri near Fort Sully. If he's not there when you arrive, he will be soon. Wait. I just don't want to miss him like Sibley did. Let him know that we're close and that we should be there before the first week in July is up."

"We'll get it to him, sir," Jesse replied. "I don't think he'll be very happy about the wagon train."

"General Sully's not very fond of General Pope," Thomas agreed. "I'm afraid that this decision won't help their relationship. But this is the hand we've been dealt by our superior, and we're dealing with it as best we can. Have a good ride and don't go seeking trouble."

"We won't look for any," Solomon offered laconically, "but it might find us anyway."

Thomas smiled. "And I have no doubt that Solomon Foot, the Daniel Boone of the Kandiyohi Lakes, the only man to fight off an attack by Sioux and save a cabin full of people, will be up to the task."

Foot laughed, "It was more than just me. Besides, I have these two little babies to take care of." He gestured at Jim and Jesse. "That makes my job tougher."

"Mr. Foot, I'm sure that Jim and Jesse will fend for themselves. Good luck to you, and I'll see you the first part of July."

∞ 14 ∞

SUMMER 1864, WASHINGTON

HE PRESIDENT OF THE UNITED STATES stood peering through an Oval Office window at the greenery below. Beyond that space, on the street passing the White House, the steady cadence of marching feet reverberated steadily in the afternoon air. The long blue line of soldiers had become an all-too-familiar sight.

"Well, Lamon, another hot one. But it'll be hotter where they're going."

Ward Hill Lamon, Abraham Lincoln's bodyguard and U.S. Marshal for the District of Columbia, sat alertly in a nearby chair. He was a large, strong man with black hair and a bushy chin beard. "It'll all be over soon, Mr. President."

"Do you think so? And who will be president when it is? McClellan?"

"You will be re-elected."

"No, Hill, for some time I've been convinced that I shall not win re-election."

"Mr. President, the soldiers will vote. They'll favor you."

"No!" Lincoln said emphatically. "I've sent too many of them to their deaths. They won't vote for me."

"I wouldn't be so sure, Mr. President. Sherman is before Atlanta. His victory there will change things. The men appreciate your attention to them, visiting in the hospitals and even on battlefields after the fighting."

"Hill, Sherman's been fighting skirmishes and battles almost continuously around Atlanta since the beginning of May. Now it's July and he's no closer to taking it."

"It's just a matter of time."

"Time, for me, might run out in the next election."

"Sir, it might be sooner than that if you don't take better care of yourself. I've seen the bullet hole in your top hat. You can't go riding off alone at night. Remember, Washington's really a Southern town."

"If someone wants to kill me, they will. Nothing we can do will stop them. I won't hide in the President's House. The people expect to see me."

"But please, be careful. Right now there might be a lull in threats because of the approaching election, but take nothing for granted."

Lincoln chuckled. "That's because no one expects me to win the election. Why go to the trouble of killing me when I'll be gone soon enough and McClellan can make peace with the Confederacy?"

Lamon shook his head. "You'll win this election, and we do have plans for your safety. Come November, a young man will be brought in from Minnesota. He comes highly recommended."

"Where is he now?"

"Fighting Indians in the Dakota Territory."

"I wish those blasted Indian troubles were over!" Lincoln was emphatic. "More than 800 whites killed in Minnesota, the western part of the state depopulated, and now we're trying to hunt down the Sioux we've driven west into the Dakotas. I'd rather have Sully here fighting the rebels than have him chasing Indians all over the territory. Not that I think he's necessary, but why wait until November to bring that well-regarded young man here?"

Lamon answered directly. "First, they want him to help finish the Indian campaign. Secondly, like I said, there's a lull leading up to the election. Finally, when this man arrives, we want it to remain a secret. Very few will know of him or why he's here. The fact that he's from Minnesota will make him even more obscure. We wanted to bring someone in from the outside, and Minnesota is about as outside as you can get. Also, working beyond the purview of Pinkerton and the Secret Service will provide us with another option for your defense."

"And whom," Lincoln inquired, "do you want to defend me against?"

"The usual suspects: Southern sympathizers, rebel soldiers, political enemies. We've got a pretty long list."

Lincoln thoughtfully rubbed a bearded cheek. "Ward, what about the Catholics?"

"We haven't concentrated on them as a group. Some suspects we're watching might be Roman Catholics. But that's likely a coincidence."

"Back ten years or so I defended a priest, Father Charles Chiniquy. Remember?"

Lamon nodded. "The priest who was sued for slander. He left the church, didn't he? Became an Episcopal clergyman?"

"Yes, we won the case, but Chiniquy felt he had to leave the church. He warned that the church, particularly bishops and Jesuits, would seek retribution against me. At the time I brushed such thoughts aside. But now I find it ironic that the only governmental entity to recognize the Confederacy as an independent country is the Vatican."

"You want us to watch out for Catholics?"

"No, not necessarily. Like I said, God's plan will be done. We can't stop it."

"Mr. President, we can try, and we will."

Lincoln sighed. "I think your efforts will be necessary, however futile, only if I win re-election. And the way things are going around Atlanta, that prospect is growing more remote each day."

❧ 15 ❧

SUMMER 1864, RICHMOND

An unassuming two-story structure with a flaking brick exterior was tucked into the heart of the Confederate capitol of Richmond, Virginia. The nondescript appearance encouraged a lack of curiosity from passersby, and no signs outside indicated anything about the business conducted within.

But once in the building and up a set of stairs, visitors encountered a small sign on a door reading "Confederate States of America Office of Secret Service." This was the center of covert operations for the Confederacy.

A reception room led to another office door which, in turn, opened to a medium-sized office. The massiveness of the man seated at his desk made the room appear small.

The man was Albert Pike, head of the Secret Service of the Confederate States of America (CSA). His physical appearance was most politely described as "impressive." Pike stood six feet, four inches tall, and he weighed 350 pounds. His dark hair hung down to his shoulders. A thick black beard covered most of his face. Some jokingly called him a devil; others thought he might really be one.

Pike hailed from Boston. He had attended Harvard University and then moved west, where he experienced a kaleidoscope of adventures. Pike became a hunter and trapper, a teacher, a newspaperman, a lawyer, and a soldier in the Mexican-American War. Arkansas became his home. While at first he opposed secession, he did support slavery. He became active in local politics and represented Indian tribes as their lawyer.

As a member of the Confederate army, Pike rose in rank to brigadier general. His Indian connections led to a unique assignment. He was named Confederate envoy to the Native Americans and was charged with the important duty of starting Indian wars on the frontier. This had taken him to the southwest and to Minnesota. Covert actions were natural for Pike. He was a man of mystery in many ways.

Now, Pike dwarfed the man sitting across the desk from him. Technically the large man's superior, Judah Benjamin was the CSA's secretary of state and the overseer of the Secret Service. His short, stocky body was topped by a face that was round but not fat. Dark hair hung past the tops of his ears.

Judah Benjamin had been born to Jewish parents, a British subject in the Danish West Indies. As a boy he had immigrated to America and had grown up in the Carolinas. His sharp mind and intelligence led to early success in life. At fourteen he entered Yale Law School, then became a lawyer in New Orleans at the age of twenty-one. He began an association with London's House of Rothschild as a commercial lawyer.

Benjamin married a Creole beauty, bought a plantation with 140 slaves and prospered with sugar cane and his legal practice. However, it was in politics where he found his true calling. Eloquent and brilliant, he became a United States senator in 1853. Once the war started, Benjamin followed his state, Louisiana, out of the Union.

President Davis appointed him attorney general, then secretary of war and now secretary of state. Unknown to the public, Benjamin held other positions as well which were not official but were every bit as important, if not more.

Pike's chair creaked loudly as he leaned backward. Benjamin looked on in alarm, fearful that it would collapse, and sighed in relief when it didn't.

"You're hard on furniture, General Pike."

"Just a consequence of being a man of substance, Judah. I have greater fears than falling off a chair. I fear for our cause."

"Our prospects grow dimmer, I agree."

"Sherman moving on Atlanta, Grant besieging Petersburg. Lee himself said that once the Union army gets to Petersburg that it's just a matter of time before Richmond falls."

"We need more men," Benjamin asserted, "the North seems to have an endless supply, we don't. I told President Davis that we should offer freedom to every slave who wishes to fight in our ranks."

"Mr. Secretary, that's not going to happen anytime soon, even though Lee backs you. I fear that when your idea is finally endorsed, it will be too late anyway. We are running out of options."

"We have a big one left. McClellan could beat Lincoln. That would change everything."

Pike shrugged. "It's a hope worth clinging to. But we must explore other avenues and other allies. Lincoln is the linchpin in all of this. It was his election, the election of a black-loving Republican, that brought about this war. It is Lincoln who has made this a war against slavery and who holds the Union cause together."

"What do you suggest, General Pike?"

"We eliminate Lincoln if he wins re-election."

"You mean kill him?"

"I don't think that needs to be our first goal. In fact, it might be to our advantage to kidnap him and hold him for ransom."

Benjamin leaned forward, his dark eyes burning with keen interest. "And what do we get in ransom?"

"We get back all of our soldiers held in Union prisons. Then we wouldn't need your slave soldiers."

Benjamin whistled. "You are a big thinker, General."

"I try. It got us Stand Waite and the Cherokee fighting for us and an Indian war in Minnesota."

"And you, General Pike, have become infamous because of the atrocities committed by Indians fighting for our cause."

"It's all a part of what transpired. We can't always control what we start. But it did help achieve our ends. Thousands of troops were sent to

Minnesota to fight Indians. Those soldiers would have been fighting us otherwise."

"How do we kidnap the president of the United States?"

"That'll require a high degree of planning. We have some time before the election. But I dare think there are many entities that would like to see the end of Mr. Lincoln. We must combine forces."

"Who do you have in mind?"

"There are some obvious ones. The so-called Radical Republicans in the North will seek retribution on us if they win the war. They view Lincoln's Reconstruction plan as too mild. Northern cotton speculators are still buying some of our cotton, then making a killing selling it to Northern markets. Lincoln has approved of cotton trading permits, driving down the price."

Benjamin nodded. "Money forces oppose Lincoln. Remember that in Louisiana I represented the banking House of Rothschild. I know European bankers offered to finance the war. They'd give Lincoln loans at high rates. He found finances in other places, one by simply cranking out more greenbacks."

"And," Pike continued, "what would Lincoln's protectionist policies do? His mild Reconstruction would allow a resumption of agricultural policy toward the South. I know the Rothschilds are betting the other way, on high prices caused by a tough Reconstruction policy. Remember also that there are sizable numbers of immigrants, Irish in particular, and the so-called 'Copperheads,' those Yankees, including some in Congress who sympathize with our cause."

Benjamin chortled at the memories this comment recalled. "It didn't take much to get the New York riots going against Lincoln's draft last year. Hopefully our plans for disruption in the North will impact the election. Our agents in the North were most useful."

"They hung negroes from lamp posts. Most ingenious, Mr. Secretary."

"General, this is all academic if we win."

"Of course it is, but we need to hedge our bets, and we need to plan now, before the election."

"So how do you plan to bring together bankers, Radical Republicans, Copperheads and immigrants to bring down Lincoln?"

"First of all, it'll take more than that." Pike rose heavily from his chair, went over to the doorway and peered into the hall. Satisfied that no one was in sight, he closed the door and returned to his chair.

"You know we have more friends available." He lowered his voice. "You know that there are secrets known to but a chosen few. We shall use them as the catalyst."

Benjamin let the thought percolate before he replied. "What about the Catholics? The Jesuits hate Lincoln. He was involved in some lawsuit and dragged them through the mud. He defended a priest named Chiniquy, who was an enemy of the bishop. The only foreign power to recognize our independence is the Vatican. The pope's on our side."

"Yes, I've thought of them," Pike concurred. "There's no love lost between the Catholic hierarchy and Lincoln, but we don't need to have them officially condone our actions. Still, they're part of my plan. Someone must be to blame for what we do. If we play this right, the Catholics will do the job without even knowing they're being used as a tool by a higher authority. They'll be blamed, and our brothers will walk away unscathed."

"You have described a very interesting scenario. You plan to cause blame to fall on the Catholic church without the church being involved at all. How do we pull it off?"

Pike raised both arms and stretched them out at head level. He twisted his wrists, tickled the air with his fingers and smirked. "Like a puppet master pulling strings."

☙ 16 ❧

SUMMER 1864, DAKOTA TERRITORY

JESSE BUCHANEN, SOLOMON FOOT, and Jim Atkinson rode hard over rolling terrain. Alkaline water was plentiful, but finding drinkable water presented a challenge. Some days this quest forced a longer ride.

The three crossed rivers, streams and prairie through blistering heat, which westerly winds drove into the riders' faces like a blast furnace. On June 23 Solomon rode ahead of the others, peering at the ground. He pulled his horse to a stop. As Jim and Jesse approached, Solomon removed a grimy red handkerchief from his pocket and wiped his face. The sweat and dust left muddy streaks across his forehead.

Foot gestured at the ground. "Look, fresh signs of horses and travois. Sioux been through here, and not long ago."

"Maybe lookin' for them." Atkinson pointed to a small herd of antelope in the distance.

Solomon shielded his eyes as he squinted at the animals. "Well, I'm hungry. But more than that, I'm tired. And my horse is even more worn out than me. Either of you up to a hard ride after them beasts?"

Jesse and Jim exchanged a glance after looking at their horses' sweaty necks.

"Nope," Jesse replied, "I'm with you. We pull up here for the day. We've got food. Jerky and hardtack might not be anything quite like fresh antelope, but we'll get by."

"More important, our horses'll get by," Jim added. "They aren't up to a gallop, that's for sure."

"Rest now, get an early start tomorrow and keep an eye out for Sioux," Solomon suggested.

The men gathered buffalo chips for a small, smokeless fire. They collapsed nearby onto blankets on the hard earth.

"How far do ya suppose we made today?" Foot wondered.

Jim Atkinson considered this. "'Bout twenty miles, I figgur."

Jesse gazed through the gathering darkness into the fiery-pink strip where ground met sky. "We need to push it. Sully didn't wait for Sibley, and he sure won't wait for us if he thinks we're late."

Solomon pulled out a pocket watch. He paused a moment and studied the picture of his wife, Ady, on the inside of the cover. In a moment of weakness, he longed to stroke her dark curls again. The next instant he resolutely shoved all thoughts of his beloved from his mind and declared, "It's nine o'clock now, let's be in the saddle at 3:30."

A short time later the exhausted men tumbled into deep slumber. The black sky filled with twinkling stars and enveloped them like a huge canopy from horizon to horizon. Only the bright flickering flames of their dying fire betrayed their existence on the huge expanse of the prairie.

They kept up a brutal pace the next three days, traveling forty-five, then forty, and then fifty miles over generally flat land with occasional hills. Grass was poor for the horses; water was even worse. There was no wood but plenty of chips to be found for fires.

Then the trio spotted growing numbers of small bands of Indians. Tension grew along with their attentiveness.

"Wish I had a stick of wood for every Indian I've seen," Solomon noted, "we'd have a regular bonfire tonight."

Jesse watched a half-dozen Sioux ride away from a quarter-mile off. "They don't seem interested in bothering us, so I see no need to bother them. Besides, Sully must be getting close."

"Hope so," Atkinson said, "I didn't ride through this hellhole for nothin'."

Two days later they broke camp at 6:30 in the morning. With trepidation, Jesse regarded the severe blue, cloudless sky.

"Gonna be a hot one," he warned, "a real scorcher."

"We'll have to quit early, maybe by a stream. If we're real lucky, maybe there'll be some shade there," Solomon hoped.

Jim wasn't optimistic. "I'd say our chances of that are slim to none."

Four hours into their travels the scouts rode onto the crest of a small rise. A sluggish stream twisted below them. But it brought not one trace of joy. A cluster of twenty Sioux lodges hugged the banks of the stream.

"Not good, boys," Solomon mumbled, "not good at all. They see us and they're comin'."

"Let's ride," Jesse urged.

Solomon's experience on the frontier told him otherwise. "No, it'd show fear to them."

Jim's response was immediate. "Well, I'm not afraid to admit that I'm a mite anxious about them chargin' up here."

"Look," Solomon cautioned, "do you really think we can outrun them? Our horses've already been in the heat for four hours. They've got a stream. They'd run us down. We wouldn't have a chance. We don't have much chance here, either, of course, unless we play our cards right."

The men waited while the charging horsemen approached. The bare-chested Indians wore only breechclouts. They were ready to fight.

"Can you speak to them?" Jesse warily asked Solomon.

"I can get by. I've been around 'em enough."

In moments, amidst a thundering cloud of choking dust, a couple dozen Indian warriors formed a circle around the white men and reined in their horses. One rode out from the others and spoke Lakota in a loud voice.

"Blast!" Solomon told his comrades. "This fella speaks Lakota, I know Dakota. Not much different though. Has to do with how they use the letter 'N.' I'll get by."

The Indian dismounted and motioned for the white men to do likewise. After several minutes of conversation, the Indian smiled and extended his hand to shake with each of the three strangers.

Solomon turned to his friends. "Sully's near. These folks ran across his men yesterday. It scared the bejeebers outta the Sioux and they ran off. I told 'em we're friendly and have nothing to do with Sully. And so, gentlemen, we're invited to dinner."

Enormously relieved by the turn of events, the three delighted in being treated to the best meal they'd had since leaving Fort Ridgely. They relished the luxury of feasting on buffalo and resting until mid afternoon. Then they thanked and bid farewell to their gracious new friends, the friends they'd made by claiming they had nothing to do with Sully.

Then they rode west. Looking for Sully.

The following day they traveled sixty miles over poor country with rolling prairie and little water. They knew the Missouri River was close, for the Indian leader had told Solomon that they would be at the river after two days of hard riding.

A grisly sight shocked them when they rode onto one of the endless crests that awaited them.

"By God! What's this?" Jesse exclaimed.

Crowning the hillcrest were the heads of three Indian men, which had been lanced onto stakes and driven into the earth.

Solomon looked away in obvious disgust. "It wasn't Indians that did this. Those are sharpened wagon staves. Sully must be near."

Jim read the note tacked to one of the stakes.

"Seems that some Sioux killed a captain of engineers, probably Sully's. This warns the Indians that if they kill a white man, this is what'll happen to them."

The irony wasn't lost on Solomon. "They must be pretty optimistic that an Indian who can read English will happen by," he noted.

Jesse stared silently and then replied sadly, "There are some that can. Remember, JoAnna taught them at Crow Creek, not that far from here."

"Sorry, Jesse. I know it's still hard."

Late that afternoon the three scouts rode into Fort Sully on the Missouri River.

ഌ 17 ൠ

MISSOURI RIVER, DAKOTA TERRITORY

T HE SCOUTS FROM SIBLEY'S ARMY found Alfred Sully's brigade camped near the outlet of Swan Lake, not far from the Missouri River. Sully himself greeted the three men when they arrived on June 30.

He placed a sketch pad onto a small table before arising from a camp stool in front of his tent. The general had a trim physique and was of medium height. He wore a mustache and full, dark beard on his chin. His cheeks were clean shaven.

"My Minnesota scouts!" he exclaimed. "Good to see you, welcome to the Missouri! Seeing as you're here, I trust Thomas isn't far behind."

"He's less than a week away, General," Jesse answered. "He wanted to make sure that the mix-up of last summer wasn't repeated."

"My supply boats were slowed down by low water," Sully recalled, "and Sibley beat me to the river and then turned around and went home after a skirmish or two. That was unfortunate."

"It didn't stop you, though," Solomon said. "You just set off after the Sioux on your own and destroyed their village at Whitestone Hill. Quite a piece of generaling."

"I'm a soldier, trained since my youth, and I try to do it well. The drawings," he pointed to his sketch pad, "are just to pass time."

Solomon, who had been able to view a variety of artwork over the years, was visibly impressed by Sully's work. "Sure better than any drawing I've ever seen anybody do."

"My father was a landscape artist. It's in the genes," Sully explained. Then he turned the topic back to the business at hand. "I was glad to have

74

you three scout for me last summer and I welcome you back. Once Thomas gets here, we'll have over 4,000 men. Then we'll move north. That's where the Sioux are. Sitting Bull's leading them. I don't know much about him, but I do know that Inkpaduta is with him."

Jim Atkinson shook his head. "Seems like Inkpaduta is everywhere there's trouble, from Spirit Lake in Iowa to Big Mound last summer. He's a troublemaker and he never gets caught or the punishment he deserves."

"Well, maybe this time," Sully responded. "Our orders are to put an end to the Sioux in this part of the country. Sibley's got the easy part, build a couple of forts, send Thomas to me and then head back to St. Paul if he wants. I get to traipse all over the territory looking for Indians."

Solomon nodded at Sully. "No offense meant to General Sibley. He's an able man. But like you said, you were born to be a soldier, West Point trained. Sibley's a fur trader and a politician turned general. There's a reason why General Pope sent you to fight and Sibley to build a fort."

Sully laughed. "Maybe you're right. Truth be told, General Pope is not one of my great admirers either. But I do eagerly await Colonel Thomas and the rest of the Minnesota boys. We'll get the job done."

Jesse turned somber. Quietly he asked Sully, "Sir, since it will be a few days before Thomas arrives, do you suppose I could ride downriver to Fort Thompson? It would mean a lot to me."

Sully hesitated. Then realization flashed across his face. "Of course you can, Lieutenant. For a moment I forgot your misfortune. I know just how hard it is to lose your love. I lost my first wife when I was in the army, and we were both very young, like you."

Sully turned wistful with his memories. "I was garrisoned in California and she was the daughter of a Spanish Don. I was about ready to give up the army and live the life of an aristocratic rancher with her family. Then she died and everything changed."

The general abruptly pulled himself back into the present. "Yes, by all means, go to Fort Thompson. But hurry back, Lieutenant. When Thomas gets here, we march."

It was but a day's ride down the Missouri to Fort Thompson. Jesse was familiar not only with the trail but also with the tragic chain of events leading up to the establishment of Crow Creek Reservation, and he was all too familiar with the ensuing tragedy which would affect him for life.

Now, riding in solitude along the trail that would lead him to the fort and the reservation, Jesse yielded to a deep yearning. He would seek comfort from cherished memories, even though they would also bring him pain.

Fort Thompson had been constructed the previous summer to oversee the Crow Creek Reservation, the new home of the Minnesota Dakota.

Signed by President Abraham Lincoln, the Indian Removal Act had required that the Minnesota Santee be removed beyond the boundary of any state. It was one consequence of losing the conflict of 1862. Ironically, most of those removed from Minnesota had not fought in the war, and many had opposed Little Crow and aided the whites.

After being confined to miserable conditions in a refugee camp on the river below Fort Snelling through the fall and winter, these people were banned from Minnesota. During the spring of 1863, nearly 2,000 Indians had been shipped by steamboat and locomotive from Snelling and their ancestral home in Minnesota to an arid, alkaline wasteland on the Missouri River.

Many other Sioux had fled Minnesota with Little Crow and other leaders. It was these bands that Sully and Sibley had pursued the year before and were still seeking retribution from, even after Little Crow had returned to Minnesota in 1863 and had been shot and killed while picking berries.

Soldiers, missionaries, teachers, and government agents tried to make Crow Creek hospitable for the Indians. The reservation was supposed to support a farming enterprise. Heat, poor soil, and lack of water made that impossible.

Jesse's fiancee, JoAnna, and their friends Nathan and Emily Cates had gone to Crow Creek to teach and minister to the Indians' needs while Jesse rode through the Dakota Territory with Sibley. Before he rode off to fight, Jesse and JoAnna had exchanged what was meant to be just a temporary goodbye at Fort Thompson. Their dreams of sharing married life had promised a bright future.

Jesse had eagerly anticipated their reunion as he returned from that mission but instead was blindsided along the trail by the unexpected sight of JoAnna's grave, adorned with the yellow bandana he'd given her. He was heartsick to learn that she had taken sick and died while he was gone.

Now, he was on that very same trail. Jesse's heart still weighed heavy at the loss, but this time he was prepared to see JoAnna's grave. Taking the very same trail to the wooden stockade fort, just as he had the previous fall, he steeled himself for what was just ahead. He prayed for strength.

The trail brought him by the graveyard outside the fort. Many new graves were scattered throughout the field. It had been another hard winter.

In the midst of the graves was a small wooden cross with a tattered, faded yellow bandana tied to it. A bouquet of purple wildflowers rested on the mound of earth. It was the grave of JoAnna Miller, the cloth his farewell gift to her.

Jesse stepped down from his black gelding and stood silently at her grave. He had so much to tell her, so much he wanted to share, but all he had in front of him now was her grave. Still, he found a strange comfort in being at her final resting place, at being so close to where they'd shared their final times together.

He knew that he would never get over the heartache of losing JoAnna and of losing all that their future together could have brought them, a happy home with children. Perhaps the pain would ease over time, but it would always be there. Somehow he would learn to live with it.

He spoke in a whisper. "I'll never forgive myself, JoAnna. I never should have let you come west. We should have married like we'd planned. Damn this war. Damn all wars! We should be in St. Paul today. I'm so sorry!"

Jesse silently rested his hand on top of the wooden cross. Then he swung back into the saddle to cover the short distance to the fort. He rode very slowly, needing transition time to negotiate the emotional contrasts between visiting JoAnna's grave and visiting his good friends, the Cates.

Nathan Cates was with his wife, Emily, under a large outdoor canopy built of sapling trees. This was his classroom in the summer. He looked up from helping a child write alphabet letters on a slate and called to his wife.

"Look, Emily, it's Jesse! Johnny," he turned to a nearby young Indian man, "keep working with the children. We'll be right back."

Nathan waited for Emily and then strode across the compound with the erect bearing of the soldier he had been. His empty left sleeve, a souvenir of Shiloh, had changed his life.

But after losing that arm, he'd gained far more than he'd ever dreamed. Circumstances of the war had brought him to Minnesota to pose as a trader on the Sioux reservation. There he had met the pretty blonde new teacher at the Redwood Agency. After almost losing her to a Dakota band of miscreants, he had rescued her from them and eventually married her.

Emily rushed into the waiting arms of Jesse. "We were so hoping you'd be here, Jesse! We knew the army was on the move. It's so good to see you!"

Nathan warmly shook Jesse's hand. "We're glad to see you. It's been awhile! Oh, Sully came through a few days ago. Did you connect with him?"

"Yes. Two of your old friends, Jim Atkinson and Solomon Foot, and I were sent on ahead. Colonel Thomas will join us with the Second Brigade in a matter of days. Then we head out after the Sioux. How are things here?"

"Not enough food, bad water, some sickness. But we get by. The children and adults are learning. Reverend Williamson is happy that the number of converts is growing. Soon we expect more to be sent here from Davenport."

Jesse shook his head. "They shouldn't have been sent there in the first place. Sure, they were found guilty by the commission after the war. But I was part of the evidence gathering with Reverend Riggs.

"I know that much of what was used against them was flimsy. Many were just soldiers who fought against other soldiers in a war. At least, that's how they looked at it."

Nathan nodded. "And they wound up imprisoned at Davenport."

"But President Lincoln's freeing them," Emily said.

"He's trying to," Jesse responded, "but for some of them it takes more than one request even from the president to get them free and sent here."

"But they were all sentenced to die," Emily countered, "the president commuted the death sentences of 265."

"Yes, he did Emily," said Nathan, "but he did order the hanging of thirty-eight, and for that he has earned the eternal enmity of these people."

Jesse stroked back his blonde hair and reminded them, "I was there and some of them deserved to die. Others did not. Mistakes were made. Think of poor Chaska. He saved the lives of Sarah Wakefield and her family. Lincoln expressly ordered that his sentence be commuted. But they hanged him anyway."

Nathan looked around the desolate compound as a moment of silence wrapped around them.

"Emily," Jesse's voice softened, "I saw the flowers on JoAnna's grave. Thank you."

"We miss her too, Jesse."

"How long can you stay?" Nathan asked.

"Just overnight. I've gotta be back soon. We pull out when the Minnesota troops arrive."

"I'll show you around the school. Johnny is here, you remember him. Traveling Star is his Dakota name."

"Of course, he rescued Emily from White Dog."

"The first time I needed rescuing," Emily rejoined. "The next time, Nathan was there."

"And White Dog will never bother anyone again," Nathan concluded.

Jesse greeted Johnny and watched while Nathan and Emily worked with their students. After a bit Johnny pulled Jesse aside. Johnny shifted uncomfortably on his feet as he summoned the courage to bring up a difficult topic.

"Lieutenant, I have some questions. I wish to talk with you."

The two moved apart from the others.

"Well, Johnny, watcha got?" Jesse asked.

"Emily and Nathan are my friends, but I cannot talk to them about this. It has bothered me and been on my heart for a long time. It is about things that I heard and saw but that I do not understand."

"Like what?"

"I saw a soldier wearing a gray uniform in Little Crow's camp just before the killing started in Minnesota. I saw him there again after all the killing."

"A gray uniform? Was he a Confederate soldier?"

"He was an officer. He was a big man with a big beard. I was told that he came here to start the killing."

"How? Why?"

"I was told that if war happened here, then Minnesota soldiers and other bluecoats from out east would be sent here to fight. There would be fewer soldiers to fight the gray coats. I heard that if this worked in Minnesota, there would be more wars started on the frontier. This is what I was told."

"Interesting. Possible, I guess. Anybody ever seen this big fellow?"

"Not since the first days of the fighting. But there is something else, something that I can talk about to no one, just you."

"What's that?"

Johnny scuffed his feet and looked from side to side to ensure no one was within hearing range. "They say that Nathan had a part. That Nathan was a Confederate officer and the big man was his chief."

"Johnny," Jesse replied in a firm voice, "there are many rumors. Are you sure you saw a Confederate officer?"

"Yes, I am sure. I even heard someone say his name. It was Pike."

"When Nathan came here he was different and he was new to Minnesota. That causes talk. But Johnny, I find it hard to believe that he could have been involved in starting the war. Someone with that goal wouldn't fight with the Union army and defend Fort Ridgely. He wouldn't volunteer for a dangerous rescue mission and bring back three captive women at great peril to his life. He rode with us and Sully last summer. Nathan was at Whitestone Hill. He was a brave soldier even though he didn't wear a uniform. And why would he come to this God forsaken spot to help Indians with the big war still going on in the East? No, Johnny, Nathan as a Confederate agent makes no sense. Who have you told?"

"I speak to no one. But it is not a secret among my people. Still, they do not talk of it. No one cares what side Nathan was on. All whites are the same to us. We do know that he was good and he treated us fairly. We see that he cares for Indian people. One thing, most of these people were not in Little Crow's village when the war was fought. There is no one who can prove that the stories about Nathan are true."

"Let them remain rumors, Johnny. Rumors die in time, and we don't want them coming down on Nathan's head. Let him do good here. Thank you for talking to me about this, Johnny. You are a good man."

Jesse joined Nathan and Emily for supper. They talked late into the night about war, Indians, Crow Creek, what might have been and what was. The subject of Nathan's past was not brought up by Jesse, nor was it believed.

Jesse did ask a question however. "Nathan, I've heard the name Pike mentioned. Who is he?"

Nathan felt an internal jolt like someone had kicked him from within. Hoping that Jesse hadn't noticed his surprise, he regained his composure and answered, "I've heard of him, if it's Albert Pike you're speaking of. He is a Confederate general and, I'm told, Director of Covert Operations for the Confederacy. Why?"

"Nothing. I hear rumors," Jesse shrugged. "Watch out for rumors and keep caring for these people. They need you. Take care of yourself."

Early the next morning Jesse bid farewell and rode back upriver to Fort Sully.

As their friend left through the gate, Emily turned to Nathan. "It was wonderful to see Jesse again. Losing JoAnna was so hard for him. And for us. Nathan," she raised her bright blue eyes to look into his, "that comment about rumors. Could he know something? Could he know Jeff Davis sent you here to start a war and then you changed sides and fought against them? Could Jesse know?"

"I don't know," Nathan replied. "If it concerns him, we'll know soon enough."

"He mentioned that awful man, Pike."

"Pike's back in Richmond last I heard. I'm sure he'll make certain I'm never welcomed back in Virginia. I'm sure he has plans. I just don't know what they are."

$\wp 18 \backsim$

FORT SULLY

ESSE'S THOUGHTS WEIGHED HEAVILY on his mind as he rode slowly along the Missouri. JoAnna, the great war to the east, the war against the Dakota two years before, and the pursuit of Minnesota warriors now in Dakota all intertwined in his mind.

Now he had more to think about. His assignment to go to Washington after the Sully Expedition to serve as an agent for the president made him excited, yet uneasy. The stories about Nathan and Albert Pike troubled and confused him. Would his path lead him to Pike?

First matters first, he resolved. He had a date with Sully and Thomas to hunt down hostile refugees from Minnesota who were now in Dakota Territory. He wished that was how it would be. But Jesse knew that General Sully wouldn't be particular about fighting Indians who had never been to Minnesota. Most of the 300 killed at Whitestone Hill the previous summer were not Santee and had lived on the Missouri. The general fought first and asked later. The village had been destroyed, but many had escaped to join Sitting Bull.

Jesse rode into the soldiers' camp by Fort Sully on July 3. Jim and Solomon greeted him and inquired about Nathan, Emily, the missionaries and the conditions at Crow Creek. They avoided all mention of JoAnna and of Jesse's visit to her grave.

Late in the afternoon a long cloud of dust was sighted stretching to the east. Solomon pointed to it and called to Jim and Jesse.

"Looks like the regiment's here, boys. No more lollygaggin'. Now we get back to work."

A couple of hours later, Thomas and his men marched to the gates of Fort Sully. General Sully, disregarding any protocol, did not wait for the colonel to report to him. The general and his staff stood outside the fort and greeted the Minnesota regiments as they approached.

Thomas dismounted a sweaty horse and slapped dust from his blue uniform with his gloves. "Reporting for duty, sir," he announced.

"You are most welcome here. I hope you're ready. Rest up tonight and we'll march out tomorrow. I don't want to waste any more time."

"General, I've got 2,000 men with me. What's our force now?"

"Colonel Thomas, we will move on the Sioux with 4,000 cavalry, 800 mounted infantry, twelve pieces of artillery, six- and twelve-pounders, 300 wagon teams, and a herd of 300 beef steers.

"Fifteen steamboats carried our supplies up the Missouri River to here. But we'll be cut off from them once we head east away from the river."

"This time you have a seasoned army, General. My boys are ready to fight. Many fought in the war in Minnesota."

"That's good, Colonel Thomas, but they are from units broken up into small detachments for frontier duty. Plus, many of your infantry are mounted for the first time. And, in its wisdom, our government decided to send us small Canadian ponies and not our regular army horses."

"I know, General," Thomas agreed. "They're faster and more nimble, but they're also smaller and not as strong."

"No matter, our superiors say they can carry big men with all their equipment and accoutrements. They'd better. But overall, it's all good. We can get the job done, Colonel."

"What's that?" Sully exclaimed as he pointed at the civilian wagon train that was gathering nearby.

"I was coming to that, General. Those are mostly miners heading for the Montana gold fields. They're going with us to the Yellowstone."

Sully's face turned crimson with rage. "By thunder they are!" he exploded. "I won't be encumbered by gold miners and their families. We're here to fight Indians. Immigrants who can't fight have no place on a combat mission! Tell them to turn back or go on alone. I won't nursemaid them!"

"General, it's not that easy. Here." He handed Sully a letter. "It's from General Pope. He orders us to see these folks safely to the Yellowstone. Without this, I would have left them in Minnesota."

Sully's face continued turning various shades of red as he looked over Pope's missive. Then he folded it, stuffed it into a pocket and ruefully commented, "Pope never will forget that I saved his ass at Bull Run. He knew this would gall me more than anything. How many are there?"

"Last count I had was 123 wagons and 250 people."

"Once they get settled, bring their leader to my office in the fort. I want to speak with him."

"Yes, sir."

A couple of hours later, Tom Holmes from the civilian wagon train was escorted by Colonel Thomas to see Sully. In the gathering twilight the general sat before a flickering campfire, his sketchbook in his hand. He rose and strode to meet the civilian.

"This is Tom Holmes, General Sully. Leader of the civilian miners."

"Well, Holmes, it shouldn't be news to you that I'm not pleased about this. We're going to march into territory where no white man has ever been. It is extremely dangerous and difficult. We might not survive. And now I've been ordered," he reached into his pocket and waved the crumbled up paper containing Pope's request, "to provide you with safe passage. To hell with orders. I should leave you here anyway. You can just take the steamboats back downriver."

"Now, Gen'rl," Holmes replied, "you know you can't do that. Orders is orders."

"You are no one to talk to me about orders, Mr. Holmes. In my opinion most of your people are heading west to avoid military service."

"Gen'rl, don't call me 'mister.' I'm Major Holmes, duly elected by the folks in my wagon train."

With disgust Sully waved a hand at Holmes. "You'll be nothing but trouble. You'll slow us down, have trouble with your wagons that you'll want help with, you'll try to tell me how to run things. You bring merchants, lawyers, farmers, and n'er-do-wells, but no fighters. Follow if you must, but stay out of my way. Now get back where you came from."

"I'm sorry, Gen'rl, that yer so cantankerous 'bout this. Gen'rl Pope seemed fine."

"General Pope is in Milwaukee. The view is different there. Now do what I say and keep to yourselves."

ON JULY 4TH SULLY'S COLUMN moved out. Immediately, though, a problem presented itself.

One of his captains rode to Sully, ready to burst with agitation.

"General, you won't believe this!" he cried. "Your supply officer didn't scnd any saddle blankets for the mules, we hadda switch to gunny sacks!"

"Do you have enough belt webbing to fasten the sacks to the mules?" Sully asked.

"That's a problem too, sir, because no webbing was sent either. All we have is pieces of hard leather about three inches wide."

Sully sighed and looked heavenward. "Then use it. We need to keep going."

The leather straps were cinched to the mules and supplies were strapped onto their backs. But the leather was not nearly as comfortable as the webbing, and gunny sacks didn't provide the protection of a thick blanket. The mules went wild. They bucked, twisted and rolled, strewing packs and supplies across the prairie.

As a result Sully had another decision to make. He informed Colonel Thomas, "We'll switch to wagons, four mules to a wagon."

"We can't haul as much that way, General."

"No we can't, therefore we'll leave behind tents and only take with us the barest of essentials—mainly food and ammunition. Captain," he turned to an aide, "see to it."

Within a week they had marched up the Missouri and established Fort Rice at the mouth of the Cannonball River. Sully left 300 men behind to finish building and man the fort. He would use it as a supply base. The expedition turned north. At periodic intervals Sully left behind smaller detachments to build smaller forts to serve as a supply line for their return.

Jim, Jesse, and Solomon rode about a mile in front of the column with the other scouts. Yellow bandanas were pulled up to cover their noses and mouths from the clouds of dust that rose up from the parched prairie with the passage of so many hooves and wheels and feet. Their main task was to find suitable camping spots and water. Neither was easy to locate.

"I thought last summer was bad," Solomon complained. "This makes it seem like a picnic."

"Find water, they say," Jim agreed bitterly. "What we do find is full of alkali and not fit to drink."

"We found a nice eight-inch-deep water hole yesterday. Maybe we'll find another today," Jesse ventured.

"Lotta good the water hole did us," Solomon said. "Even after Sully posted guards around it for the night, the animals stampeded into it, and by morning it wasn't fit to drink."

Jim reminded them that not all was bad. "At least we'd filled our canteens first. And we've been finding some buffalo and some antelope ever' now and then. That helps."

"Maybe," Jesse concluded, "but I'd give all the gold in the Yellowstone for a glass of lemonade right now."

Solomon wiped the muddy sweat from his forehead. "We all would, Jesse, and I'd love to be swimming in the Kandiyohi Lakes right now, too. But we're here, in a place all burned up and scorched."

"Solomon, do you ever wish you were back East fighting the rebs?" Jesse wondered.

"Once, maybe," Foot answered, "but I've had about enough fighting the last few years."

"What about you, Jesse?" Jim asked.

"I think I'll be going east when this is over."

"What regiment, ya think?"

"I don't know, Jim." Jesse hesitated. "They might have something different for me. Do you think President Lincoln could be in danger?"

"Prob'ly," Solomon replied. "Lotsa people blame him for the war and all the misery it caused. I'm sure there are folks who'd like to put a bullet in him. Why do you ask?"

"Just thinking. I'm just thinking."

❧ 19 ❧

JULY 1864, BOSTON, MASSACHUSETTS

HREE MEN FROM CANADA REGISTERED at the Parker House Hotel in Boston on July 26, 1864, using aliases to conceal their true identities. Their real names were George Sanders, Clement Clay, and Jacob Thompson. Thompson and Clay, officially known as commissioners, headed Confederate clandestine operations in Canada.

Another name appearing in the register that day was that of J. Wilkes Booth.

The four met in a small upstairs room. Two sat on chairs and two on the single bed.

Sanders began. "Mr. Booth, we welcome you to our cause. After your induction into the Knights of the Golden Circle and your exploits as a courier, we decided you may be uniquely suited for a special assignment."

"Mr. Sanders, weren't you the organizer of a peace conference at Niagara Falls last month?" Booth wanted to know. "The one the Confederacy attended, but no one from the Union?"

"George was being too cute by half," Clay answered. "It was a political move."

Sanders continued, "I knew the Yankees wouldn't come. That would show Lincoln as a warmonger right before the election. Horace Greeley of the *New York Tribune* fell for it, though. He even showed up."

"Unfortunately," Thompson added, "George was working at cross purposes with our efforts in Canada. Our objective was to create fear and instability in the North. We wanted to force Union troops out of the South by having guerilla raids on northern cities and prisoner of war camps, by sabotaging railroads, disrupting shipping and creating a general terror throughout the union. The draft riots in New York were one result."

"People were confused," Clay continued. "Did the Confederacy want peace or war?"

"It worked," Sanders claimed defensively, "Yankees blamed Lincoln for the failure of the conference. Greeley criticized him in an editorial, and his popularity is at a low point."

Thompson snorted. "Short term, maybe. But our strategy must be used in the long haul. Even now we have yellow-fever-contaminated clothing being sent into Union territory in trunks from Canada."

"Can people catch yellow fever from clothing?" Booth wondered.

"Our Dr. Blackmun says so," Clay responded.

Booth paused in a dramatic pose before asking, "Why do you need me?"

Thompson answered. "You're a famous man. You have access to all sorts of places and venues that others don't. You're trusted and admired."

"And you're devoted to our 'cause,'" Clay interjected.

"So?" Booth murmured.

Sanders continued. "Something bold must be done. I'm in favor of killing Lincoln and having it done with. In the Dahlgren raid last March, we found orders on him to kill President Davis and other government officials. Thank God, we killed the Yankee bastard. But I say tit for tat. Kill Lincoln. Others have a milder plan, but still potentially quite effective. They want to kidnap the president."

"What would that accomplish?" Booth inquired.

"The Confederacy is in sad shape. Our armies are greatly depleted. Many are held in Union prison camps," Thompson explained. "We don't have the immigrant hordes to draw from that Yankees do. We propose to kidnap Lincoln and ransom him for our imprisoned soldiers."

"Let me ask the obvious: how, when and where?"

"Mr. Booth," Thompson said, "the 'when' is within the next six months. The 'where' seems to be Washington City. Lincoln is careless about his personal well being. The 'how' is open to discussion and planning. If you choose to take this on, you would work with our contacts in Washington."

"You would also select your own team," Clay added.

Sanders threw in an enticement. "It would make you more famous than anything you could ever do on a stage."

But Booth was not convinced. "This is not without risk and it could be costly. Is there funding for this?"

Thompson was direct. "Mr. Booth, there's five million dollars ready if you need it."

That opened his eyes. "I thought the Confederacy was short of funds."

"There are people and organizations with great wealth who don't believe that a victory by the North or a continued Lincoln administration is in the best interests of a world economy and their particular interests." Thompson considered a moment and then continued, "Our Canadian efforts are going well. President Davis sent Thomas Hines to aid us further. He is to take charge of escaped Confederate prisoners from Yankee camps over the border and to carry out appropriate enterprises of war against our enemies. There will be raids into Union territory from the north. Davis wants it done.

"On his way here, Hines was to confer with leading persons in the north who are friendly to us, or who may be advocates for peace. Knights of the Golden Circle are among them."

"John Wilkes Booth," Sanders intoned, "you are a member of a great brotherhood. The Knights were spawned by Masonic rites. There are great forces at work here, forces beyond all of us that seek a goal greater than any man or nation or groups of nations. You have been called to a great service."

"Gentlemen," Booth said solemnly, "I will answer the call."

ɞ 20 ଔ

JULY 1864, DAKOTA TERRITORY

HE EXPEDITION CONTINUED to make good progress despite miserable conditions, averaging twenty miles a day through rough country. Breaking camp at 3:00 or 4:00 each morning and camping in early afternoon to escape the worst of the heat, Sully pushed the men on.

On July 24th they reached the Heart River in the northwestern part of Dakota Territory. General Sully called for an officers' meeting on the banks of the sluggish, meandering stream. He was dressed in his customary campaign attire of brown corduroy pants, white shirt, and a slouched white hat.

"Gentlemen," he began, "my Nebraska scouts have brought word that the Sioux are close, less than 100 miles away. We'll lay over in camp tomorrow and get ready for a fight. Take seven days' rations on the pack mules. We'll leave the rest of our supplies and retrieve them later."

He turned to one of his men. "Sergeant Jones, we weren't able to use artillery to its maximum effect at Whitestone Hill. I expect your battery to play a significant role in the upcoming fight. Be ready."

"We will be, sir," answered the full-bearded, burly veteran of Fort Ridgely, the only regular army soldier who had fought there and whose cannons had saved the day.

Captain Brackett wondered, "What about the immigrant train?"

Sully responded crisply. "We leave them behind, with 300 men. That's all I can afford. We've already left nearly half my army scattered in outposts from here to Fort Sully. I've got only about 2,000 left for battle. We could be facing five to six thousand Sioux according to our scouts' report."

"Major Holmes won't like it," Colonel Thomas advised.

"He shouldn't be here anyway. He'll have to like it. He has no choice."

"We move out on the 26th," Sully continued. "If we do this right we'll put an end to the Sioux as a fighting force in this part of the territory."

The army went into camp on the banks of Heart River. Writing at a camp stool in his tent, General Sully heard his sentry announce, "Gen'rl, sir, Major Holmes from the wagon train, he wants ta see ya."

Sully stepped through the tent flap into the dimming sunlight of early evening. Holmes was clearly agitated.

"All right, Sully, what in God's name do ya think yer doin'?" he blustered, paused and continued without waiting for a response. "Yer leavin' us almost defenseless whilst you go traipsin' off. There be thousands of reds out there. What if you miss 'em and they find us?"

"Major," Sully responded, "I told you before we started that this was a military operation and that you shouldn't come with us. You've developed a sense of security because thousands of soldiers have been near.

"The 300 men I'm leaving behind should be more than enough to protect you. I can't spare any more. I have a battle to win. That's why I was sent west."

"You could be givin' us a death sentence. Yer leavin' us ta die."

"I think not," Sully dismissed. "You'll be here when we get back. If it makes you feel any better, prepare some defenses. If you didn't know what you were getting into, you certainly should have."

Sully stood and called out, "Corporal, please escort this man back to his wagons."

"I'll see Pope hears about this," Holmes warned.

"You do that," Sully countered, "it'll make no difference to anything."

The next day Sully watched in disgust as the immigrants dug rifle pits and prepared to shoot their horses so they could hide behind the carcasses if Indians attacked.

Come morning the expedition moved out. Sully called back to his men, "We have Indians to find. Forward!"

The three Minnesota scouts were joined by a dozen more, including six friendly Indian scouts as they rode ahead of the column.

The scouts' captain cautioned his men, "Indians are up ahead, we want to find 'em 'fore they find us. Keep yer eyes peeled for yerself and yer friends. We'll split up and head in different directions. Meet back here tonight to report."

"What about the Indians the Nebraska scouts spotted yesterday?"

"That was just a couple dozen. When Brackett's men moved on 'em, they disappeared, not to be found. Maybe we'll find 'em. They're out there. We know that."

Jim, Jesse, and Solomon formed one unit of scouts and continued north.

"I don't like this," Jim said warily. "All these hills . . . they could hit us anytime."

Solomon laughed. "Come on now, Representative Atkinson, these fellas can't be much more of a threat than those Democrats in the state legislature."

"Two years of that was enough for me, but I didn't have to worry about keeping my hair there." He chuckled in spite of himself. "Come to think of it, with your thinning hair, Solomon, you don't have to worry about it here."

Jesse joined in the laughter.

Solomon shrugged. "Fine, when they come after you two with your fine heads of hair, I'll just be grinning. They'll leave me alone."

"Look up ahead," Jesse pointed, "what's that at the base of the mountain?"

In the distance the ground rose sharply forming a low mountain range. Solomon peered intently.

"It's a village," he declared. "We've found 'em, dagnabit! That's just what we're lookin' for!"

The three men sat silently astride their horses studying their discovery.

"How many?" Jim asked.

Solomon contemplated. "Hmm. It's pretty big. Sully talked about five to six thousand, and it's all of that."

Jesse wanted a better view. "Let's get a little closer."

But a mutual surprise lay just over the next rise. A young Indian man who had killed a buffalo was butchering the enormous animal on the prairie. His pony was tethered some distance away along the bank of a creek. Startled from his task, the Indian spied the horsemen and bolted for his steed.

Jesse spurred his horse and galloped toward the fleeing Indian. He quickly made up ground and, just as they neared the creek, came alongside the Indian. The soldier leaned over and whacked him with his rifle butt, sending the Indian tumbling off his pony. Jesse leaped off his mount to the ground.

In the next instant the pursued became the aggressor. The Indian brandished his bloody butcher knife and charged straight at Jesse.

The young lieutenant sidestepped his attacker, who appeared to be little more than a boy. He grabbed and twisted the youth's wrist, causing the knife to drop. A solid punch to the mouth sent the Indian sprawling to the ground.

Jesse pounced on him, drew his pistol and held it to his head. "Settle down or I'll shoot!" he cried. "Solomon, tell him."

"I hear you." The Indian spat out hate-filled words.

Solomon and Jim grabbed their captive by the arms and pulled him roughly to his feet.

Jesse leveled his pistol at the Indian and demanded, "Are you Santee?"

"I am Yankton."

"Who is there?" Jesse pointed at the mountain.

"Many bands, Santee, Teton, Hunkpapa, Blackfeet, Minneconjous and Yankton. More than ever have before came together to fight. More than the trees at Pa Sapa, the Black Hills."

"You're awful free with yer information," Solomon noted.

"It is because we know who you are and where you are. Sully is coming. He will pay for Whitestone Hill. We will kill you."

"Big talk for someone not much more than a boy," Solomon replied.

Jesse wanted to know more. "Are there many Minnesota Santee here?"

"Some, not as many as other bands."

"Who leads you?"

"Sitting Bull of the Hunkpapa. Inkpaduta is here as well."

"Just once I'd like to get my hands around that bastard's neck!" Solomon exclaimed. "I came so close at Whitestone."

"He is too smart for you," the boy retorted.

"What is this place?" Jesse kept throwing out questions.

"Tah-kah-ha-kuty, some call it Killdeer. It is where you will die."

"What we gonna do with him?" Jim wanted to know.

"Take him with us, I guess," Jesse figured.

Solomon released the young man and reached down to pick up his knife. The Indian, sensing that Jim had relaxed his grip just a little, wrenched free and in an instant leaped onto his pony from behind. The animal bounded ahead into a gallop. Jim raised his pistol to shoot.

Jesse reacted immediately. "Let him go!"

"He'll let 'em know we're here."

"If you shoot, they'll know we're here, too. Either way it makes no difference. They've been watching our army. There's no surprise. No sense killing a boy. Sully will be here soon enough, and the battle both sides seem to want will finally happen. Let's get back to the other scouts and Sully."

The scouts traveled back south to reunite with Sully's advancing army and met them camped on the Knife River. Jesse delivered his report to the general.

Sully's eyes gleamed with excitement. "It's on for tomorrow, then. Colonel Thomas, we'll move out at 3:00 in the morning. I want to be able to rest the men before we fight."

EARLY THE NEXT MORNING the army moved out as scheduled with the scouts out front. A faint pink glow in the eastern sky signaled the coming dawn and another day of blistering heat. Pushing north were 2,200 cavalry and artillery.

The scout detachment paused on high ground in the brightening day and waited for sight of the column.

"Here they come!" Jesse cried.

"Look at that," Solomon announced, "I thought the general would be ready for bear."

At the front of the column rode Sully on a prancing iron-gray stallion, his war horse. He was dressed in a clean blue uniform with buttons gleaming in the sunlight.

"Battle dress," Jim Atkinson noted, "no white shirt or corduroys today."

"The general's ready, I hope the men are," Jesse noted.

Solomon squinted into the sun. "We'll know soon enough."

ᴔ 21 ᴕ

KILLDEER MOUNTAIN

T 9:00 A.M. SULLY CALLED A HALT to the march. The men rested while scouts ventured ahead. An hour later Solomon reported to the general.

"The Sioux are still there in front of Killdeer, massed and ready for us. I've never seen so many Indians in one place in my life. There must be 6,000 warriors."

"Thank you, Mr. Foot. Men," he called to his officers, "it's time to head to Killdeer Mountain. Solomon here tells me that the Sioux are waiting for us. I don't want to keep them waiting any longer."

By 11:00 a.m. Sully's force was within a couple of miles of the low mountain. As the troops were positioned for battle, Jim Atkinson pointed onto the prairie between them and the precipice.

"Look, a party of Indians're comin' this way. They wanna talk!"

"Jesse," Solomon called, "ya better tell Sully."

A half-dozen Indians rode slowly on spotted ponies toward the soldiers. They wore eagle-feather headdresses, and their faces and nearly naked bodies were smeared with war paint. About midway from the mountain they halted.

Sully mounted his stallion and brought four officers and Solomon Foot with him.

"Dust yourself off, men. Sit straight in your saddle and look sharp. We want to make an impression."

The Sioux remained mounted as the soldiers approached. When Sully and his men reined in before them, they were met by insolent stares. Foot, brought along to interpret, offered a greeting from Sully. Then he asked their names.

"General," Solomon relayed, "there are only two names here that mean anything today. The fella with the brown hair, lighter than the others, is Sitting Bull. You might know the older one, he's Inkpaduta."

Solomon spoke to the Minnesota Indian and then conveyed to Sully, "I just told him that I missed talking to him at Whitestone Hill. He ran off without even saying hello."

"Tell Sitting Bull that I want Inkpaduta and the Minnesota Santee, and I want him to take his people and go west out of the territory."

Solomon translated the message to the Sioux, waited for their answer and then passed it on to Sully.

"Well, General, I'm afraid they're not gonna take ya up on yer offer. Sitting Bull here wants you to pack up and go home. He has no intention of giving up this part of the country."

"What did Inkpaduta say?"

Solomon hesitated. "He's a little more direct. He asked why we came here to die. He said of you, 'If he has no ears, we will give him ears. If he has ears, we will cut them off.' Not real neighborly."

"Give them one more chance, Solomon. Tell Inkpaduta he'll be treated fairly."

Solomon repeated Sully's comment. Inkpaduta responded in a derisive tone. Then, without waiting for Sully's reply, the Indians wheeled their horses around and trotted back toward Killdeer.

"What did he say?" Sully asked.

"Basically, he told you to go to hell, that you'd be fair to him right up to where you'd hang him. The point is this—they want to fight and they say they're ready for us."

"They'll see how ready they are shortly."

At the base of the mountain the women, children, and old men gathered to watch their warriors make good on their boast that they would annihilate the white men. Sully gave instructions to his officers.

"We will make no demonstration. Have the men dismount and form a skirmish line. Every fourth man will stay behind the line holding his horse and three others. We will advance, but there'll be no charge. I do not want hand-to-hand combat.

"Captain Jones, the show today will be yours. Move your cannon to the flanks. There you'll have a sweeping view of the flats before the mountain. Train your guns so that you can sweep through the entire Indian line from the side."

"In other words," Jones agreed, "rip into them from the side instead of just punching a hole in their line from the front. Cause more damage."

"Exactly. Any questions?" Sully looked at his officers. When none responded, he issued the order. "Get into position, move on my command!"

Within fifteen minutes Sully's skirmish line was in place. A few warriors rode out from Killdeer. Once within firing range, they turned and galloped back to a mass of waiting mounted warriors.

General Sully stood at the skirmish line with Solomon Foot at his side. Peering through binoculars, he made his assessment. "Wooded cover. High, rugged hills. Nearly impassible ravines. This won't be easy. But I know Minnesota boys are great fighters. I led the First Minnesota at Bull Run, and they saved the Union center at Gettysburg. Now the Eighth Minnesota has a chance to avenge 800 deaths from the uprising last summer. I know they'll fight like devils."

"They killed my brother, Silas."

"Fight for Silas, Mr. Foot. Colonel Thomas, give the order to advance."

It was a strange battle scene: quiet, no bugles, no war cries from either side. Both soldiers and Indians were like spectators, deathly silent and motionless. It was as if a funereal cloud shrouded the battlefield.

Then thunderous sounds erupted, the rumble of thousands of horses' hooves and the steady tread of soldiers advancing on foot. Hell broke loose after a few random shots rang out from the Indian line. The warriors charged pell mell at the soldiers' line. The air became charged with screams of men and horses, gunfire and battle yells. Bullets whizzed past the advancing soldiers. Jesse, with the Eighth Minnesota, fired his carbine with steady aim.

A nearby soldier jerked his arms into the air and dropped backward with a thud. Jesse rushed to his side, but it was no use. The man had died before he hit the ground.

The measured fire of the soldiers drove the Indians back.

Jesse yelled to Solomon, "They're running away. Should we pick up the pace?"

"No! They'll be coming back. Keep the pace slow and steady. We've got to keep moving forward!"

As Solomon predicted, the Sioux fell back, reloaded and charged again. This time Jones's cannons ripped into the Indian line from both sides, inflicting serious casualties. Indians fell like grass under the sweep of a scythe. Within a few minutes at least 150 warriors were killed.

Panic swept the attackers and those in their camp, where the onlookers had been so confident that they hadn't prepared for an escape. The soldiers advanced to within half a mile of the settlement before the retreating warriors raced into it and shouted for all to follow them.

In a desperate exodus, old men, women, and children grabbed what they could carry and followed the warriors away from the mountain. The lodges in the camp were left standing.

"Colonel Thomas," Sully yelled above the din, "send four companies of the Eighth Minnesota and clear any Sioux off the top of the mountain."

Jesse, Solomon, and Jim mounted their horses with the other soldiers and thundered up the sloping mountainside. Once atop the summit, they watched as thousands of Sioux raced to the west into the Badlands.

"Look at 'em go," Atkinson commented. "Do you think Sully will head after them?"

"Hard telling," Jesse answered. "They're in sad shape. The casualties they suffered are one thing. But look at the camp below us. It's obvious they didn't have time to take much with them. The Sioux have headed into the Badlands without food, clothing, or shelter."

As he had at Whitestone Hill, Alfred Sully surveyed the destruction of the Indian camp after his troops had attacked. Thomas, Brackett, and Jones accompanied him.

"General," Thomas asked, "will we pursue into the Badlands?"

"I've been considering. The men are played out. It's been a hard march. We've covered 172 miles in six days. We'll rest here tonight and bury the few men we lost. We can use the Indian lodges for shelter if we wish and then burn them tomorrow. I don't want the Sioux coming back here for any reason. Burn everything of value they've left behind."

"Then we head after them?" Jones inquired.

"I'd like to return to Fort Rice and rest up the men before resuming pursuit. But there's the little matter of that damn immigrant train. We can't leave them out here, and I have orders to get them to Yellowstone. A steamboat with supplies is scheduled to rendezvous with us there. So we go back to the Heart River, gather up our miners and settlers, and then go after the Sioux."

The Sioux had fled to the northwest corner of the territory, which they planned to leave and head into Montana. Sully's army endured a tortuous march. Unbearable heat driven by westerly winds blasted their faces. The dust cloud raised by the soldiers and the wagon train mingled with dirt and sand driven by the winds, coating everything.

Sweat turned to mud. The heat swelled soldiers' and settlers' tongues so that by midmorning no one could speak intelligibly. The route became littered with animal carcasses, as spent creatures collapsed along the way. Such animals were shot right where they lay.

Sully ordered reveille at 3:00 each morning and commenced the march by 5:00. After twenty miles a halt was called, usually by 3:00 in the afternoon when the temperature was highest. The general knew that his exhausted troops could go no farther even if he wanted them to.

The advance to the west had brought the army in contact with the Heart River again. Solomon. Jim, and Jesse sought refuge along its bank, submerging their heads in the tepid water and savoring the relief it brought.

Too tired for a campfire, the men chewed jerky and hardtack as they sprawled along the riverbank.

"The Badlands are close," Solomon noted. "We'll be there tomorrow. They pretty much run north to south on the western edge of the territory."

"This is all Inkpaduta's fault," Jim complained. "If it wasn't for him and the Minnesota Santee, I think Sully woulda just let the rest of 'em go."

Jesse disagreed. "That might've been true, if it wasn't for the immigrant train. Pope ordered him to see them safely to the Yellowstone. That's on the other side of the Badlands."

"Well, I know one thing," Solomon proclaimed, "when this is over, I'm done. I'm going back to Ady and the little Foots and finding a less adventurous kind o' life."

"Civil War's still on," Jim countered, "I expect I'll keep soldiering. I'll go east if that's where orders take me. What about you, Jesse?"

"I guess I'm going east, too. But my job's a little different. I met with Governor Miller before the expedition started. They've got plans for me that don't involve the type of fighting you're talking about, Jim."

"Then what?" Solomon wondered.

Jesse put his finger to his lips. "Shhh, it's a secret. Someday, we'll talk about it. When it's over."

Solomon managed a weary grin. "The big secret on the Badlands. I'm lookin' forward to hearing about it someday."

"You will, my friends, just not today."

On the afternoon of August 5th the expedition reached the eastern edge of the Dakota Badlands. Sully and Thomas stood on the rim studying the desolately beautiful spectacle.

Sully emitted a low whistle. "Forty miles across, 600 feet down to the basin, full of canyons walled in by buttes that are nearly impossible to climb. This is something. I've said it before about this country and I'll say it again, this truly is hell with the fires burned out."

Thomas nodded. "No water, no vegetation. I don't even think we can get a mule through some of those narrow canyons. But look at the colors in the rocks and those magnificent rock formations."

Captain Brackett spoke up. "General, we can't go into that. It's impossible."

Thomas Holmes's ears caught the remark. He briskly strode up to the rim, took one look and proclaimed, "You ain't takin' us down there! You'll kill everyone in the wagon train."

"Then turn around and don't follow us," Sully rejoined. "I have orders to cross to the Yellowstone, and I will. How did you think you'd get to the gold fields without crossing this? Come with us or find your own way. It's up to you. Frankly, I don't care what you decide. Either way, I'll destroy the Sioux or make sure they can never come back to Minnesota or the territory and attack again in force. I will complete my mission."

The expedition was followed by the immigrant wagon train. The procession lurched down a twisting trail to the basin below, where an arduous, back-breaking crossing began. At times, much to his disgust, Sully had to call a halt to cut roads for the immigrant wagons to pass over.

Riding with the scouts, Solomon observed, "Well, I don't see the hellfire, but the brimstone's sure here. The only water's rain that's collected in holes."

"Something else is here." Jesse pointed up at the high buttes. "Sioux. The buttes are full of them."

"And just watching us, Jesse. Why don't they do something?"

"They're too high up. We can be worried when we pass lower ground. I'll let Sully know."

Jesse's apprehensions were well founded. When they passed lower buttes, the sky darkened with arrows raining down on them. From atop the buttes and on lower ledges, warriors found footholds and whizzed arrows at their prey below.

Sully ordered, "Keep moving, don't bother to shoot back, it just slows us down. You can't hit 'em anyway."

"We could charge!" Brackett urged.

"The buttes are too steep. Captain Jones, if you can find places wide enough for your cannon, set up and let 'em have it. Artillery will get their attention."

Occasionally Jones was able to fire up into the cliffs, but the impact was minimal.

Sully, to his chagrin, became sickened by rheumatism and dysentery and was forced to ride in a wagon because his illness made riding horseback difficult. Despite this setback, the general led his force on, through the ravines and over steep embankments. Men and animals alike tumbled to the ground when the trail brought them onto the top of a butte.

On August 7th the Sioux gathered on a nearby 500-foot butte. As the military and civilian procession passed beneath them, the Indians once again opened the sky with arrows. The column became penned into a gorge too narrow for the wagons to maneuver.

Holmes angrily accosted Sully. "Look what yer doin' ta us. Look at my people!"

Sully maintained a calm exterior as he turned toward the wagons. The column had lurched to a halt as people attempted to protect themselves. Amid an onslaught of screams, horses reared and scraped against the rock wall. Jones fired his cannons with little effect.

"What should we do, General?" Captain Brackett called.

"Wait here. It'll be dark soon. That will be our salvation."

Night gave Sully the opportunity to plan. He called his officers to his wagon. The general remained on the wagon seat in obvious discomfort, but his eyes gleamed as he addressed the men.

"Colonel Thomas, have everything ready to move at 6:00 in the morning, in perfect fighting order. Put one of your most active field officers in charge of a strong advance guard, and you'll meet Sioux at the head of the ravine and have the biggest Indian fight that'll ever happen on this continent. There'll be no frontal attacks. Tomorrow it'll be flank and maneuver. The Sioux are masters of it. But we'll beat them at their own game."

Jesse approached Thomas after the meeting broke up. "Colonel, I'd like to lead the advance guard tomorrow."

Thomas briefly considered the request. "It's risky."

"Colonel, it's risky standing under a hailstorm of arrows, too. I want to be part of this."

"All right, Lieutenant, it's yours."

Before 6:00 the next morning Jesse stood with his line of troops. Sully came to inspect them, looked them over. He turned to Thomas. "Those fellows can whip the devil and all his angels. Hold them well in hand, but push for the Indians' camp, if you can find it. They'll fight for their families. Protect your flanks and I'll protect the rear. You must make history today."

The ravine before them was narrow, hardly wide enough for a wagon to pass. Jesse led his mounted troopers over a trail that ascended gradually until they reached a high plateau.

Ahead of the soldiers lay a wide plain. Just as Sully had predicted, the Sioux were gathered there in large numbers. Where the trail crested the plateau, the Indians began to fire.

"Slow, men, fire slow and make each shot count!" Jesse hollered. "Keep moving step by step!"

The soldiers inched forward. Meanwhile, the Sioux gathered on three sides of the column. Behind them Jones and his artillerymen struggled mightily as they strained to pull and tug the cannons up to flat land.

"Hit the weak spots!" Jesse commanded, arrows flashing by. "Then back off and look for another opening."

Solomon had joined Jesse. He shouted, "Force them between the hills! Brackett's men are on top and can fire down."

A maelstrom of screaming, gunfire, and yelling enveloped the ravine. Then Jones's cannons roared and blasted rocks and Indians into the air.

SULLY, LISTENING TO THE BATTLE, barked a quick order to his aide. "I've got to see what's happening. Help me on my horse and help me to the top of the plateau."

They rode to the crest. There the aide helped Sully dismount and maneuver into a sitting position with his back propped against a rock.

Thomas found his commander. "What do you want us to do, General?"

"You're doing wonderful. Huzzah to the Second Brigade! The advance is pushing the devils back. The Indian camp's up ahead, there by the far butte. We can take it, but there's still some fighting to do."

The battle went back and forth for over twelve miles. Finally, at nightfall, the Sioux disappeared like the last rays of the sun. The soldiers located the camp where Sully said it would be, but the Indians had all left.

The next morning Sully made a painful ride with his lead officers as they looked for remnants of Sitting Bull's warriors. They found only small bands and, after an hour's skirmish, the Sioux dispersed in all directions.

General Sully grimaced as he twisted in his saddle. "Men, in a lot of ways this was unfortunate. I really don't hate the Sioux. At one time I was married to one. We had a child. They're even superior to us in some ways. But they were in the way of progress, and I had a job to do. I did it."

A count of the previous day's battlefield totaled 311 dead Sioux and an estimated 650 wounded. There likely had been 8,000 warriors. Sully's troops had lost 9 killed and 100 wounded.

It was for a frank talk that Sully summoned Holmes to his tent. "Major, you have been a pain in my ass. The Yellowstone River is a few days away. We will get you across and see you on your way. A steamboat is waiting there to re-supply me. Then this army is turning back and going home."

"Yer sure it's gonna be safe?"

"You're a fine one to worry about safety now. You'll be on your own once we turn back. I'll tell you this: the Indians are broken up and scattered all over. They're going to have to get through the winter without lodges. Everything they stored up for the winter—food, provisions, warm clothing—is gone. Their horses are used up or dead. They'd better pray to their 'Great Spirit' for a mild winter. The fact is that future large expeditions against the Sioux in this part of the country will be unnecessary. The only thing that'll make this more complete for me is when I'm done with you."

On Sunday, August 14, the expedition and the wagon train crossed the Yellowstone River. Several men drowned crossing their wagons. The ford attempt also claimed a dozen mules.

At the riverbank Jesse bid farewell to Jim and Solomon. "Sully tells me that he expects the brigades to get back to Minnesota by the end of September. I'm supposed to be back before then. I showed the general my orders. I'm released from duty now."

"You're going back alone?" Solomon was alarmed.

"Don't worry, old man. I'll make it. You just get back to your wife and kids. You'll hear from me again."

"Who ordered you to leave early?" Jim asked.

"Governor Miller. If you get to Washington, look me up."

"Where should I look?"

Jesse couldn't hold back a grin. "The White House."

↪ 22 ↩

SEPTEMBER 1864, BALTIMORE

OHN BOOTH WAS BACK IN HIS HOME state of Maryland. He checked into the Barnum Hotel. The clerk knew who their famous guest was at first sight.

"Mr. Booth, welcome!" he exclaimed. "No room is too good for you. I saw you in *Richard III*. You were tremendous, so athletic and energetic!"

"Thank you, my man. I'm glad you were entertained. There'll be several visitors to my room. Please see that they reach me with no trouble." He flipped the clerk a gold coin.

"Anything for you, sir." The clerk beamed.

The next day two young men rapped on Booth's hotel door. They were boyhood and school friends. Michael O'Laughlen had lived across the street from the Booth family's Baltimore townhouse. Age twenty-four, he had served in the Confederates' First Maryland Infantry and had been a Knight of the Golden Circle.

Samuel Arnold, twenty-nine years old, had attended school at St. Timothy's Hall with Booth. He too had served in the CSA First Maryland Infantry but had been discharged for disability after First Bull Run.

Both men were fit, dark haired and handsome. Each wore a mustache that drooped down at the corners.

Booth greeted each of them warmly with a hug. He offered drinks and cigars, and the three reminisced about old times and growing up together.

"As I recall," Arnold remarked, "you did much better in athletic pursuits than academics."

Booth concurred. "Fencing, shooting and riding suited me better."

"How ever did you become an actor?" O'Laughlen asked.

"It's in the family genes, of course. The physical part was natural. But I have to admit that I struggled with my voice and learning my lines at first. I've overcome those obstacles."

"What do you think, Sam? We're in the presence of greatness."

They all laughed again. Then Booth turned serious. "My friends, I have a very special mission for you. Grant has stopped exchanging prisoners, and the Confederacy is running out of manpower."

"What can we do about that?" Arnold asked.

Their famous friend explained. "Abraham Lincoln lives away from the White House in warm weather. He lives in the Soldiers' Home on the outskirts of Washington. Sometimes he rides horseback, sometimes in a carriage. Since often he's unguarded, he can be easily kidnapped and held for ransom. Our ransom will be all Confederate soldiers held in federal prisons."

"You don't mean just us?" Arnold was incredulous. "How ever could we accomplish that?"

"Others are involved, especially in the escape with Lincoln into Virginia. I'm forming my team. You two are the first. More will be added."

"How do you know so much about Lincoln's habits? You haven't been in Washington since when . . . sometime last year?"

"November of 1863. I have contacts who know Lincoln well."

The scheme had begun to entice O'Laughlen. "How do we get him to Richmond?"

"We'll take his carriage or get him on horseback and rush to lower Maryland. There we'll find a boat already moored and a boatman waiting for us. Cavalry will meet us as an escort. In less than a day we can deliver the Black Republican to President Davis."

Arnold was pensive. "I don't know about you, Mike, but I'm willing to play along with this and see if it works out."

"I can't fight anymore, but just maybe with this I can still make a difference."

"A major difference, men," Booth interjected. "We can win the war for the Confederacy. I have another recruit to meet in southern Maryland. I'll be in touch with you later. You must not speak of this to anyone else. Does each of you swear to absolute secrecy? Do you swear to God?"

"I swear to God," Arnold affirmed.

O'Laughlen made it unanimous. "I swear to God."

"Excellent. You'll hear from me soon. Stay close to Baltimore."

This plan given to Booth had originated elsewhere. Benjamin Ogle Tayloe was a Harvard graduate and son of one of the nation's richest families, scions of Maryland. He currently lived on the east side of Lafayette Square in Washington, where he could benefit from a top-notch view of the comings and goings at the White House.

Ogle Tayloe resided in the nation's capitol, but his loyalties remained unswervingly with the Confederacy. The Tayloes had vast land holdings in Charles County, Maryland, as well as in King George County, Virginia.

Tayloe knew well the Reverend Kensey John Stewart, an Episcopal pastor. Stewart, married to Hannah Lee, a first cousin of Robert E. Lee, served at a church across the street from the Soldiers' Home. Reverend Stewart met Ogle Tayloe at this time and joined the Confederate Secret Service.

They comprised a formidable team. Together they had intimate knowledge of the roads north and east of Washington. Together they had the geographic and personal knowledge needed to kidnap the president of the United States.

But the plan needed an instigator, a catalyst. That man was a master spy, Thomas Nelson Conrad. Conrad spied in Washington and watched Lincoln's solitary rides to the Soldiers' Home. Needing knowledge of the surrounding area, he brought Tayloe and Stewart together to flesh out the details of his plot.

Conrad brought the scheme to Richmond in late 1863. He reported to Albert Pike in the nondescript brick building tucked away in that city. Following protocol, the director of covert activities referred him to Secretary of War Seddon and Confederate President Jefferson Davis.

Pike welcomed the approval of those higher in the chain of command, but he was determined to follow through regardless. He waited until the timing was right and then revealed the plan to Judah Benjamin.

"Can it work?" Benjamin asked.

"It's most certainly worth a try, and with Dahlgren's bungled attempt to kill Davis, we are justified. It's mapped out pretty well."

"Whom do we enlist to carry this out?"

"My choice is our agent in Washington who brought this to me, Tom Conrad. But I fear that our old friend George Sanders also has knowledge of this plan. God knows what he's up to."

"For all we know, Sanders has launched his own kidnapping plot."

"Two different plots?" Pike mused. "Interesting. Maybe it doubles our chance of success."

"Or dooms both to failure. I guess time will tell."

"I'll talk to Conrad. He's met with Davis and Seddon, they approved of the plan. Not that we needed their approval. When all is ready we should act."

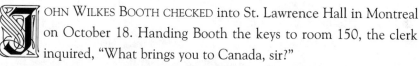

$\text{\large $\wp$} 23 \text{\large $\wp$}$

OCTOBER 1864, MONTREAL, CANADA

OHN WILKES BOOTH CHECKED into St. Lawrence Hall in Montreal on October 18. Handing Booth the keys to room 150, the clerk inquired, "What brings you to Canada, sir?"

"I'm here to ship my theatrical wardrobe to Richmond."

"Why did you travel here for that? Wouldn't it have been easier from the States?"

"Not with a blockade. I'm expecting guests. Let them know I'm waiting, please."

Booth's eyes swept over the hotel parlor en route to his room. He was not surprised to recognize several faces. St. Lawrence Hall was like little Richmond, the unofficial Confederate headquarters in Montreal, the gathering spot for southerners who needed a place to pick up mail, catch up on news about the war, or meet friends and acquaintances.

Booth slipped into his room and waited. The room seemed large and comfortable to him. He moved four chairs so they formed a circle. After a series of three raps on the door, Booth swung it open.

Three men entered. They were the Confederate Commissioners to Canada, Jacob Thompson and Clement Clay, along with agent George Sanders.

"Welcome to the Richmond of the North," Sanders grinned.

After the men shook hands, Booth motioned to the chairs. "Sit down, gentlemen. We have much to discuss."

"Indeed," Clay replied, "it's been a few months since you accepted the Lincoln mission. What have you accomplished?"

"The former senator thinks he's still in the Senate," Sanders remarked. "You are before his committee."

"My team is being assembled. The plans are being laid."

"Don't delay, move ahead quickly," Clay urged.

"Clement, this takes time," Thompson cautioned. "I'm sure he's short of funds. That's one reason why he's here. We started him on this. We have to back him."

Thompson reached into a coat pocket and removed a pouch, which he flipped to Booth. The bag clinked as the actor caught it.

"Gold coins, they should get you by for awhile. More are coming."

"The former United States Interior Secretary is more diplomatic," Sanders explained. "Pretty soon we'll have a whole government up here. Take a look around, we've got former senators and congressmen all over.'"

"John, did you get your trunk shipped?" Clay wanted to know. "That's ostensibly why you're here."

"Captain Martin has taken it aboard the *Marie Victoria*. Our favorite blockade runner will get it to Richmond."

"When do you expect to act?" Thompson asked.

"Sooner, now that I have the money," Booth replied. "It shouldn't take much longer to put things in place."

Sanders grew restless and shifted in his chair. Clay regarded him.

"George is about to burst. Don't hold it in, my friend, we know that you have a different approach in mind. Spill it."

"We should forget the kidnapping. It's involved, it's messy, and it probably won't work. Mazzini advocated the 'Theory of the Dagger.' Tyrannicide is justifiable. I say, kill Lincoln. It's clean and it'd throw the Union into chaos."

"This isn't new to George," Clay noted. "While he was a consul in England, he advised the killing of Louis Napoleon. It got him kicked out of Europe."

"At times, George, you work at cross purposes with the rest of us," Thompson asserted.

Booth was thoughtful. "I find his words worth considering."

"Be careful, John. You have the money and the plan. Stick to it."

"What if Lincoln loses the election?"

Sanders snapped, "The election be damned, win or lose, take him out! It'll turn the Union upside down and inside out."

For the next ten days Booth remained in Montreal. Sanders stayed in the room next door and regaled the younger man with stories of Mazzini, secret societies, clandestine operations and the assassinations of political tyrants.

"Chaos and disorder can fell the greatest of countries and the greatest of men," Sanders proclaimed. "Five million dollars has been appropriated by the Confederate Congress to our secret service. There is great fame and wealth ahead for you, John Wilkes Booth. A great stage awaits your greatest performance. But you must slay the dragon and not just put him inside a cage."

"I shall remember your words, Mr. Sanders. My orders are to kidnap Lincoln, not to kill him. But I shall not forget what you've said. You inspire me."

"No matter what path you take, Wilkes, you may hold the key to our country's future in your hands. Don't let us down."

❧ 23 ❧

NOVEMBER 1864, WASHINGTON

N OVEMBER 8, 1864, WAS ELECTION DAY. The fate of the nation hung in the balance as Americans in the Union states chose between Abraham Lincoln and the general who Lincoln had twice named head of the Army of the Potomac and twice dismissed for his failures.

The president was committed to staying the course. Saving the Union at all costs had become his mission. McClellan's commitment to preserving the Union was not nearly as steadfast. He was saddled with a defeatist Democratic platform. Both men counted on the votes of the soldiers in the field, who numbered 850,000.

The members of the army had been devoted to McClellan. Their general showed great concern that his men be properly trained and given the food and tools needed to do the job required of them. The soldiers recognized that McClellan cared, and they genuinely appreciated his efforts.

Lincoln came to believe that, while his general had created a great army, he also was afraid to use that army. It was like getting a new toy at Christmas, then putting it on a shelf and never playing with it.

The president commented on McClellan's delays in deploying his troops and not making decisive moves in battle by saying, "McClellan has the slows." After his second dismissal by Lincoln, the general went into politics and became the Democratic candidate for president.

Lincoln predicted a McClellan victory in the campaign.

Election day in Washington was dark and gloomy. A drizzle compounded the misery as streets and grounds turned slick and muddy. Ward

116

Hill Lamon was surprised to find Lincoln alone at midday in the President's Mansion.

"Where is everyone, Mr. President?"

Lincoln's spirits were every bit as bleak as the weather. "Seward has gone home to New York to vote. Stanton is sick at home. Hay will be here soon. Lots of folks are out voting, not that it'll make a difference."

Lamon intentionally softened his normally booming voice as he offered encouragement. "Abe, you're going to win. I have no doubt."

"I fear your optimism is in the minority. I'm enough of a politician to know that I would get the Republican Party nomination again. But about this election I'm very far from being certain. I wish I were certain."

"Do you wish we were back in Illinois?"

The comment elicited a weak smile and a nod from the president. "Practicing law, Lincoln and Lamon, I enjoyed our years practicing together. But there was a greater calling, and I needed you here with me."

"I did all I could to get you here."

In spite of himself, Lincoln laughed. "You packed the convention hall with Lincoln men who gained admittance with counterfeit tickets printed by you. They shouted down my opponent's supporters."

"It seemed like a good idea, Mr. President, and it worked."

"And look what it got us." Lincoln turned somber again. "If we lose, we have just over four months to save this country. McClellan will take over in March. We must win this war before our beloved nation is taken over by those who would let it be forever ripped apart."

"Sherman did take Atlanta. That'll help us, Abe."

"'Ours and fairly won,' his telegram read. After four years, I think the people expected more. They wanted this war over long ago."

Lamon asserted, "We had it harder than they did. We had to win the war and we had to invade the South. All the Confederates had to do was play things out. The longer the war goes, the more our people tire of it."

"A war of attrition," Lincoln agreed, "drag it out until we give up and let them go. But it won't happen as long as I'm president, even into March.

"What of my protector from Minnesota? I hope he hasn't left yet. It would be a shame for him to make the trip and then have to turn around and go back."

"I've received word from Governor Miller that he's on his way. Perhaps he has more confidence in your chances than you do."

"I've looked at some dispatches about him. He seems to be a good soldier and a fine young man. He managed to impress General Sully, and that's not an easy thing to do."

"His fiancee died. That's another reason why he appealed to us," Lamon explained. "He has no attachments in Minnesota."

Sadness crept across Lincoln's face and into his eyes. He sighed. "Then he and I have something in common. Hill, you know that my first love, Nancy Hanks, died back in New Salem. I felt so miserable that I almost ended it all."

"Thank God you didn't."

Lincoln brightened as he put the discussion back on course. "Well, the campaign against the Sioux is over. Sully has seen to that. I don't expect they'll ever pose a threat to Minnesota again."

The president paused and stroked his bearded cheek. "Hill, I often wonder if agents from the South had a connection with causing the Indian uprising in Minnesota. All seemed to be going well there. Then this war started, and things fell apart out west. There were so many coincidences that led to war in Minnesota."

"Possibly," Lamon concurred, "but we'll likely never know."

The two friends continued in conversation for much of the afternoon. At times Lincoln was thoughtful, sometimes melancholy. On occasion he joked and his eyes lit up when he told stories about his young son, Tad.

Late in the afternoon, John Hay arrived in the Oval Office. Technically a clerk in the Interior Department, Hay was one of two private secretaries who served Lincoln. The young man from Illinois was twenty-six years old, youthful in appearance and clean shaven except for a long mustache.

"Are we going to the War Department?" Hay inquired.

"That's where the nearest telegraph is," Lincoln responded. "Are you coming with us, Hill?"

"I'll be over presently. I have a couple of things to tend to here first."

As the clock in the ante room sounded seven loud *bongs*, Hay and Lincoln began the mucky, muddy trek to the War Department and the telegraph—their link to election results and the future of the nation.

En route Lincoln commented, "It's a little singular that I, who am not a vindictive man, should have always been before the people for election in canvasses marked for their bitterness."

The War Department was aglow with lights and activity. Orderlies, government personnel and clerks scurried from room to room. The president took a seat near the telegraph and prepared for a long vigil.

Before long the steady *tat-tat-tat* of the telegraph revealed early results. They were all positive.

"Sir," Hay exclaimed, "our Republican margins are bigger than ever!"

Lincoln felt a tinge of relief. "Johnny, please carry the news to my wife at the White House. She's very anxious about this night."

Moments later, Secretary of the Navy Gideon Wells arrived. The white-haired, bearded, rotund official was beaming as he cried delightedly, "Mr. President, have you seen the results from Maryland? You're doing very well there.

"And Winter Davis has been defeated for re-election to Congress! The Radicals have lost a leader, and you have lost a thorn in your side!"

"Poseidon," Lincoln replied, using his favorite moniker for his Navy secretary, "you have more of that feeling of personal resentment than I. A man hasn't time to spend half his life in quarrels. If any man ceases to attack me, then I never remember the past against him."

Lincoln's margin continued to widen throughout the night as state after state gave him their majority.

"I'm still worried about New York," Lincoln demurred, "the Irish immigrants there have not been favorable to me."

CONSPIRACY!

By midnight, a supper of fried oysters was served up along with results fresh from New York. There was no doubt that President Abraham Lincoln had been re-elected. McClellan had prevailed in only three states: New Jersey, Delaware, and Kentucky.

John Nicolay, Lincoln's other secretary, burst into the room. "Mr. President, I know you worried about the soldier vote. It's still just an estimate, what with figures still coming in. But it looks like you got eighty percent of it. Seventy percent of McClellan's former command, the Army of the Potomac, voted for you! It is a smashing victory!"

Hill Lamon held up a scrap of paper. "The Electoral College total is Lincoln 212, McClellan twenty-one, popular vote margin about 400,000. Thanks be to God! The country is saved!"

At 2:00 a.m. Abraham Lincoln and Hill Lamon stepped into the fresh night air. The rain had stopped, and small groups of people huddled along Pennsylvania Avenue.

"Now you can finish what you started, Abe."

"Thanks to Sherman and Grant, we're getting closer."

"Please be careful, Abe. You're in even more danger now."

Lincoln simply looked at his friend. A smile played at his lips.

A crowd gathered around them as the two men walked. Unprompted the onlookers sang:

> The Union forever, hurrah, boys, hurrah.
> Down with the traitor, up with the star.
> While we rally round the flag, boys,
> Rally once again,
> Shouting the battle cry of freedom!

"It's a great song, Abe."

"It's an even better song tonight, Hill."

≈ 24 ≈

WASHINGTON

PRESIDENT LINCOLN SAT ALONE at his desk on the morning of Friday, November 11. Moments of solitude in the Oval Office were few and far between for this most accessible of presidents. Office seekers, military personnel, politicians, and just ordinary civilians all received this president's attention.

But it was still early, and Lincoln relished the chance to be by himself. He had endured several mood swings since his victory the previous Tuesday. He was alternately pleased and buoyed by the great support shown him by the electorate, then weighted down by the enormity of the work before him, the task yet to be finished.

He stretched his long legs and winced. His feet hurt. "Darn bunions," he muttered, loosening his shoes. A moment later a rap on his office door led to the sight of Ward Hill Lamon escorting a young man into the office.

The man was in his twenties, wearing a blue officer's uniform with lieutenant's bars. He was trim, athletic and handsome. Sun-bleached blonde hair and bright-blue eyes contrasted sharply with his well-tanned face.

"Mr. President, I'd like to present Lieutenant Jesse Buchanen of Minnesota. Your new bodyguard."

Lincoln rose and walked around his desk to shake the young man's hand. "Welcome to Washington. Do you really want to help protect this old bag of bones? I wonder if it's worth the effort."

The young soldier studied the commander in chief's face while matching his firm handshake. The pictures and descriptions hardly

121

matched the man in person. *Not a handsome face, but a good face*, Jesse thought, *and his eyes look like he's carrying the weight of the world.*

"Mr. President, I'll help however I can."

"How are Minnesota and the Dakota Expedition? I know that Sully has won several battles."

"The Sioux are done as a military force in Minnesota and in the Dakota Territory east of the Missouri, sir."

"Good, we need the troops here. Governor Miller has promised more Minnesota regiments now that the Indian business is over."

"Yes," Lamon surmised, "but we might need to send them to Canada. We were just attacked last month at St. Albans, Vermont, by Confederate raiders. They obviously have a Canadian base."

"One belligerent at a time, Hill. I'm not about to bring the British into this."

"Congratulations on your victory, sir," Jesse said.

"I don't think you'd be here today if it had turned out otherwise. Please sit down."

The three men took seats at a small round table in front of the president's desk.

"Lieutenant," Lamon began, "I'm the president's official bodyguard. He's also protected against any sinister activities by the Pinkerton Agency and the military."

"That seems like plenty. Why do you need me?"

"Frankly, Mr. Lincoln's a little hard to keep up with. He has a penchant for doing what he wants without thinking about his security."

"Gentlemen, if someone wants to assassinate me, they will. They won't be stopped."

"Mr. President," Lamon admonished, "you don't have to taunt fate. Remember when you returned at night, alone on horseback, from the Soldiers' Home? There was a shot, and a bullet narrowly missed you."

Lincoln turned ruefully to Jesse. "Someone ruined my new hat with a bullet hole. The point is, they did miss. It wasn't my time."

"Lieutenant, we have to save this man in spite of himself," Lamon continued. "You're here because no one knows you. You're from the frontier and come highly recommended with an exemplary record. You'll wear civilian clothing. You'll stay in the background, away from the Pinkertons and the military guards. Watch what's happening. Be diligent and vigilant. Report only to me. Only we in this room and the president's secretaries, Hay and Nicolay, know who you are and why you're here. Report any threats to me immediately, small or large, real or remote, treat them all as being serious. We'll sort things out from what you report."

"Where do I begin? Who poses a threat today?"

"It might be easier to say who doesn't," Lincoln quipped.

Lamon explained. "Confederate agents are logical suspects, but we have enemies in the North as well. The president's policies have infuriated banking interests and immigrant groups as well as southern sympathizers in the North."

"Anyone specific?"

"Well, Lieutenant," Lincoln advised, "I've been warned about the Catholics. You see, I defended a priest once against the wishes of his bishop. Things didn't turn out well for the church or the Jesuits."

"Any formal threats, sir?"

"No, just that the pope recognized the Confederate government."

"The Catholic Church has a history of political involvement and intrigue," Lamon added. "Church sanctioned assassinations and coups go back to medieval times. It would not be out of character for them here, either.

"We have nothing concrete, but the Catholic Church may be one place to start looking for threats."

"By an odd coincidence," Lincoln commented, "the priest I defended is currently in Washington City. I'm scheduled to meet with him. I think you might learn something from Father Chiniquy."

"I'll make contact with him."

"Hill," Lincoln concluded, "this is all well and good. But I'll do what I must to perform the duties of my office. Lieutenant, please don't get in the way of what I must do. I believe that fate has already determined what

123

will happen to me. It's long been my belief that I won't survive this war. I can't hide in my office. The people and my soldiers expect me to be among them."

"Well, Lieutenant," Lamon shook his head, "see what we're up against with this man? Do your best. I don't mean to give you added pressure, but the future of our country is in this man's hands. We need him alive."

"You'll have my best effort, sir."

"Fine, I'll put you in touch with Chiniquy."

TWO MEN BROUGHT JOHN WILKES BOOTH to church at Bryantown, Maryland, on November 12, 1864. They attended mass at St. Mary's Catholic Church, but their true purpose there was to meet a local doctor and loyal Confederate sympathizer, Dr. Samuel Mudd.

After church services they gathered in the shade of an oak tree. Mudd shook Booth's hand enthusiastically. "Mr. Booth, I'm honored to meet you. I've seen you perform in Washington several times. I really am honored."

"The honor is mine, sir. I'm told you support the southern cause."

Mudd glanced furtively from side to side. "Yes, but keep your voices low. Not everyone around here is on our side."

"Thank you for meeting me."

"Normally I go to the Church of St. Peter. It's near my home, and that's just some eight miles away."

"It's the location of your home that brings me here, Dr. Mudd. It is on a route that we might be using for an endeavor in support of our cause. If it happens that you're needed, might I have the convenience of using your home as a refuge?"

"Certainly, Mr. Booth, I'd be pleased to help you."

"The time may come. Be ready."

$\mathscr{so} 25 \mathscr{os}$

RICHMOND, VIRGINIA

LBERT PIKE AND JUDAH BENJAMIN rode their horses well ahead of a troop of cavalry. They were on the outskirts of Richmond. In the distance a low rumble of cannon fire could almost have been mistaken for thunder had not the sun been shining in a cloudless sky.

Pike rode a big, strong war horse capable of carrying a big man. Benjamin, the Confederates' secretary of war and overseer of the Confederates' Secret Service, rode next to him but was a foot lower.

"I really thought we had a chance," Benjamin complained, "I thought McClellan would win the election."

Pike shifted in his saddle and looked back toward Petersburg and the sound of cannons. "I didn't share your optimism, but I was hopeful. It seems the Yankees are a little more invigorated by news of Lincoln's victory. More cannonfire than usual today."

Benjamin's laments continued. "Even the Union soldiers voted heavily for Lincoln, I really thought they'd vote for McClellan. He offered a quick end to this war."

"It bodes badly for us, Mr. Secretary. It shows that the Yankee soldiers are prepared for a long haul. They've passed on a chance to end it. They'll fight until they win or we find a way to defeat them."

"Have you come up with any new ideas? Thompson's idea to raid St. Albans from Canada didn't come off as well as planned, but it sure shook up the Yanks."

"They managed to burn only one building, and the Canadian government returned the $88,000 they took to the St. Albans banks. But remember," Pike reminded him, "we do have friends, and we have a plan that's been shelved until needed. I think now is the time."

"A plot to kidnap the president?"

"That's one option. We must prepare contingencies as well."

"General Pike, do you really think the Yankees would empty their prison camps of our soldiers in return for Lincoln?"

"I do, but if not, what have we lost? We hang Lincoln and turn the Yankee government into chaos. Vice-President Johnson is from Tennessee. Deep down inside he's really a Southerner. More recently his actions have been most unsouthern—he's been a traitor to his place of his birth—but at heart he has sentiments we can cultivate. It'd be good for us either way."

"What ideas do you have for putting this together?"

"Wheels are already in motion, Mr. Secretary. We have many agents working with multiple groups."

The Confederate secretary of war was caught off guard, puzzled not to have been privy to this information. He realized with a start that Pike had the inside track.

The large man continued his revelations. "Judah, this is about much more than slavery or state's rights or our war for independence. What happens in the next six months will have worldwide significance. It'll change the order of things forever."

"What do you mean?" Judah's uneasiness was mushrooming.

"There are many who want to see President Lincoln removed, and the Confederacy be victorious. As the plan comes together, you'll be informed."

The last part of that comment was too much for Benjamin. "General Pike, I shouldn't have to remind you that I am your superior! I am the one in charge of the Secret Service. Don't you think that the details of your action should be given to me? I am entitled to know."

"And you will, sir, but it's important that pieces start to come together first. I'm not going to give you puzzle pieces one by one until you can guess the picture. Eventually you'll be informed. But right now, it's best you leave this up to me."

Benjamin was not persuaded, but he also surmised quickly that he had little choice. Now it was a matter of saving face. There was one graceful way out. "General Pike, as a brother Mason, I trust you. Do not deceive me."

"I won't despoil our brotherhood. I value your trust. You do know of the plan and its goals. Leave the details to me. I tell you this, we will start with dupes who'll have no idea of our ultimate mission."

"I believe I know who."

They continued the ride toward Richmond in silence.

ℰ𝒪 26 𝒞𝒳

NOVEMBER 1864, WASHINGTON

THOMAS CONRAD PEERED THROUGH BINOCULARS from the Tayloe mansion's porch across the square from the White House. He watched as a lone horse trotted with its rider northward into the gathering twilight.

"Lincoln, alone again," he muttered. "We can do this."

Ogle Tayloe stood behind the spy. "Are you ready?"

"I think so. Reverend Stewart has constructed a boat of rubberized cloth and saplings. It's waiting for us on the banks of Nanjemoy Creek. Mosby's cavalry will be in the northern neck to escort us."

"Union spies are monitoring our troop movements. Won't they suspect regiments being transferred so close to Washington?"

"No," Conrad responded, "because regiments aren't being transferred. Soldiers from the northern neck and surrounding areas in Virginia are being sent home. They'll all be in proximity to each other and ready to move when needed. But no discernible hole will be evident in our forces.

"I have a copy of Secretary Seddon's order. It states 'Lt. Col. Mosby and Lt. Cawood are hereby directed to aid and facilitate the movements of Captain Conrad.' Cawood is the senior Signal Corps officer in the northern neck. They have been put on notice to be of service."

"Will you follow the escape route Stewart and I outlined?"

"Take possession of Mr. Lincoln. Then move him through southern Maryland to the lower Potomac in Charles County. Cross the river and deliver the prisoner to Mosby's Rangers for transportation to Richmond."

"What about the upper Potomac?"

128

"Still a possibility. This is my third trip to Washington on this. It's taken time to figure out Lincoln's movements. Between here and the Greene Mansion on Constitution Avenue, I see pretty much all I need to. He usually travels early evening or early morning. We're about ready to act."

ACROSS THE SQUARE THE WATCHER was being watched. As the president trotted his horse toward the Soldiers' Home, Jesse Buchanen surveyed the surrounding area. His binoculars caught Conrad watching Lincoln from the Tayloe house.

"I've got to find out more about that man. He's up to something," Jesse murmured.

Taking a circuitous route, he crossed LaFayette Square toward the mansion on the other side. Jesse was surprised to see a man resembling the man from the Tayloe house walking toward him. It had to be him. The man was tall with short brown hair and a mustache.

Conrad had begun the war as headmaster at Georgetown College near Washington. On his final day there, he had ordered the Marine band not to play "The Star Spangled Banner" but to play "Dixie" instead.

The provost marshal was alerted and Conrad put under watch. He was arrested on charges of recruiting for the Confederate Army on August 2, 1862, and sent to Old Capitol Prison. Just one month later he was released and exchanged for a northern prisoner with merely one stipulation: Conrad was to keep out of Washington.

As Jesse neared Conrad, a police officer accosted the spy.

"I know you!" the officer exclaimed as he drew a pistol from his belt. "You're Conrad, that 'sesesh' teacher spy. You're s'posed to stay out of Washington. Get your hands up! I'm taking you in."

Thoughts flooded Jesse's mind. The policeman's back was to him, facing Conrad. Jesse darted behind the officer and cracked him soundly over the head with his pistol. The man crumbled unconscious to the ground.

Conrad gestured for Jesse to follow as he hurried across the square.

"Thank you, sir," the spy said, "I didn't expect a friend of the 'Cause' to happen by. It was certainly fortuitous."

Jesse, wanting to nurture Conrad's apparent misconception, searched quickly for the right words. "I heard what he said to you. I don't want any more of us holed up in prison."

Conrad was wary. "You don't sound like a Southerner."

"I'm not, but I am Peace Party, and I hate the man in the White House. He has to go. There are many in Washington who feel like me."

"So I've heard. How interested are you in doing something?"

"About what?" asked Jesse.

"Lincoln."

Jesse nodded affirmatively. "I'm interested."

Conrad continued to gauge the man's believability. "Then I may be in touch. Where are you staying?"

"I just took a room on H Street, next to the Surratt Boarding House."

"You have me at a disadvantage, I believe you heard my name. What's yours?"

"Mr. Conrad. Yes, I heard. I'm Jesse Miller."

"There's a bar on H Street, McGovern's, not far from where you live. It's a less conspicuous place and I'm not likely to be recognized there. As it is, I can't remain in Washington much longer. They'll be looking for me." Conrad reasoned that much was safe to share. "I'll meet you there tomorrow about this time."

"I'll be there."

Jesse walked back to H Street with competing thoughts wrestling for domination. The inward battle raged. *Did I do the right thing? I could have caught a spy. But if something bigger is going on, this man could lead me to it. I saved Conrad from the police; I hope that earned me trust. But still, should I have helped the policeman instead? Somehow this seemed too easy. Too late now,* he ultimately determined. *I'm into something and I can't let go.*

Passing the Surratt Boarding House, Jesse noticed a couple of priests entering. He had heard that Catholics frequented the establishment.

Owner Mary Surratt was a devout Catholic and catered to those of her faith.

The hotel where Jesse was staying was but a couple of buildings past Surratt's. As he reached the front stoop, he noticed a small man with graying hair, a bushy beard lining his jawbone. The glow from a lantern on the hotel porch shimmered down onto the man in the early evening darkness.

"Lieutenant Buchanen?"

"I'm sorry, sir, you are mistaken. My name's Miller."

"Are you sure? My name's Charles Chiniquy. I was told we needed to meet."

"Let's walk aways. Darkness is a friend when it's important to keep things between ourselves."

The tall soldier dressed in civilian clothes and the short priest hung in the protection of shadows as they slowly moved along the street.

"Let's be as vague as we can. The darkness can also hide big ears. Yes, you know who I am," Jesse explained quietly, "but it's best I use another name here. And, yes, I was told to meet with you. Do you have something to tell me?"

"Lamon sent me to you because things are getting very tricky. I met with the tall man from Illinois today. Ever since he defended me at Urbana, he's been marked for retribution by the Jesuits. I warned him this afternoon that he'll fall to one of their assassins if he doesn't pay attention and protect himself."

"What did he say?"

"He reminded me that I'd warned him in Urbana in 1856 and that nothing had happened. Then he told me . . ." Chiniquy hesitated as if testing his memory, then continued. "He said, 'Man must not care where and when he will die, provided he dies at the post of honor and duty.' Then he added, 'But I have a presentiment that God will call me to Him through the hand of an assassin. Let His will, and not mine, be done.'"

"There are many of us determined to keep him safe," Jesse assured Chiniquy. "Do you have anyone in particular I should look out for?"

"Watch the house run by Mary near your hotel. It's a den of Catholic iniquity. The comings and goings there could be eye opening."

"Thank you, Father, if you find out anything pertinent, please let me know."

∽ 28 ∾

WASHINGTON

HE NEXT MORNING IN THE GREENE MANSION overlooking the White House and Constitution Avenue, Tom Conrad welcomed a guest in the library, Lieutenant Benjamin Franklin Stringfellow, described by Union Secretary of War Edwin Stanton as "the most dangerous and daring spy in the Confederate army." A reward of 10,000 dollars hung over his head.

The tall, clean-shaven man had a full head of wavy dark hair. His face was pleasant but solemn.

"The plan is about ready. I'm glad you're here," Conrad greeted him.

"General Lee thought you might need me."

"You're under his command now?"

"I report directly to him."

"Good for you, but it's not the same, is it?"

"I was with JEB Stuart from the beginning as his personal scout and chief clandestine operative. He was my friend. I miss him."

"The whole Confederacy misses him. It's been nearly a year."

"May 12, 1864, at Yellow Tavern. He can't be replaced. He was General Lee's eyes. When do you plan to act?"

"Most things are in place. The mining of the James River needs to be finished. I believe the how and the where are set; the timing remains to be decided. It depends on some other pieces falling into place. But I expect that'll happen within the next two months. Is Mosby ready?"

"He will be soon. General Lee wanted me to give you a bit of information. It seems that another plan may be brewing to kidnap the president. John Wilkes Booth, the actor, is also involved."

133

"What sense does that make? Lee permits this?"

"It comes from our Canadian operatives. Sanders is heading it up. Likely nothing will come of it, but General Lee views it as a fallback position. You are the first option. Booth hasn't even finished lining up his team, and you're ready to go. But we thought you should know. We don't want you stumbling over each other."

"Fine, we'll be done before he's ever needed."

"Is your Washington team ready?"

"Yes, and I may have added another man yesterday. But I'm not quite sure yet."

"Who?"

"A local. I'd be more suspicious, but he clubbed a policeman who was onto who I am, and he helped me escape. Still, I wonder about him. I have more checking to do."

"Be careful, Tom. You need to get out of town for a while. Come back when everything's a go."

"I plan on leaving tomorrow. You need to get out, too. You're the one with the big price on your head."

"We can leave together, but now give me the details of your plan."

JESSE WATCHED OVER LINCOLN throughout the day. The president spent most of the time with Stanton in the War Department, leaving Jesse to explore nearby areas in the city. During the afternoon he sent a telegram to Governor Miller in Minnesota. He wanted a letter printed in the *St. Paul Pioneer Press*. He also visited Daniel James, a Lincoln agent posing as a Copperhead leader.

Early in the evening he headed down H Street toward McGovern's Bar. Ahead on the walkway was a woman on her hands and knees, searching for something with her hands.

Jesse stopped. "Can I help, ma'am?"

The young woman glanced up at him with lustrous, teary blue eyes. Long dark hair framed the most beautiful face he had ever seen.

"Yes, please! I've lost my bracelet. It's a family heirloom. I just have to find it!"

Jesse knelt down and helped in the search. A short time later he smiled triumphantly and held up a gold bracelet. "Here!" he exclaimed. "It fell into a little crevice."

"Oh, thank you, sir!" the woman cried as she gratefully wrapped her arms around Jesse's neck. Then, embarrassed, she released him and stammered, "I'm sorry for being so forward, but my bracelet means so very much to me. Thank you for finding it!"

"I'm not offended. My name's Jesse, Jesse Miller."

"I'm Kate Thompson. I'm pleased to meet you, sir."

Her voice was soft with a slight French accent. To Jesse it seemed musical. He was glad he was ahead of schedule for his meeting at McGovern's. It would be nice to get to know this woman a little better.

They exchanged small talk on the street until Jesse motioned to a nearby bench in front of a closed storefront.

"Do you want to sit and talk awhile?"

Kate reddened slightly. "That would be fine, sir."

"Jesse, please call me Jesse," he said as they sat down.

"What do you do here?" she asked.

Jesse hesitated. He obviously couldn't tell the truth, and his cover would not impress the right lady. He deflected her question. "I come from the West, from Minnesota. I wanted to be where the action is. I've been helping in the hospitals."

"There was an Indian war in Minnesota. Did you fight?"

"I did some fighting. What about you? Are you from here?"

"My family was Acadian. Most were banished to New Orleans. Grandfather came to New York. I was raised there. Now I'm studying to teach. I'd like to get a job here, but things are so unsettled. I wish that McClellan had won. If women could vote, I would have voted for the Peace Party."

Jesse felt an attraction to this independent, outspoken woman. And, he reasoned, her political tendencies could be helpful. He decided to go ahead with his cover story. "I support the Peace Party, too. The war's wrong. My fighting's been against Indians, not Confederates."

Kate smiled. "I'm glad."

They continued to chat until Jesse realized that the time had come to meet Conrad. "I'm sorry, but I must go. May I see you again?"

"I'm staying at the Willard. You can find me there."

"Tomorrow," Jesse smiled.

As he hurried away to McGovern's, Jesse felt a pang of guilt and borderline disloyalty. But JoAnna would have understood.

Tom Conrad was seated at a corner table in the smoky tavern. Jesse peered through the haze for the man he had come to meet and joined Conrad.

"Mr. Miller, good to see you. I was hoping you wouldn't forget."

"Of course I wouldn't."

"I have a project in mind. But, frankly, I need to know more about you. Where are you from?"

"Minnesota."

"Why didn't you go south to fight rebels?"

"We were busy fighting Indians. But the more the war went on, the more I came to realize that Lincoln and the Republicans were wrong. I want peace. I came to Washington hoping I could help find a way."

"How do I check on you? What references do you have?"

"Check the *St. Paul Pioneer Press* newspaper. Talk to Daniel James."

"The Copperhead Peace Party leader? Yes, I know him."

"Talk to him."

"I will. If your stories check out and you're willing, I'll involve you in something big."

"Like what?" Jessie said, giving Conrad a look of excitement.

"That'll have to wait. I'm leaving town for a while tomorrow. Meet me here again at noon. I may have my answers then."

ɛɔ 29 ങ

WASHINGTON

THE NEXT MORNING JESSE OBTAINED a horse from a nearby stable and rode a few miles to the Soldiers' Home. Dawn was just breaking into a pink smear on the horizon when he arrived. But the president was an early riser and would soon be on the trail back to Washington.

He waited alongside the road and soon heard a steady *thump, thump* of hooves on the earthen road. Lincoln, wearing his customary black coat and high hat, soon rode past. He nodded at Jesse but said nothing.

Jesse waited as ordered, staying on the fringes of the president's movements, watching but keeping out of the way. He followed until Lincoln reached the War Department office. Knowing that the president would spend several hours there, Jesse decided to drop by the Willard Hotel. It was as good a place as any for breakfast.

The Willard, the National, and the Kirkwood were the premier hotels in Washington. Vice-President-elect Johnson stayed at the Kirkwood. General Grant was known to stay at the Willard. Jesse entered the Willard's dining room and was pleasantly surprised to see Kate Thompson seated at a small table awaiting breakfast.

"Good morning, Kate. Mind if I join you?"

Kate's smile displayed even white teeth. "I'd enjoy your company very much. Please sit down."

"How did your meeting at McGovern's go last night?"

"It was short, but I accomplished what I needed to do."

"How long do you plan to stay here? Do you have family in Minnesota?" She looked down, lowered her eyelids and asked more softly, "A wife?"

Jesse was flattered by the last part of question. "I'll probably be here until the war ends. My parents are in Minnesota. I'm not married. I came close, though."

"What happened?"

"She died, sickness."

"I'm sorry, Jesse. And I don't mean to appear forward. I just like to get to know people before I . . ." Her face reddened.

"Before what?"

"Oh, I guess I meant to say that I just like to get to know people who are becoming my friends."

Jesse answered with a smile. The two continued to enjoy breakfast and conversation, and time flew by until Jesse realized that he needed to get to McGovern's to see Conrad.

"I'm sorry, Kate, but I must leave. I'd like to see you again."

"And I you, Jesse, but I'll be gone for a while—family matters in New York. In fact, I fear that I'll have to be back and forth quite a lot in the coming months. My mother is ill. I'll leave a message for you when I return here."

She stood as Jesse did and reached up to brush his cheek with her lips. "So you won't forget me," she whispered.

His face flushed as Jesse felt tantalized by her touch. "There's no danger of that. I hope you're back soon."

A SHORT TIME LATER JESSE ENTERED the smoky tavern on H Street. Conrad was seated at the same table as the night before. They exchanged a handshake as Jesse sat down.

"Mr. Miller, I've done some checking. Mr. James speaks very highly of you. He says that you're a valuable ally in the peace movement. There also is a letter in the St. Paul newspaper dated last month, but for some reason just published, in which you attack our dear Mr. Lincoln quite harshly. Maybe I do have a use for you."

It's working, Jesse thought silently. The telegram to Governor Miller with a bogus letter and a request that Miller arrange to have it printed had been successful. The meeting with James, a Union Secret Service plant in the Peace Party hierarchy, had also produced the desired results. They believed his bogus identity.

Conrad's voice broke into Jesse's thoughts. "I have to leave town and, frankly, you're still being checked out. But I'll tell you this much. We're assembling a team that could impact the government of the United States. Are you interested in being a part of it?"

"I'd be most interested."

"Good. I'll be gone a couple of weeks. When I return, I'll get in touch with you. By then I'll have determined if you can be trusted."

"If it's about ending this war and making sure that Lincoln's policies are ended, then I'm all for it."

Conrad replied with a grim smile. "You might be on the right track with your thinking. But there's much more to what is intended. You may be hearing from me or from one of my associates quite soon."

THAT AFTERNOON JESSE REPORTED to Ward Hill Lamon. "Something is in the works, Mr. Lamon. I believe Conrad's planning something very big."

"Any idea what?"

"Just that it involves the government. It's risky. Maybe we should have arrested him. He's left for a couple of weeks now."

"Maybe, Jesse, but that would've blown your cover, and we still wouldn't know what's going on."

"Thanks for your help with James. Conrad believes my story."

"Good, for now all we can do is watch and wait."

LATER THAT SAME AFTERNOON John Wilkes Booth left for New York. There he purchased two seven-shot Spencer carbines, three pistols, ammunition, daggers, and two sets of handcuffs. When he returned to Washington, Booth dropped the weapons off with Sam Arnold in Washington.

❧ 30 ❧

DECEMBER 1864, BALTIMORE

FTER LEAVING THE ARSENAL WITH ARNOLD, Booth returned to Washington on December 17. He brought with him a nineteen-year-old prostitute, Ella Starr, and left her in a bordello on Ohio Avenue. He felt guilty because he had become recently engaged to Lucy Hale, daughter of a United States senator, but he didn't feel guilty enough to leave Ella in Baltimore.

Several days later, more important things occupied Booth's mind. He left Washington for Bryantown, thirty miles to the south in Maryland. The following day he met Dr. Samuel Mudd in a tavern there. They were joined by Tom Harbin, a Confederate Secret Service agent from King George County, Virginia. The three went to an upstairs room for a private conversation.

Booth opened with dramatic flair. "Mr. Harbin, this will be one of the great moments in world history. The stage we play upon today is the stage of the world. Shakespeare will be but a scribbler, compared to what we write."

"Mr. Booth," Harbin responded, "this isn't a play. This is serious, dirty business, and you've got to come down here with the rest of us to get in the mud. Now, what do you have in mind?"

Booth was taken slightly aback. Somewhat deflated, he continued. "One question is paramount. Are you prepared to assist in the capture of Abraham Lincoln?"

"This has been discussed with my superiors in Richmond and the answer is, yes, I will assist you. What do you need?"

"Help in assembling my team. I have two so far, trustworthy men who have been loyal friends since boyhood. We need more."

Dr. Mudd was a sturdily-built medical doctor. He sported a mustache and dark hair that fringed a retreating hairline, which reached almost to the crown of his head. He interjected, "There's a fellow in Washington, a John Surratt. He lives at his mother's boarding house on H Street. I think he'd be willing to be part of this and would help Mr. Harbin find others."

"I know John Surratt. He's a courier for us, traveling between Richmond and Montreal with messages, the lucky dog," Harbin replied.

"Why do you say that?" Booth wondered.

"Because he escorts another more experienced courier, Sarah Slater, the most beautiful woman I've ever seen. Surratt is as devoted to our cause as anyone, but he's not quite twenty years old. Miss Slater's only a few years older but much more experienced in the business of espionage. We do find male accompaniment to be valuable for the safety of our female agents."

"When you return to Washington," Mudd suggested, "I'll take you to Surratt. When will you return?"

"I'll be there in two days, on the 23rd. I stay at the National Hotel."

"I'll meet you there."

"Then send Surratt to me," Harbin finished. "We have work to do."

JOHN SURRATT WAS JUST REACHING WASHINGTON with Sarah Slater. Slender and of medium height, Surratt had dark hair that was already starting to recede in front, leaving a high forehead. His beardless face was long with slightly sunken cheeks. Sarah Slater was indeed beautiful with dark hair and blue eyes.

Surratt left her at her hotel. "Sarah, I'm staying at my mother's boarding house. You know where to reach me."

"When another dispatch is ready, I'll let you know, John. Before long we'll have to go to Richmond."

"I'll be ready."

John Surratt's plans changed on the evening of December 23rd when he and Louis Weichman, one of Mary Surratt's boarders, encountered Booth and Dr. Mudd along the street leading to the boarding house.

"John," Mudd cried, "what a coincidence, we were coming to get you! This is John Wilkes Booth. He wanted to meet you with a proposition."

"The famous actor!" Surratt exclaimed. "I'm honored. This is my friend, Louis Weichman."

"The pleasure is mine," Booth replied. "Come, let's return to my room at the National where we can talk."

Once there the four immediately retired to Booth's room. They sat in a tight circle on wooden chairs and, at Booth's urging, spoke in low voices.

"An ear at the door could spell big trouble. We must be careful," the actor advised. Then he proceeded to verify the newcomers' loyalty. "John, Dr. Mudd's told me good things about you. As a courier you're trusted and know the right people on the inside of the Secret Service."

"And he knows every back road in southern Maryland," Mudd added.

"What about Weichman here? Is he one of us?" Booth demanded.

"Louis's loyal to the Confederacy. We can talk," Surratt affirmed.

"Then here it is." Booth laid out his plan. "We'll capture Lincoln and hold him for the ransom of our captured soldiers. Will you help us?"

Surratt's response was energetic. "I will. What do you want?"

"We need three to four more men to assist us at various tasks. Tom Harbin'll help recruit, but we need you to help form the team as well. Do you know Harbin?"

"Very well."

"He'll meet you on January 14th at Port Tobacco."

"I'll do it. Some costs may be involved."

"I'll see to them. In the end there'll be great reward, not only to our country but to all involved. I'll make you rich. Dr. Mudd, we'll be in contact with you as well."

THAT NIGHT KATE THOMPSON SENT a message to Jesse that she was back in Washington. Pleased to renew their budding relationship, Jesse met her at the Kirkwood.

He was surprised when Kate greeted him with a quick hug. "I've missed you, Jesse."

"And I missed you. How's your mother?"

"Better, but I may have to leave again in a few days. She isn't out of the woods yet. How are things with you? Is the war any closer?"

"No closer. I may have some prospects."

"Like what?"

"It's best not to talk about it, Kate. Not now."

"Do you see the president very much?"

"Sometimes I see him riding the streets, mostly out to the Soldiers' Home, I guess."

"Do you ever think about really taking a side in this?"

"What do you mean?"

"Some Copperheads are actively helping southern sympathizers."

Jesse considered his response. "Maybe I would, if the right chance came along."

"Enough about wars and politics. I want to talk about pleasant things. Don't you?" Kate's melodic tones sounded alluring to Jesse.

IN RICHMOND, ALBERT PIKE, and Judah Benjamin met in Pike's office.

"Things are starting to shape up nicely, Judah."

"We have two separate plans unfolding to accomplish the same result. I'm surprised that Lee and Davis approved of Conrad's scheme."

"Come now, Judah, why should you be surprised? We devised the plan, and we have the power to make sure it gets implemented."

"But, Albert, what about this actor, Booth? It came out of nowhere."

"Sanders is one of us. He sees the golden grail. He found Booth, who is a Knight of the Golden Circle."

"All Knights aren't Illuminati."

"We can be thankful for that, Judah. Too many cooks spoil the broth. As Mazzini wrote me long ago, there must be a separate rite above all others. It's from them that change will come. Our efforts are disguised by the lower degrees of Masons. We may be aided by men who happen to be Masons. But this is not of Freemasonry. There is and must be no sanction or our efforts by them."

"We need more money, Albert. The requests are coming in."

"Involve your Rothschild friends. They already fear Lincoln's protectionist policies. They don't want depressed prices."

"I've heard that Lincoln went to them to help finance the war," Benjamin said. "Bankers were asking twenty-four to thirty-six percent interest. Lincoln got Congress to print 450 million dollars in greenbacks instead. Interest-free money to support the Union cause is not what the Rothschilds want."

"Englishmen believe that British free trade, industrial monopoly and human slavery travel together. Lincoln's policies will destroy the Rothschilds' commodity speculations."

"Albert, the Rothschilds view Lincoln as a threat to the established order. They want him out of the way. I've contacted August Belmont, the Rothschilds' northern agent. He'll see that we have the funding necessary."

Pike pondered before commenting, "I've heard from Conrad that they need better maps through the escape route."

"Lieutenant Blackford and our topographical engineers are at work on it. He'll have good maps," Benjamin assured him.

"Good. Conrad's torn between taking Lincoln through Maryland to the lower Potomac and crossing, or going to the upper Potomac and delivering the prisoner to Mosby for transport to Richmond. The map will help him decide."

"Mines are being placed in the rivers to impede boats from helping in the rescue."

"Judah, the pieces of our plan continue to move into place."

"Most of our leading players are Catholic, with more to come."

"Even Booth?"

"He's attended mass with Mudd, and he knows what needs to be done.

"Yes, Albert. It's God's will."

"Or Satan's," Pike concluded.

IT WAS ON CHRISTMAS EVE THAT SAM Arnold delivered Booth's weapons by buggy to the Surratt Boarding House in Washington. The weapons were later taken to Surratt's Tavern, where John Lloyd was told to hide them until they were needed. Another piece was set in place.

ॐ 31 ☙

JOHN SURRATT DETERMINED THAT THERE were two obvious needs in Booth's plan. They required a boatman to get Lincoln across the Potomac, and they required some muscle. None of the participants so far had impressive physical strength, which might be needed in a struggle with the powerful president.

Surratt met Tom Harbin at Port Tobacco in Charles County, Maryland, on January 14. Surratt knew this spot well from his travels. Port Tobacco was on an old canal that ran into the lower Potomac River. It had secluded creeks and inlets all around, making it an ideal haven for blockade runners and for the comings and goings of Confederate agents.

Harbin and Surratt were there to buy a boat to carry Lincoln across the river into Virginia. They also hoped to find an experienced blockade runner to join their plan.

Surratt purchased a large flat-bottomed boat from Richard Smoot and James Brawner for 250 dollars. Next they needed a boatman. They tracked down George Atzerodt.

Surratt introduced Atzerodt to Harbin. "He does a good job, Tom. He's carried me as a courier and also other Confederate agents, mail and couriers across the Potomac. He's an expert on the river around here. Also, the creeks and small hiding places, George knows 'em all."

Atzerodt was a short, stocky, nondescript man. A scraggly beard spread over his chin. He was thirty years old and had come from Germany at the age of eight in 1843.

"What did you do before becoming a boatman?" Harbin wanted to know.

"I vas a carriage repairman," Atzerodt replied in a German accent. "But I like da river."

"We have a special passenger coming for you," Surratt said. "Can you get him across?"

"Wit dis boat I'll take the whole army across." Atzerodt smiled with tobacco-stained teeth.

Surratt grabbed the German's hand in a firm grip to seal their pact. "Welcome on board. Hide the boat here. We'll contact you. You'll make more money than you can imagine if you do this right."

He handed Atzerodt a gold coin. "A down payment for you."

"Where's Mosby?" Harbin asked.

"Go into da northern neck," the boatman answered. "Dey vill find you."

"Will you take us across?"

"You've made a bargain. I vill take you."

Within minutes Atzerodt and his new compatriots were traveling down the canal away from Port Tobacco and to the Potomac and the northern neck beyond.

John Singleton Mosby and his Rangers had been ordered to the northern neck of Virginia, the northernmost of three Virginia peninsulas bordering the Chesapeake Bay, with the Potomac River on its north and the Rappahannock on the south.

The "neck" would be traversed as part of the kidnapping escape route. Mosby was there to provide an escort when called upon.

Surratt and Harbin left Atzerodt on the south bank of the river and walked into the greenery of the wooded finger of land. They strolled aimlessly through tangled underbrush.

Harbin recalled, "When I was a boy I read books about Robin Hood. This reminds me of Sherwood Forest and the sheriff's men wandering around until Robin and his men found them."

"I expect we'll make a similar encounter," Surratt suggested.

Not long afterward a voice rang out. "Ya'll lost? Hold where ya are iffn ya wanna stay livin'!"

The two men stopped dead in their tracks and waited. Moments later four men materialized from the brush, their rifles leveled at Harbin and Surratt. The men looked forlorn and disheveled, their tattered butternut-colored clothing seemingly held together by patches. One man had no shoes. Despite their resemblance to mangy mutts, the men carried themselves with the menacing air of guard-dog authority as they defended their turf.

"Hold on, boys, we're Confederate!" Harbin cried. "We came here to see Colonel Mosby."

One of the soldiers spit a stream of brown tobacco. "S'pose the colonel don't wanna see ya?" he challenged.

"Tell him we are agents from President Davis," Harbin replied.

"And I'm President Jefferson Davis, hisself," the head soldier mocked. "Yer better git outta herea afore we start fillin' you with lead."

His buddies scowled assent as they edged closer to Harbin and Surratt.

"Please, our mission is urgent. We must see Colonel Mosby." Harbin stood his ground.

The gunmen remained unconvinced. "Why should we believe ya'll?" one snarled.

"You don't have to," Harbin bargained. "You outnumber us. You're in control. Take us to Colonel Mosby, and you can take care of us there if it turns out we're lying."

"Come with us," the soldier ordered.

After negotiating a twisting horse trail for half an hour, the small party of men entered a clearing. A cluster of faded gray tents filled the opening. Before one of them flapped a guidon, a small flag, of a colonel.

Before them stood the "Gray Ghost" of the Confederacy, master of hit-and-run raids, John Mosby. His gray uniform was wrinkled but clean. His dark beard was trimmed, as was his brown hair. The colonel's diminutive frame contrasted with his reputation for oversized feats of valor and boldness. Mosby waited while Surratt and Harbin were led before him.

"What brings you to the 'neck'?" Mosby inquired.

"Colonel, I'm Tom Harbin and this is John Surratt. We're Confederate Secret Service. You were sent here to help deliver a package to Richmond," Harbin continued cryptically. "We're part of the team that's going to wrap the package and bring it to you."

"I see." Mosby studied them. "When will the package be delivered?"

"We're still wrapping it, Colonel. But within a month or so."

"What do you need from me?"

Surratt replied, "The team's almost complete, but we need a final member. Frankly, we need muscle. We were told you might have the man we need."

Mosby scrutinized them at enormous length as he silently debated their credibility. Understanding the colonel's need to be certain of their identity, Harbin and Surratt exercised patience.

Eventually Mosby completed his deliberation and turned to a man standing guard next to him. "Sergeant, get me Powell." Mosby turned back to his visitors. "The man we're bringing in for this is fearless as he is strong. He could be a great help to you."

Moments later the sergeant returned with a powerful-looking man who stood over six feet tall, with dark complexion, black hair, blue eyes.

"This is Lewis Powell, sometimes he goes by Paine. Private, these are Secret Service agents Harbin and Surratt. They have a need for you."

Harbin was direct in his approach. "Private, we're involved in a secret plan to kidnap the president of the United States and to ransom him for our comrades in Yankee prisons. Will you join us?"

Powell looked at Mosby, who nodded. "Yes, sir," Powell agreed, "I will."

Harbin and Surratt concealed their enormous relief. "Thank you, Colonel. This will benefit all of us," Harbin replied in a level tone.

Within the hour Harbin and Powell were being rowed across the Potomac and back to Maryland by Atzerodt. John Surratt, accompanied by Colonel Mosby, left them and continued on to Richmond for an appointment with Judah Benjamin.

Secretary Benjamin had requested that Surratt give him an update on their plan to take Lincoln. He and Mosby were ushered into Benjamin's office.

"John, I'd like a status report on our Lincoln plan."

"Our team's been rounded out. We now have the men we need and are nearly ready to act."

"Can you cross the river?"

"We're set with a boatman and a boat. Colonel Mosby, here, is ready to escort them safely to Richmond. We're ready and waiting, Mr. Secretary. The men are anxious to get this underway."

"Make sure this stays quiet. I hate that so many people know."

"Word can spread in an army, sir. I'm trying to keep this quiet, but the sooner we act, the better."

"Colonel, is the mining done on the rivers?"

"The James is done. Any ship coming in to disrupt our mission will meet a bad end. The other nearby rivers will be mined shortly."

"What else do you need, John?" Benjamin inquired.

"Have the Signal Corps camps along the lower Potomac been alerted that they need to be ready to receive our 'guest'?"

"They have been told," the secretary confirmed. "All is ready on our end."

"We'll be ready soon. Booth is pushing. I'm sure we'll act before long."

"Good luck, John. The whole future of our nation may rest in your team's hands."

Benjamin chose not to mention the other team and Conrad.

"Sara Slater is here. I want you to escort her as far as Washington. I'm sending her with your report and what needs to be known about this to Thompson and Clay in Canada. We need everyone on board."

≈ 32 ≈

JANUARY 1865, WASHINGTON

UPON HIS RETURN TO WASHINGTON, John Surratt stopped at his family's tavern just twelve miles from the capitol. John Lloyd, a former Washington policeman, had leased the building from his mother for 500 dollars a year. Mary Surratt had moved to Washington in November to open her boarding house.

Sarah Slater took her place on a bench outside the establishment and waited as John entered the building. Sarah maintained that, although she was a spy, a proper woman would not go into a bar without dire justification.

It was early evening and a good crowd was merrily tipping back liquid refreshments. Surratt spotted a familiar face near the bar. It belonged to Davy Herold, who had frequently patronized the tavern while on bird-hunting trips. Recently he had become a frequent visitor to the boarding house on H Street.

"Good to see you, Davy!" Surratt cried. "How are things in Washington?"

The twenty-two-year-old beamed with gapped teeth showing. "Hey, just fine, Johnny! I'm getting tired of my job, though."

"How long have you been working at the pharmacy?"

"Just about a year. Seems like ten. It pays the rent, though. I have to help out my mother and sisters, ya know."

"Too bad your dad died."

"Yeah, but he wasn't making much anyway, and he was a drunk."

John reflected a moment, then asked, "Say, Davy, I've got a job for you, if you're interested. It can pay pretty well, too."

"What is it?"

Surratt lowered his voice to just above a whisper. "I know you're on our side, Davy. Join our team to capture Lincoln and hold him for ransom."

"What!" the young man exclaimed, his jaw dropping open in shock.

"You heard me. Don't be loud, and don't talk about this. We can use you."

"Who's pushin' this?"

"We're led by John Wilkes Booth."

Herold struggled to contain his excitement. "I'd get to work with the great actor, with one of the most famous men in America, north or south!" He shook his head with disbelief at his sudden good fortune. "I'll do it! When do I start?"

"You're officially part of the team as of now. Come by my mother's house. Your part will be explained."

Surratt reached his mother's boarding house to find that two visitors were already engaged in conversation in the small sitting room, Tom Conrad and John Wilkes Booth.

"Welcome, John," Booth greeted. "Was your trip successful? This is Tom Conrad. He's sharing something most interesting with me."

"Our team's complete, Mr. Booth."

"Excellent. It seems that we and Mr. Conrad have both been engaged in similar endeavors. Conrad's also preparing to kidnap the president."

"What? How!" Surratt blustered.

"It seems that our friends in Canada and Mr. Conrad's friends in Richmond both conceived of plans to do the same thing. While our efforts have been kept separate, I wouldn't be surprised to hear that there were those who knew of both plans, using one or the other of us as a backup, if you will."

"I heard some talk, put some things together and came to talk to Booth at the National," Conrad explained. "He suggested we meet here."

"A little more out of the way," Booth pointed out.

"So now what do we do?" Surratt was still trying to grasp the turn of events.

"Mr. Conrad and I have reached a consensus. While our team is selected, the members are not all here yet. Conrad's men are all in place. He plans to act within days. He gets first crack."

"You'll be kept informed," the spy asserted.

"Mr. Conrad, if you're successful, you won't have to tell me anything. The world will know."

After Conrad left, Surratt demanded, "Honestly, now, where does this leave us?"

Booth was reassuring. "Just waiting a little longer. I don't think he can pull it off. Where's Miss Slater?"

"At her hotel. Oh, I added one more member to our group, Davy Herold."

"I've met him here. Is he needed?"

"He'll come in handy. Did Harbin arrive here?"

"Yes, with Lewis Powell, that very impressive young man you've recruited."

"It's all set."

"When Conrad fails, we shall be ready."

THAT NIGHT JESSE ONCE AGAIN MET Conrad at McGovern's. The Confederate spy determined that, because of Booth, he needed to act soon, so he took Jesse into his confidence.

"I've asked around about you. James led me to other Copperheads who know you."

Other plants, Jesse figured silently.

"So, are you ready for an important mission for peace?"

"Of course. What is it?"

"Come outside. I'll tell you there."

Secluded in shadows away from the building, Conrad revealed the plot to kidnap President Lincoln.

"Ingenious!" Jesse blurted. "It could end the war."

"More surely than the Hampton Roads Conference or any other such political gambit." Conrad spoke of a recent attempt between Union and Confederate negotiators to reach a peace settlement that failed because Lincoln would not recognize the Confederacy as a separate country.

"In the end, warriors bring more peace than pacifists. Count me in," Jesse agreed. "When do we act?"

"Lincoln will be heading to the Soldiers' Home day after tomorrow. We'll take him on the way."

"Done. What do you want from me?"

"Jesse, you'll be part of the squad of captors. We'll leave from the stable behind the Kirkwood at 4:00 a.m. You sure you're on board?"

Jesse nodded, "Yes, of course!"

"Then be there and keep your mouth shut."

JESSE WALKED BACK TOWARD THE WHITE HOUSE dumbfounded. Somehow he had uncovered a conspiracy against the president. He had accomplished what he had been called to do. Now he had to alert Ward Hill Lamon.

Realizing that he might be followed, Jesse opted to take a circuitous route to the mansion that should shake anyone on his trail. He had planned to have dinner with Kate at the Willard, but that would have to wait.

After traveling in and out of alleys, backtracking and surreptitiously observing his surroundings, Jesse was convinced that no one was watching him. He reached the White House and rapped sharply on the door. It soon swung open, and an elderly doorman beckoned Jesse to enter.

Lamon himself approached from an office.

"Mr. Lamon," Jesse burst with excitement, "I have news!"

Lamon motioned to an office door and ushered Jesse into the room. "What have you learned?"

"There is a plot to kidnap Mr. Lincoln, day after tomorrow."

"What? Explain!"

Jesse detailed Conrad's plan to Lamon, whose emotions ranged from shock to fear to joy.

"Excellent!" he cried. "I'm concerned that they know so much and have progressed this far in their plans. But we know what they're doing. We assigned you for this very purpose, and our strategy has succeeded."

"So, you'll keep the president away from the Soldiers' Home."

"We'll do what needs to be done. Thank you so very much, Jesse. Stay with Conrad. We can learn more."

FROM THE WHITE HOUSE JESSE WALKED to the Willard Hotel. Most tables were empty. But Kate Thompson waited at a small, round table with white cloth set for two.

"Jesse!" She appeared relieved. "I was worried something had happened to you."

"Something did delay me, but nothing serious. I'm sorry."

"It's all right. I'm just glad that you got here."

She wrapped her arms around Jesse and kissed his cheek.

Jesse returned the embrace and gazed into her deep-blue eyes.

"Kate, there's no problem so great that I couldn't surmount it to get to you."

Kate reached over and took Jesse's hand as they sat at the table. "Do you miss JoAnna?" she asked gently.

"I think of her every day. Probably will for the rest of my life. But I'm starting to think of you more. Sometimes I feel guilty."

"JoAnna would understand. No man is meant to be alone, Jesse."

Over their meal the two continued to talk about the past, their present and the future. Kate spoke of a future without war and without Lincoln. Jesse agreed, still playing his role, although he found it was becoming more difficult to deceive Kate.

"I have to leave again tomorrow."

"Kate," he protested, "you just got here."

"My mother really needs me. I won't be gone long."

She stood and took Jesse's hand. He rose to stand beside her.

"Goodnight, Kate," he said.

Kate held tightly to Jesse's hand and walked to the stairway with him. Then she stopped and whispered into his ear, "Come with me. I want to say a proper goodnight."

Jesse stifled a gasp and grabbed the railing to steady himself. *This is moving so fast. Too fast*, flashed through his mind. As he hesitated, Kate's gorgeous eyes and seductive smile melted his resistance.

Hand in hand they crept up the stairs together.

✂ 33 ✂

JANUARY 1865, WASHINGTON

A DAMP CHILL HUNG IN THE AIR as Jesse joined seven other men in a stable a block behind the Kirkwood Hotel.

"Thought you might not make it," Conrad called. "Are you ready?"

"Of course, I am. I'm ready to see that warmonger put away."

"Good. Men, here's what we do. Nothing's really changed from our plan. We stop him on the way to the Soldiers' Home. Don't be overly rough. Use only what restraint is necessary. Try not to hurt him. If Lincoln is in a carriage, we'll take him and the carriage. If he's on horse, then just him with the horse. Then we'll hurry to the Potomac by the lower route, cross over, and it's on to Richmond."

"Ain't that what Yankees keep sayin'?" a man said laconically.

"Yes, Jeffers," Conrad smiled, "but this is in a good way. We can be there by tomorrow."

"Then let's get going," a man called.

A half-hour later four men on each side lined the road leading up to the Soldiers' Home. Before another half-hour was up they heard the drumming of horses' hooves.

"Too many hooves," Conrad mumbled.

Moments later cavalry troops galloped past, surrounding a carriage containing Lincoln.

"Damn! He's got an escort! They never did this before. Did they know about this? How?"

The men gathered in the brush off the roadside. Conrad scrutinized each of his men and stared especially hard at Jesse.

157

"How? There's only one thing different from before." His eyes remained focused on Jesse.

One of the men spoke up. "I din't say nothin' before 'cause I thought it wuz hearsay. But I wuz told that Mosby's troopers bin talkin' at Surratt's Tavern. Some bin blabbin' that they be here to take Lincoln. I bet the wrong person heard 'em."

"I'm not surprised! But this really tears it."

Grateful for the timeliness of Conrad's noisy retort, Jesse tried to stifle the deep exhalation of relief that needed to escape his mouth.

"What now?" Jeffers asked.

"I'll let you know tomorrow. Let's go to Surrattsville for now."

By mid-morning the eight men had reached the tavern, where more news upset Tom Conrad. The caretaker, Lloyd, handed him a newspaper.

"This beats all!" Conrad exclaimed as he waved the paper at his men. "Grant's reversed himself, the prisoner exchange is back in effect! They won't be holding our boys locked up until the war is over."

"Isn't that one reason why we were trying to kidnap Lincoln?" Jeffers asked in wonder.

"Yes, and due to today's events, I'm going to make a recommendation. Lloyd, get me a pencil and paper."

Conrad wrote in detail of his efforts to capture Lincoln and his failure in doing so. He concluded by writing, "I don't see any use in continuing this project or of staying here any longer. As far as I'm concerned, this finishes it."

He turned to one of his men. "Take this to Richmond via the Signal Route. It's over. We have to find other ways to win this." Then he surprised the men with a chuckle. "Hell, maybe we'll just blow it up."

"Blow up what?" one of them asked.

"Just you wait."

As the men dispersed and rode east, Jesse bid them goodbye and headed back to Washington. He considered himself exceptionally lucky.

34

FEBRUARY 1865, WASHINGTON

HE BALLROOM CHANDELIER BLAZED brightly, glowing down upon the finest couples in Washington. The National Hotel reverberated with live music from the bandstand as luminaries abounded on the dance floor. Amidst this wonderland were Jesse and Kate, for he had succumbed to her wishes and accompanied her to this gala event.

Beautiful women were twirled about in their wide hoop dresses. They had spent weeks planning and gathering their finery, down to the very tiniest of details, for this was a chance to dazzle, to be in the spotlight. The men were resplendent in dark-blue dress uniforms or their finest suits.

John Hay and John Nicolay, the president's assistants, welcomed the attention of young ladies and cheerfully accompanied them to the dance floor. Robert Lincoln, the president's son, danced with Lizzie Hale, daughter of Senator John Hale, the abolitionist from New Hampshire. Sam Arnold traversed the floor with a young red-haired woman in his arms.

But all eyes were riveted on the couple in the very center of the room: the dashing John Wilkes Booth and the other daughter of Senator Hale, Lucy. While the women in the crowd admired Booth, the men found Lucy most alluring.

At twenty-three, she had saucer-like blue eyes, luminous dark hair and a striking, although slightly full, figure. Her mind, charm, and humor attracted eligible bachelors like moths to a flame. The flame burned hottest for Booth.

Hay and Captain Oliver Wendell Holmes, Jr., watched the pair dance with disgust. "Oliver, there's no one with her charm and ability to steal hearts."

159

"She seems quite taken with that actor Booth, that popinjay!" Holmes was scornful. "A war's going on, and he plays on the stage. How can a woman like Lucy, who is passionate about the war and a staunch abolitionist, be so enamored of someone who plays on a stage while others are fighting and dying?"

"Bad judgment," Hay replied.

Jesse and Kate watched with bemusement.

"The glamour couple have attracted a lot of attention," Kate observed.

Jesse held her tightly as they swept by. "She's the second-most-lovely woman in the room," he whispered into Kate's ear.

She smiled. "And I'm in the arms of the most handsome man."

"Watch this," Jesse cautioned, "Robert Lincoln's cutting in on the actor."

The tall, dark-haired, mustached son of the president deftly tapped Booth on the shoulder. Startled and clearly irritated, the actor stepped aside, and Lincoln took Lucy in his arms.

Red-faced with rage, Booth found Sam Arnold. "Of all people, the son of the devil himself takes my beloved in his arms. I'm of a mind to challenge him."

"John, be careful," Arnold advised. "You have bigger fish to fry, and you can't fight a duel with the president's son. In a moment the music will stop and you can rejoin her."

"The hands of that ape's son have touched my Lucy."

"Wait until the music stops. Do nothing stupid."

Jesse watched in amusement. "Kate, Booth seems perturbed."

"I won't share my dance partner," she whispered back, "and he doesn't want to, either."

The music stopped, and Booth reclaimed his prize on the dance floor.

"It pained me to be apart from you for even that little time," he told her.

"What will you do when my family takes me to Spain?"

"Die a little every day. Why can't he continue as a senator? Why does he want to be Minister to Spain?"

"My father wants a change in his life."

"Lucy, perhaps he believes your consorting with an actor is a social step backward for you, and that your ardor for me will cool in Spain."

"It won't work, John. My ardor for you will never die."

Kate and Jesse stepped outside to escape the heat and the stale air in the ballroom.

In the cool darkness of the evening, Kate reached up and gently kissed Jesse's lips.

"I have to leave again tomorrow, Jesse. I won't be gone long. But once again I'm needed in New York."

"I wish I could go with you. But I must stay in Washington."

"It's all right. I'm better off going alone. I'll be back within a week."

"My days are full, but my nights will be empty," Jesse replied. He held her close in a tender embrace.

INSIDE THE NATIONAL'S BALLROOM the band played its final song. Booth bade Lucy goodnight as her father's assistant, acting as an escort, departed with Lucy and Lizzie.

Arnold and Booth left together. They meandered slowly along the street, which was full of carriages taking finely-clad couples to their homes.

"Sam, you seem out of sorts," Booth observed. "Is something wrong?"

"Just this," the frustrated Arnold muttered, "when are we going to do something? Our team is set and I've seen at least two good chances to grab Lincoln come and go with no action. The month of January has passed and we've accomplished nothing. And you, John Wilkes Booth, you traipse around with women like Ellie Starr, Sarah Slater, and particularly Miss Lucy Hale. You squander money and have to go to New York for more, you live high and carelessly. Will February be like January? I've talked to O'Laughlen, and he shares my concerns. If we're going to do something, we must do it soon. Richmond is besieged, and the South cries for you. We have placed our hope in you. Don't let us down!"

Booth chuckled in spite of Arnold's condemnation. "Sam, I'm the actor, and you're spewing drama! Oh, the irony! I must go to Philadelphia next week, Sam. When I come back, the time to take action will be near. All isn't ready. We have some loose ends to tie up. Surratt's still carrying messages and escorting Sarah Slater through Union lines. He needs to make sure the boat and Mosby are ready for us. But be assured, Sam, it's almost time."

"It better be, Wilkes. It seems to me like you're intentionally delaying. I, for one, am about ready to leave this venture as an exercise in waste and futility."

"I said soon, Sam." Booth was firm. "It'll be soon, and we'll have Lincoln in our grasp."

"I saw Sarah Slater there tonight," Arnold commented.

"Did you? There were so many people, I'm afraid I missed her. I guess I only had eyes for Lucy."

"That's not like you, Wilkes. You usually have eyes for all beautiful women."

"I'm focusing on one. Who was she with?"

"I don't know, someone I've never seen before. He's not a soldier; at least, he wasn't in uniform."

"Well, we know who she'll be with soon. John Surratt."

❧ 34 ☙

FEBRUARY 1865, PHILADELPHIA

BOOTH TRAVELED THROUGH PHILADELPHIA on February 10 en route to a meeting in New York City. While there, he stopped to visit his sister, Asia Booth Clarke.

Asia had dabbled in the theater when younger but had left the Booth family "business" to devote herself to her husband and family. She was also devoted to John, who was three years her junior.

"Johnny!" She squealed her delight and embraced him lovingly as he appeared on her doorstep. "What a pleasant surprise! Come into the sitting room, I have tea. What brings you here?"

"I'm on my way to New York and decided to stop off here to visit you."

"I'm so glad you did! Are you going to perform in New York?"

"No, I've suspended my acting for a while for other ventures."

"Like investing in oil wells. How is that working?"

"I've sold off my Pennsylvania stock. It wasn't the boon I expected."

"Johnny, I want to tell you again how much I enjoyed watching you and your brothers last November in New York. The Booth Brothers in *Julius Caesar*. It was magnificent!"

"The only time Junius, Edwin and I have ever performed together. It's too bad your husband couldn't have performed as well."

"John was engaged in another play that night, or it could have been a complete family affair. But you were all tremendous."

Booth revealed a large envelope with a packet of papers and handed them to Asia. "Put these in your safe, please. One deals with my oil transactions, others are of a personal nature."

163

"Why do you give them to me?"

"I move all around with no permanent home. I want them kept together all in one spot, where I know I can access them."

"Then they'll be safe here," Asia agreed.

"Look at this." Booth unfolded a sheet of paper containing an alphabetical square.

"What is it?"

"It's a cipher, a way to decode messages."

Asia looked at the paper in alarm, her hazel eyes widening. "This is the type of thing spies use. I shall have nothing to do with it."

"Please, Asia, I may need to use it to communicate about money."

"No, John. I won't allow it to remain in my house. You must take it with you. I haven't talked to you about your other 'ventures,' and I've no wish to know."

"I can't leave it with Edwin, the abolitionist fanatic."

"All the Booths favor abolition except you, Johnny. Your argument with Edwin did not set well with Mother."

"Edwin blamed fires in New York on southern sympathizers and prayed for the re-election of the tyrant Lincoln. I could not let that rest."

"Politics and this war must be kept out of family discussions. Edwin won't speak of it, and you promised Mother that you wouldn't split the family by actively supporting the South."

"And I regret it every day."

Asia found herself regretting that her brother had just shown her the sinister-looking paper, whose image refused to leave her. Much as she feared what she may learn, Asia feared for her younger sibling's well-being even more. She felt compelled to question him.

"What are you doing, John? Please, tell me the truth."

"I have smuggled precious drugs to the Confederates."

Startled, Asia searched for hints of a joke in his expression and detected none. But, of course, he was an actor by profession, and a superb one at that. Or was it acting?

She plunged ahead in her quest for the truth. "Why would you do this? Do you really obtain drugs and smuggle them to the other side? Aren't you afraid of getting caught? Is this a bad joke?" She prayed that it was.

"My fame has allowed me to obtain passes that give me a certain freedom of range," he replied without apology.

Asia's world tumbled upside down at the horrible realization that her brother actually was doing evil, and that he was capitalizing on Booth fame in order to do so.

She recoiled in shock. "You really are a spy, like Benedict Arnold and John Andre!" she gasped.

"Don't think badly of me, dear sister, I'm a patriot."

"No, John, there must be nothing in those packets of a Confederate nature, including a cipher!"

"Don't worry." He kissed his sister's cheek. "My family won't be involved in any of my affairs."

Asia did not see it that way. "We're Booths. What each of us does affects all of us. The Booths are known North and South."

"Don't worry, Asia. You will be proud some day."

BOOTH LEFT TO COMPLETE HIS JOURNEY to New York, where an important rendezvous had been arranged. It was a summit on the enterprise planned for Lincoln. The site for the meeting was the Fifth Avenue Hotel, a six-floor, state-of-the-art structure completed just seven years earlier.

At the appointed hour he rapped on the meeting room door. When it opened, Booth entered into a light haze of cigar smoke. He recognized some of the men there, CSA commissioners to Canada Jacob Thompson and Clement Clay, along with John Surratt and George Sanders.

The actor did not know three other men. One was tall and slender. Another was equally tall but heavily built, like a square block of granite. A third was short, slight and balding. One woman there he knew well, Sarah Slater.

Sanders spoke. "Welcome, John, I believe you know most here. Surratt and Miss Slater have given us dispatches to bring to Montreal."

"Meeting you in New York shortened up the trip considerably," Sarah remarked.

"Giving Surratt more time to help me," Booth pointed out.

"I've done my recruiting and planning, Mr. Booth. It's up to you to fulfill the mission. And that, in part, is why we're meeting," Sanders said. "These gentlemen are Colonel James Gordon and General Albert Pike. That short one is Roderick Watson. He's the nerve center of our clandestine operations in New York."

All sat on chairs except for Pike, who stood to address them.

"I've been sitting back and watching, watching you try to disrupt the Union with raids from the north, watching you plan and try to kidnap Lincoln, start disease epidemics. I've watched you arrange futile peace conferences. I've watched, and it hasn't been all bad. But it hasn't been good enough. As our fortunes continue to dwindle, we must be bold and decisive. Conrad has abandoned his plan to kidnap Lincoln. But there is an alternative plan still to carry it out." Pike nodded at Booth.

"Things have changed. The exchange of prisoners has been reinstated by Grant. Lincoln was re-elected. We need a master stroke to throw the Yankees into chaos. Capturing Lincoln can do this. It's like cutting off the head of the snake."

"Mr. Booth," Sanders interjected, "it's up to you."

The actor was pleased. "When I have the maps, a ready boatman, and an escape escort in place, I shall be ready," he announced. "Are the river mines all in place?"

Pike answered, "I think you could proceed tomorrow. I have no doubt that by March first there can be no excuse."

"And am I truly the only option?"

"Obviously, we still have armies in the field. There are even other kidnapping plots. Lieutenant Stringfellow insists he can capture Grant. Maybe Mr. Watson can help organize another riot in New York. We also are employing the good graces of our Torpedo Bureau. Who knows, if all else fails, we may blow up the White House. But, Booth, you're the main option at this time. You can end this thing. Have you obtained passes for the inaugural?"

Booth smiled. "I had two sources, Senator Hale and, believe it or not, Vice-President-elect Johnson. I joined him and his assistant for a night of debauchery in Nashville a couple of years ago. Johnson can consume impressive amounts of alcohol and has a fine taste in women, too."

"I still say just shoot Lincoln and get it over with," Sanders snapped impatiently.

Pike's sinister gaze turned to ice. "It's not the time for such talk, not yet."

The tall, slender man, Gordon, spoke up. "This venture requires desperate men in desperate times. It will require great caution and skill as well. I'm glad you haven't been hasty, Mr. Booth. Make this work."

"Surratt and his mother are good Catholics, what about the rest of your team?" Pike asked.

"I'm not sure." Booth looked at Surratt, "John, who are the Catholics?"

"Arnold, O'Laughlen, and Atzerodt."

"Mr. Booth," Pike continued, "don't you think it's about time you attended the mother church?"

"I've been to a mass. What does that have to do with anything?" Booth dismissed.

"There's a plan that's beyond what you think or know. Let's just say it offers a symmetry to our operation. Miss Slater, how goes your work?"

"Richmond to Montreal, Montreal to Richmond with stops in Washington and New York. Surratt knows the way and gets me there safely."

"Gentlemen, how goes Canada?"

Thompson replied, "We have tacit support from England. The country offers a haven to Confederate sympathizers. We've launched raids to disrupt the border."

"Blockade runners continue to operate," Clay concluded, "but it's getting harder."

"Time is running out," Pike declared. "All must do their utmost for the cause."

As the meeting concluded, Sarah sidled next to Booth. "Are you sure that devoting so much attention to a senator's daughter is helpful to our cause?"

"She's the love of my life. Yet, I'll sacrifice all for the cause of the South."

"You may have to, John."

That night Booth stayed at the home of his brother, Edwin. He stayed up most of the night working on Valentine's Day cards for Lucy Hale.

❧ 35 ❧

MARCH 1865, WASHINGTON

ARCH BLEW INTO WASHINGTON cold and wet. Jesse shivered in the early morning mist as he watched President Lincoln ride in a carriage toward the War Department, where the president had become accustomed to spending most days.

Following Conrad's failed kidnapping attempt, Jesse had warned that more violent actions could await the chief executive. He had requested additional help, but Lamon and Stanton had decided that would draw too much attention to the president.

Jesse didn't agree. Conrad had come back to the city and had contacted him again. Something was brewing, perhaps even bigger than before. Convinced he needed help, Jesse had made a contact and was anxiously awaiting an arrival.

The presidential carriage was usually accompanied by a cavalry detachment, although Lincoln still managed to go off without them occasionally. Now Jesse watched as Lincoln unfolded his long body from the buggy and strode up the stairs and through the War Department doors.

That afternoon, as gray skies blanketed Washington, Jesse waited at the train station. A locomotive chugged in from the west and clattered to a stop. When the passenger cars opened, an athletic-looking man with one arm stepped out and onto the platform. It was Nathan Cates.

Jesse rushed to see him and wrapped his strong arms around Nathan, greeting him like the long-lost friend he was.

"Nathan, thank God, you've come! I needed someone like you here."

"You wrote a compelling and intriguing letter, my friend."

"How are things back west?"

"The campaign in the Dakotas is over. Solomon and Jim have gone back to Minnesota. I'm back at Crow Creek. Emily's still there, and I'll return there from here. How are you handling things, Jesse?"

"My life here and my assignment are much different. I'll explain later. I've met a girl, Nathan. It's hard to let go of JoAnna, though."

"Move on, Jesse. You have to."

As the two men made their way along the wet, muddy street, Nathan turned to his friend. "You know, you left me little choice but to come here. You raised some questions in your letter about my past."

"Nathan, your past is safe with me. I don't know what's true or not. I do know if even part of what was said is real, that you can help me here."

"What do you think you know?"

"When I came to Crow Creek, your Indian ward, Johnny, asked me if I knew if a Confederate spy had come to Minnesota to start the Indian wars. He said that a Confederate officer had been seen in Little Crow's camp and that he was your superior. I find that hard to believe, after how hard you fought with our army against the Dakota and how you continue to serve as a teacher and missionary to the Indians."

Nathan sighed. "Let the past be. Things happened that I'm not proud of. I'm trying to make things better."

"I can let that all go, Nathan. I don't know what you were or what happened. I do know who you are now, and I'm glad to call you a friend. I have other problems here and, if you do have Confederate contacts and background, I need your help."

"What are you trying to do?"

"I'm trying to protect the life of Abraham Lincoln, and I'm being drawn into a web of Confederate agents. You may know these people or know of them. Can you help me?"

"I've come to believe this war's wrong and fought for the wrong reasons. What happened in Minnesota was wrong as well. As long as we don't talk about the past, I'll help you with the present," Nathan agreed.

"There's just one thing. If this involves Confederate agents, I can't be seen with you. I'm not sure how much my activities in Minnesota are known here, but if Albert Pike is part of this and he becomes aware that you're with me, it would be your death warrant."

"Who's Albert Pike?"

"Director of Covert Operations for the Confederacy. He's a big man both in bulk and height, with a heavy black beard and near shoulder-length hair."

"I haven't seen him."

"I think he's centered in Richmond. But he does venture out. I found that to be the case in Minnesota. You need to keep me in the background. I can advise you."

"Thank you, Nathan. Maybe we can save the president."

ON MARCH 1ST JEFFERSON DAVIS brought Benjamin Stringfellow into the Confederate Executive Mansion. The handsome soldier with wavy, dark hair was ushered through an ante room and into the office of the president.

Davis, lanky and gray-haired with a goatee on the chin of his narrow face, motioned for Stringfellow to be seated.

"First off, Lieutenant, I want to compliment you. Your work with General Stuart and now General Lee has been exemplary. I want to reward you for that work with a promotion. You are now a captain."

No emotion cracked his serious demeanor as Stringfellow replied simply, "Thank you, sir."

A distant rumble carried through an open window. "Damn cannons!" Davis snapped. "Don't those Yankees ever run out of ammunition?"

"It seems that Petersburg is getting closer," the new captain drawled laconically.

"I don't know how much longer we can hold on," Davis said, "Grant keeps trying to slide around Lee's right. Lee has to keep stretching his flank. Eventually he'll run out of men to stretch."

"How can I be of service to you, Mr. President?"

"Captain, I've looked over your letter to General Lee. Magician that you are, I don't think Grant can be captured. I don't even think it advisable right now. We have another target."

"You mean Lincoln. Conrad gave that up."

"Yes, but we're still proceeding with another plan."

"I could have killed Grant, you know."

"Explain."

"I was behind Union lines seeking information. I came upon Grant. His back was to me, my rifle was in my hand."

"What stopped you?"

"I'm a religious man, sir. I wouldn't shoot a man in the back."

"But you would kidnap him."

"With your approval, Mr. President."

"I have a different mission for you. We're about to launch a new phase of the war."

"What's that, sir?"

"Through the auspices of the Torpedo Bureau, we've been mining rivers. Now we have a more dramatic plan. We'll plant a bomb in one wing of the White House and blow it up.

"General Rains of the Bureau will coordinate the plan. He has an excellent man working with him."

"Harney?" Stringfellow wondered.

"Yes, Harney."

"I've heard of him. Everywhere he goes it seems that explosions cost Yankee casualties and loss of equipment."

"He does know his way around explosives."

"What is my mission?"

"Twofold. The actor John Wilkes Booth is still proceeding with a plot to kidnap and ransom Lincoln. The plan to bomb the White House is also in the works. Coordinate them. Booth's in Washington. He stays at the National Hotel. He also frequents the Surratt Boarding House with his associates. You know John Surratt, our courier."

Stringfellow nodded.

"It's his mother's establishment. We have agents and sympathizers in New York City pushing the bombing plan."

"You want both plans to come off."

"If Booth is successful, we may not need to blow up the White House. But Booth's dragging his feet. Prod him. Conrad'll be back in Washington, but he wants to concentrate on the bomb. He's given up on the capture."

"So you'll still have the chance to kidnap a Union power, even if it isn't Grant."

"What's my cover?"

"You're to be a dentist. We've set up an office for you."

"I've always wanted to pull Yankee teeth. I don't plan to use any anesthetic. Complete Victory." Stringfellow relished the thought.

"Or Come Retribution," Davis finished.

∽ 36 ∾

MARCH 1865, WASHINGTON

HE MORNING OF MARCH 4, 1865, was drizzly and miserable in Washington. It was also Inauguration Day. Vice-President Andrew Johnson had been sworn into office in the Senate chamber.

Johnson gave a long rambling speech filled with outbursts and self-aggrandizements. Embarrassed senators hid their faces behind programs.

Secretary of the Navy Gideon Welles remarked to War Secretary Edwin Stanton, "Johnson is either drunk or crazy."

"The man's deranged," Stanton asserted. "Our unity man—a Tennessee senator who stayed with the Union. His reward'll be our punishment."

Johnson shouted, "I'm a-going to tell you . . . here today . . . yes, I'm a-going to tell you all that I am a plebian! I glory in it! I am a pull-E-bian! The people . . . yes, the people of the United States, the great people have made me what I am . . . ." Johnson grabbed the Bible and kissed it.

Lincoln turned to the parade marshal and whispered, "Do not let Johnson speak outside."

A platform had been erected on the eastern front of the capitol. The cheers of a great crowd below greeted the re-elected president as he took his place on the platform. The band began to play. Above and behind him and to his right was a balcony. Booth, having received a pass, stood on the balcony with Lewis Powell and watched in anticipation.

Jesse watched from in front of the viewing stand. He was vigilant but was comforted to know that many other sets of eyes were on the lookout for danger as well. Union snipers lined high vantage points all around.

Nathan stood apart from Jesse with his coat collar turned up. In another time and place, his one-armed status might have made him feel conspicuous. But all around were soldiers with obvious effects of battle, including those with lame or missing limbs and assorted wounds and scars.

Lincoln strode slowly to the lectern, gazed into the slate-gray sky and unfolded his speech. At that instant clouds parted and the platform was flooded with sunlight, like a spotlight on a stage.

Powell whispered to Booth, "Ya want me to shoot 'im? I got a good shot from here. Can't miss."

"No, Lewis. He still has more value alive than dead," Booth responded.

The president was not triumphant in tone. He spoke of wrongs being done on both sides. He balanced that by saying that slavery was an unmistakable evil and was justly ended.

It was a short speech. Lincoln gazed out into the faces of his audience now washed in sunlight. He finished by proclaiming, "With malice towards none, with charity for all, with firmness in the right as God gives us to see the right, let us strive to finish the work we are in; to bind up the nation's wounds; to care for him who has borne the battle, and for his widow and his orphans; to do all which may achieve and cherish a just and a lasting peace among ourselves and with all nations."

Booth turned to Powell and said bitterly, "Maybe I should have let you shoot him."

When it was over, Nathan joined Jesse back at his hotel room. "There were Confederate agents there, all right. I saw Tom Conrad. You knew he'd be there. He had a couple of men with him I didn't recognize. I think he felt safe in the crowd."

"I'm sure Conrad will come to see me again soon. Something is in the works again. I know it," Jesse said.

"I've been watching Surratt's Boarding House," Nathan replied. "A lot of strange comings and goings there. First off, it seems to be a haven for priests staying in Washington. I've seen Confederate agents there, but also a group of men who seem to come and go together."

"Couldn't they just be guests at the boarding house?"

"They don't go there to sleep. It seems like they meet and then leave. Most are pretty nondescript, but they don't appear to have much in common. Some are well dressed and groomed, but others look rough like common laborers.

"The man who seems to be their leader is polished and dresses well. He looks familiar, but I can't place him. In time I will."

"Thanks, Nathan, keep your eyes open. I need the help."

THE NEXT DAY, MARCH 5, BEN STRINGFELLOW reached Washington to confer with Conrad, Arnold, O'Laughlen, and Booth. They were joined by John Surratt, recently back from delivering dispatches in Montreal.

Stringfellow was direct. "Booth, all is ready for your mission. Whether you go by the upper or lower Potomac, boatmen and escorts are ready. I just passed through on the way here and checked on it myself."

"I must make arrangements for horses to escape Washington. I'll get Herold on it," the actor said.

"We've waited long enough, Wilkes," Arnold complained. "Much longer and it'll be too late. O'Laughlen and I are going back to Baltimore. Send for us when you decide to do something. How bad is it in Richmond, Captain Stringfellow?"

"Grant's tightening the noose. When Petersburg falls, it'll be all over. We think we can hold on until maybe April tenth or the fifteenth. An escape route for Lee's army and supplies is being readied. If we move on the road first, we'll chew it up. When Grant follows, he'll be slowed down. Lee should be able to join Johnston in North Carolina and keep fighting. We don't need a capitol to wage war. We need an army. Mr. Booth, we need you to cause disruption in Washington."

"You know I don't think this will work," Conrad reminded them, "I tried. I prefer the torpedo idea, and I'm working on it with our New York contacts. That'll cause real chaos."

"Sanders sent word from Canada, 'Just kill Lincoln and get it over with,'" Surratt reported.

"I don't care who does what," Stringfellow snapped, "let's get this moving!"

37

MARCH 1865, SURRATTSVILLE

OM CONRAD SENT FOR JESSE and asked that he travel twelve miles south of Washington to meet at Surratt's Tavern. The two sought a table in a back corner of the noisy, smoky bar.

"The way station of the Confederate Secret Service," Conrad said expansively, "a haven for agents and spies between Washington and Richmond, a place where I feel much safer than I do twelve miles to the north."

"Why does Lloyd run this place?"

"Surratt died. His wife, Mary, and son, John, made a go of it for a while, and then Mary sought greener pastures at the boarding house in Washington. She still owns this place and leases it to Lloyd. Both are friendly to us."

"Why did you send for me?"

"Our attempt to kidnap Lincoln failed. I'm off to New York to discuss plans for another option. We're bringing in some experts for this, but we'll still need people like you. I want to make sure you plan on being around Washington through March. I'll be in touch when the time comes."

"What's the plan?"

"It's big, and will really shake things up here," Conrad chuckled. "But for now it's best if knowledge of the details is left to a few. You'll know about this when you need to know."

Moments later John Surratt entered the tavern with a woman at his side. Conrad called, "John, Sarah come over here. I want you to meet someone."

Conrad proceeded with the introductions. "This is John Surratt, who I just spoke of, and this is Sarah Slater. Don't let her beauty fool you. She is our best courier and the finest female agent in the Confederacy. Sarah and John, this is Jesse Miller."

Jesse stared with wide-eyed astonishment. He opened his mouth to speak and managed, "Pleased to meet you." The woman before him was Kate Thompson.

After a quick flash of her eyes, Kate maintained a cool demeanor. "Pleased to meet you, sir." She extended her hand and squeezed Jesse's harder than usual.

The two sat at the table, joining Jesse and Conrad.

"How did you make the acquaintance of Mr. Miller?" she asked Conrad.

"He rescued me from a Washington policeman. One thing led to another, and he has aided our cause. He has been a part of my team."

"Very interesting," Kate demurred.

"How was Montreal?" Conrad wondered.

"Still chilly for March. I prefer the South. Our agents there are getting restless."

The four continued talking until Conrad and Surratt broke off into a conversation of their own. Jesse only caught one word, "Booth."

Kate leaned toward Jesse and spoke in a hush. "What are you doing here? I can't believe this!"

"Might I say, I share the same surprise. How's your mother?"

"All right, you've found me out. This is who I am. But it doesn't change how I feel about you. Are you really who Conrad says you are?"

"It would seem we are both surprised."

"Please, come to the Kirkwood tomorrow. I must talk to you."

"Tomorrow then," Jesse said as he stood to leave. He nodded at the two men. "Goodnight, gentlemen. I'll await your contact."

Jesse mounted his horse and rode back toward Washington, glad that darkness cloaked his face. He was overflowing with anger and confusion.

He had fallen in love with a Confederate spy who thought he was a Confederate agent. It was all too much for Jesse to even begin a strategy of how to work this out. The truth was impossible. The lie could lead to disaster. His stomach churned as if he had eaten too much greasy salt pork from Sibley's mess tent.

He gazed toward the heavens. "Please help me find a way out of this," he prayed.

↔ 38 ↔

MARCH 1865, WASHINGTON

HE NEXT MORNING AFTER WATCHING Lincoln go into a meeting in the White House, Jesse went to the Kirkwood Hotel. He knocked on the door of his friend's room. He waited, knocked again and turned to leave. In a way, he thought, it was best. He had many questions but didn't know if he wanted the answers.

Then the door opened. Kate had obviously just gotten out of bed. Her hair was disheveled, and she had thrown a robe over her night clothes.

"Jesse," she called, "please come back."

Jesse retraced his steps to her door. "Good morning, Kate, or is it Sarah?"

"It's Kate to you."

He stepped into the room and she closed the door.

"I'm sorry for how I look. It was quite late when I got back from Surrattsville."

"You're still beautiful."

"Jesse, I'm sorry you found out about me the way you did."

"I don't know how I feel about this. You're a spy."

"We all serve however we can. Many women work as nurses or for the Sanitary Commission, the Hale sisters, for example. I was asked to carry messages between Montreal and Richmond. It's easier for women to pass through enemy lines, particularly when they have an escort. Mine is John Surratt."

"I'm confused," Jesse admitted. "I'm not sure about this at all."

"Why, Jesse? We're on the same side, aren't we? I know you've worked with Tom Conrad and you say you hate Lincoln."

"It's more complicated than that, I just can't . . ." Jesse sadly shook his head and turned to leave.

"Lieutenant Buchanen," Kate called, "I think we should talk more."

Jesse stopped abruptly, then wheeled around to face Kate. "You know? How?"

"I'm a spy, and I do my job well. We have contacts in Minnesota and I used them. You pulled the wool over Tom Conrad's eyes. But I had a deeper interest in you, and I looked more closely into who you are and who you might be. The name JoAnna was a clue. So was the name Miller. You're a spy, too, for the Union."

Jesse's mouth hung open.

"Do you know what made me suspicious?" Kate asked, cocking her head at him. "You *said* you hated Lincoln, but it just wasn't in your eyes. There was no hatred there."

"I didn't come here to spy, Kate. I'm one of Lincoln's bodyguards."

"But you wound up posing as one of Conrad's men and then exposing his plans."

It was true. "So, we're spies, the two of us . . . for different sides. Have you told Conrad?"

"No one knows anything about this except you and me."

Jesse waited for her to continue, trying to anticipate where this momentous discussion would lead.

"I have ideals, but I'm also a pragmatic," Kate continued. "After I got back last night, I spent hours trying to sort through all this. Eventually I determined that what you're involved in doesn't affect what I do. Primarily, I deliver messages. I'm a courier. You're trying to protect the president's life. As devoted as I am to the Confederacy, I don't see how the murder of Lincoln will change anything. The war's lost. That fact's plain to any rational person. Killing Lincoln won't change that and may only make it worse. Therefore, your efforts to protect the president serve my personal beliefs. I'll finish this war as a courier."

"What about us? For so many reasons, we can't be together now."

Kate moved to Jesse, wrapped her arms around his neck and kissed him. "Until this war is over, yes, it's best we stay apart. Wait until it's over. I do care deeply for you, Jesse."

He held Kate in a tight embrace and murmured, "And I for you, but I'm still confused."

"Jesse, my mother does in live New York. I do stop en route to Montreal to see her. But she's not sick."

Jesse smiled ruefully and kissed Kate's cheek. "Until it's over, Kate. May it all end soon."

"It will be, Jesse."

Jesse left the Kirkwood with confoundedly mixed emotions. Kate immediately collected her belongings and checked out of the Kirkwood.

❧ 39 ❧

MARCH 1865, WASHINGTON

OOTH WAS WRACKED WITH INDECISION. He had reveled in the planning and in the admiration of his little corps of accomplices. As mid-March neared, his team had partly dispersed.

Arnold and O'Laughlen were back in Baltimore, as was Powell. The boatman, George Atzerodt, was staying in a dive hotel just off Pennsylvania Avenue. Booth paid for the room. Davey Herold was in Washington, living with his mother and two sisters near the Navy yard.

Finally, by March 13, after a conversation with his "dentist" String-fellow, Booth decided it was time to act. He sent a telegram to O'Laughlen, "DON'T FEAR TO NEGLECT YOUR BUSINESS. YOU HAD BETTER COME AT ONCE." The next day O'Laughlen and Arnold boarded a train for Washington.

John Surratt sent a telegram to David Preston Parr, a Baltimore china dealer who had worked as Powell's clandestine superior. Parr gave the message to Powell, "GO TO WASHINGTON."

Atzerodt and Herold were quickly and more easily summoned. They would all gather at Gautier's Restaurant at 252 Pennsylvania Avenue for planning. But first, a select few would attend the play, *Jane Shore*, at Ford's Theater.

Booth had reserved the President's Box, combined boxes seven and eight. Surratt and Powell were to watch the play from there. The real purpose was to become acquainted with the theater layout and the balcony box. They invited two boarders from Surratt's to lessen suspicion: seventeen-year-old Honora Fitzpatrick and ten-year-old Mary Apollonia Dean. The latter was a student at the Catholic School for Girls.

As the play transpired, Booth visited the box several times to speak with his two compatriots. During that time he also visited with the cast and crew backstage. When the performance was over, Booth gathered his principals at Gautier's. The young ladies had been brought back to Surratt's Boarding House at midnight.

The men met in the private dining room and talked amidst oysters, alcohol, cigars, and cards. With Booth were Atzerodt, Surratt, Herold, Powell, O'Laughlen, and Arnold.

Booth's two childhood friends knew nothing of the meeting until Herold came to get them. They had never met any of the other conspirators. In fact, they didn't know that anyone else was involved.

Once everyone had settled in, Booth outlined his plan. Actor that he was, he determined to use the theater.

"We will kidnap Lincoln while he watches a play," Booth explained. "I have rented the stable behind the theater. Our horses will be kept there. We can use the back exits from the theater. When I signal, Herold and O'Laughlen will turn out the gaslights. Arnold, Atzerodt, and I will rush the box, fasten Lincoln's hands together and lower him by a rope to Powell on the stage.

"A carriage will be waiting out the back exit. We will race to the Navy Yard Bridge, where Surratt will be waiting to help us escape into Maryland. Mosby will provide an escort, and by morning we will be in Richmond."

Arnold was dumbfounded. "Wilkes, have you gone absolutely mad!" he exclaimed. "This has no chance of working. The president has guards, there are soldiers all around. Do you expect everyone to just stand around while you do this? This is insane!

"For months Mike and I have been waiting to do something big for our cause," Arnold continued. "I turned down jobs because I was waiting for this. FOR THIS? I can't believe it!

"We agreed to help capture Lincoln on a country road, not in a theater full of people. Remember, the whole purpose of this was to make Grant resume the prisoner exchange program. He already did that."

"Sam, men, please understand." Booth waved an arm in a dramatic pose. "Capturing Lincoln is still best for the Confederacy. It will cause chaos in the Union. It will help in the peace negotiations."

"I don't care," Arnold rebutted, "I'm done with this."

Booth glared at his friend. "Do I need to remind you that you took an oath? Do you understand that you are liable to be shot?"

Arnold stubbornly returned the glare. "You're the one who has broken a compact. This is not what we agreed to do. If you feel inclined to shoot me, you have no farther to go. I shall defend myself."

Silence hung like a stiff, heavy curtain in the room. The realization hit Booth that he was in danger of losing his whole action squad unless he relented.

Exhaling deeply, Booth agreed. "All right, we'll go back to the original plan. We'll take Lincoln off the road."

Arnold still had an announcement. "Gentlemen, I grew tired of waiting for Wilkes to act, and I found employment elsewhere. I'm to start next week. Today is Thursday. Wilkes, you have three days. Gentlemen, if this isn't accomplished by the end of this week I forever withdraw from it."

Booth delivered the promise Arnold wanted to hear. "Within three days you'll all hear from me and we'll act. Davy, we'll be going by Surratts-ville after the capture. Is all ready?"

"Two double-barreled shotguns, two Spencer carbines, one pistol, ammunition, a knife, a sword, a rope, and a monkey wrench. All hidden in the tavern."

"Good, we'll need it all."

The men rose to leave the room. Booth glared at Arnold's back as he left. He privately vowed he would find a way to tend to Arnold later.

On March 17th Booth heard that Lincoln was going to attend the play, *Still Waters Run Deep*. It was to be performed for wounded soldiers at Campbell Hospital near the Soldiers' Home.

Nathan, who had taken on surveillance of the Surratt Boarding House as a prime mission, watched as seven men gathered in front of the establishment. The leader was the same mustached, dark-haired man he had seen before.

He hurried to find Jesse, who was standing guard outside the White House. He spotted him stationed at a discreet distance from Lincoln, who was walking down the War Department steps to a waiting carriage.

185

"Jesse! Where's the president going?" Nathan cried.

"To see a play near the Soldiers' Home. Why?"

"Stop him! I'll explain later, but I'm convinced there's a plot to kidnap him on the road today."

Without asking any more questions, Jesse raced to Lamon, who was helping Lincoln into the carriage. "Mr. Lamon, I believe the president's in danger if he goes to the play today. You must change the plans."

"Are you sure?"

"I have good reason to believe it. Was I wrong last time?"

"No, you weren't. He won't like this. Mr. Lincoln doesn't like to back down when he's made up his mind to do something."

"Is there something else he could do?"

Lamon thought a moment and then snapped his fingers. "At the National Hotel there's a ceremony honoring the capture of a Confederate battle flag. I can convince the president it's more important he show up there."

Moments later Lincoln's carriage turned down the street to the hotel.

On the road to Campbell Hospital, seven men waited impatiently until they realized with disgust that Lincoln had changed his plans.

"That's it! We're done!" Arnold exclaimed to Booth. He and O'Laughlen boarded the next train to Baltimore.

Surratt surmised, "The Yankees must have heard about this somehow. The war's lost. I'm getting a job, too. Mr. Booth, the weapons are hidden between the walls of the tavern in Surrattsville."

"I've got a job," Davy Herold announced, "Starting the first of April I'll be a clerk for the Army of the James."

Atzerodt looked at Booth. "Long as ya keep payin' my room and board, I'll stick with ya."

Powell nodded at Booth. "I'm with ya."

"Times like this let one know who his real friends are," the actor reflected. "Lewis, we go to New York."

$\wp 40 \infty$

HE NEXT NIGHT, MARCH 18, BOOTH appeared in a play for the last time. He had the lead in *The Apostate* at Ford's Theater. Three nights later he boarded a train for New York with Lewis Powell.

Booth and Powell sat silently in a private compartment. The slow *chug, chug* of the engine became more rapid as the locomotive picked up steam. The rhythmic *click, click* of the wheels passing over the rail joints quickened to a rapid *clickety-clack*.

Powell leered at Booth. "So, are ya gonna look up Annie Horton again while we're in New York?"

"No, Lewis, I'm done paying for women. I'll stay true to Lucy."

Powell wasn't convinced. "Yeah, we'll see about that."

"This is a business trip," Booth countered. "We have a meeting with some gentlemen, and then we return to Washington."

The two checked into the St. Nicholas Hotel in New York, where a meeting took place with the New York operative, Roderick Watson, and one of his accomplices from the riots of July 1863, Hennessey.

Watson hefted a pouch of gold coins and dropped them onto the table. The money rattled and clinked with the impact. "There's more where that came from," he announced. "Our friends still want Lincoln out of the way. They want you to try again."

"How many Knights are involved in this?"

"Some, but that number isn't important. Your brothers and those of the highest rank want this done."

"Mr. Watson, I've tried. It failed and now my team has dispersed."

"Put them back together."

"I don't know if that's possible."

Watson reached onto the table, held up the bag of coins and dropped it again.

"Come now, Mr. Booth. Don't you think this can buy what you need?"

Powell's eyes gleamed. "Well, I think it'd sure help."

"I'll give it one more try."

"If you fail again, there's one more alternative."

"Sanders's way."

"The Tyranny of the Dagger."

Booth turned to Powell. "I need to tie up some matters here in New York. Go back to Washington and stay at the Herndon House."

"Remember, Mr. Booth, I don't know my way around Washington very well."

"I'll get the address for you. I'll send a telegram to Wiechmann at Mrs. Surratt's. In it I'll ask John Surratt to line things up for you at the Herndon. Start putting the team back together. I'll help when I get back."

"Good luck, Mr. Booth," Watson said, "Complete victory."

"Or come retribution," Booth finished.

Booth went into the hotel telegraph office and sent a message to Wiechmann. After seeing Powell off at the railroad station, he returned to the St. Nicholas. In the lobby he spied a familiar face, Sarah Slater.

"Sarah, my dear," Booth cried, "what brings you to New York?"

Kate moved close to her actor friend and spoke in a low voice. "Not so loud, Wilkes. I'm on my way to Montreal. My escort, Augustus Howell, was arrested by federal troops at the Surrattsville tavern. John Surratt is being sent up here to take his place and get me to Canada."

"What? I need him in Washington."

"You've been overruled. He's to escort me."

"Blast! They want me to do something and then raid my team."

"I'm sure you have others to help you."

"John is my most dependable." Booth hesitated. "Sarah, would you like to come up to my room?"

"All of that's in the past, Wilkes. Aren't you engaged to Lucy Hale?"

"Not exactly, not officially yet, anyway. We haven't announced anything."

"Does Miss Hale think you're engaged?"

"I suppose she does."

"I have interests of my own, Wilkes."

"Who?"

"A mysterious man who you don't know. Say hello to Mr. Atzerodt for me. He's taken me across the river many times."

"He's most captivated with you, as am I." Booth held her hand gently in his. "I shall miss you, Sarah Slater."

"Will you miss me as Kate Thompson as well?"

"Of course. Good luck to you. I hope to see Lucy soon," he smiled. "But for tonight, I don't think I'll pass up on Annie Horton."

The following day Booth paid a visit to his sister Asia and to his brother Edwin. He tried to avoid politics and discussed plays and family matters.

On March 24th he boarded a train to Washington, where he planned to revive his kidnapping plan. Kate continued on to Montreal with John Surratt with dispatches for Jacob Thompson, Clay, and George Sanders.

41

MARCH 1865, WASHINGTON

BOOTH WALKED DOWN H STREET until he reached 604, the Surratt Boarding House. It was a sturdy, four-story structure of gray brick. Mary Surratt had taken possession of it after leaving Surrattsville on October 1, 1864.

He entered the street level door, which opened into a large dining room. A large crucifix was fastened to a back wall. The room was empty save for Mary Surratt, who at once smiled and rose from a chair to greet her visitor.

"Mr. Booth, thank you for coming." Mary was forty-five years of age with a pleasant face and black hair worn at mid-ear level. "John isn't here. He had to leave on a mission."

"I heard. Do you know when he'll be back?"

"I'm not sure, it could be weeks this time. He had to take Sarah Slater after Howell was captured. Stay away from my tavern for now. LaFayette Baker and his men are watching it closely."

"Baker?"

"The union counterintelligence agent. The devil take him. He's the one that got my boy Johnny dismissed from his postmaster job at Surrattsville. Not loyal enough, they said. We were depending on that salary."

A young priest walked into the room via an upper level stairway. Mary furtively signaled Booth with a finger to her lips. Then she introduced the two.

"Father is from Minnesota. He's here to study. Father, this is the famous John Wilkes Booth."

"A pleasure to meet you, Father. How long are you staying in the capitol?"

"I'm honored, Mr. Booth. I'm from an abbey near St. Joseph, Minnesota, and must return there before the middle of April."

"Be careful here," Booth said playfully, "this is a southern town, you know. There might be rebels about."

"Strange you should say that," the priest responded, "but St. Joseph is known for its southern sympathies."

Booth laughed. "There are more folks who think that way than people realize. But not Mrs. Surratt and me." He winked at Mary. "We are firm Unionists. I'll take my leave now, Mrs. Surratt. I'll speak with you again about a matter, and do let me know if your son returns."

On March 27 Booth sent a telegram to O'Laughlen. "Get word to Sam. Come on, with or without him, Wednesday morning. We sell that day sure. Don't fail."

Arnold and O'Laughlen were not interested and did not show up on Wednesday. They did visit with Booth on Friday. The two men reaffirmed with Booth that they would not participate in any future plans.

"Lincoln isn't even in Washington," Arnold explained. "He's on board the *River Queen* at City Point in Virginia. There's a final assault brewing on Lee's army. Lincoln wants to be there with Grant."

"It's over, isn't it?" Booth lamented.

O'Laughlen comforted his friend. "Wilkes, it's about time you realized it and got on with your career again."

"I'll never act again. There must be a way."

On the first of April, Booth told Atzerodt that he was taking the evening train to Canada. Instead he got off in New York. Two days later he embarked for Boston and a meeting there.

The Commons in Boston was just starting to green in the April sunshine. Booth stood in the park and watched as pigeons flocked where a farmer had spilled some seed.

"Very pastoral, isn't it." The voice came from behind.

Booth turned to see George Sanders. "You're early."

"Maybe you're late. Does it matter? This won't take long, but I needed to talk to you. Courier messages won't suffice. It's just you and me here and I'll be direct. Watson and others in New York have gone over the plan of blowing up the White House. An attempt will be made soon, probably between April tenth and fifteenth. We think Richmond can hang on that long. We have time to get explosives and explosive experts to Mosby.

"The colonel has been instructed to infiltrate a team into Washington to work with you. Done properly, it could kill Lincoln. It'll certainly cause a great deal of concern and confusion in the capitol either way. If it doesn't work, there's a surer way."

"What's surer?" Booth asked.

"Something that I've been advocating all along. A bullet in the tyrant's head."

"You want me to shoot him?"

"Not just Lincoln. Throw them into mass confusion. Kill the vice-president, kill Secretary of State Seward. You have enough men with you. It can be done."

"Is this just your idea?"

"Higher-ups in the Confederate government have endorsed this plan. Especially if the bombing falls through, which I expect it will. John, you will be a hero in the South. There will be statues to you. Parades held in your honor. You may be our last hope."

Appealing to his vanity was a certain way to get to Booth, and Sanders knew it. Booth took the bait. "I'll do it."

"Wait to be contacted by the explosives team. Even if Richmond falls, you must act. It's still vital to the final outcome."

"Sir, I will not let my people down. The South be saved! Complete victory!"

"Or come retribution."

ᔍ 42 ᔎ

APRIL 1865, RICHMOND

ON APRIL 4TH THE PRESIDENT of the United States left the ship at City Point and walked with his young son, Tad, through the haze and smoke of still-smoldering Richmond, Virginia. It was one day after Lee and Davis had abandoned the city.

Former slaves lined the streets and cheered as Lincoln walked past. It was like Jesus coming to Jerusalem on Palm Sunday. Some slaves began to kneel before the president for a blessing.

Lincoln was embarrassed. He shouted, "Don't kneel to me. You must kneel to God only and thank Him for the liberty you will hereafter enjoy."

Later the president and his son boarded a carriage and rolled through the streets of the Confederate capitol. Ten sailors and four officers acted as their commander-in-chief's guards.

Confederates had instituted a scorched-earth policy; they burned or destroyed anything that could be of value to northern troops. Abandoned cotton and tobacco barns were still burning as Lincoln passed by. He stopped the carriage at two prisons where Union prisoners had been held, Castle Thunder and Libby.

When they approached the home of a Confederate general, George Pickett, Lincoln ordered a halt. He left the carriage and with Tad walked the brick pathway to the front door of the house.

Before he had a chance to rap, the door opened and Mrs. Pickett warmly greeted her visitor. The president was also happy to see her.

"Did you know that I recommended George for his cadetship at West Point?"

"I do, Mr. President. My husband told me. He thinks well of you."

A baby's cry sounded in an adjoining room. Mrs. Pickett disappeared a moment and then returned cradling a child in her arms.

Lincoln's face lit up as he looked down at the baby. "May I?" he asked.

"Of course you may, sir."

The president leaned down and kissed the little one on his forehead.

"May he grow tall and straight, inside and outside," Lincoln wished as he smiled at Mrs. Pickett.

His next stop was at the Confederate White House. A housekeeper, left behind by the South's leader, ushered President Lincoln into Jefferson Davis's office. Lincoln took a seat at the Confederate's desk and met with officials seeking an interview with him.

No one told Lincoln that a few hours earlier, a Union soldier had examined Davis's desk and found a bomb in the shape of an imitation lump of coal left on the desk top. Confederates had used these devices to throw into the coal bunkers of ships. This one was targeted at Lincoln.

Knowing that the war was virtually over, an agent in the Torpedo Bureau, Richard Snyder, sought to forestall further deaths. He went to the Richmond occupation headquarters of General Edward Hastings Ripley.

"General," Ripley explained, "I've gotta tell ya something. You need ta know this."

"Tell me."

"A party's been sent from the bureau. They've got a secret mission. I don't know what it is, but they're gonna blow something up."

"Where?"

"Don't know fer sure, maybe Washington."

"What's the target, Mr. Snyder?"

"I think President Lincoln's in great danger. Please tell him ta take better care of himself."

Ripley raised his eyebrows. "Thank you for the warning. I'll talk to the president, but I don't know if it'll do any good. He has a mind of his own. I'd like you to take an oath and swear what you've told me to be true."

"Whatever ya want, sir."

ON APRIL 5, RIPLEY BOARDED A SHIP, the *Malvern*, where Lincoln was quartered. The general told his commander in chief, "I've got a statement here from a former Confederate agent. Let me read it to you."

After Ripley read Snyder's warning, he asked the president to meet with the Torpedo Bureau agent.

Lincoln refused, saying, "I can't bring myself to believe that any human being lives that would do me harm."

❧ 43 ❧

APRIL 1865, WASHINGTON

OOTH RETURNED TO WASHINGTON on April 7th after his trip to New York and Boston. He sent for George Atzerodt and explained in frustration, "We need to put a plan in motion, George. There are people in New York who'll get the president if we don't."

"What they goin' to do?"

"They want to mine the end of the President's House near the War Department. If we don't get him, they will."

"What's yer plan?"

"There are two projects—revive the kidnapping or blow up the mansion. They can work in tandem. If one doesn't work, we have a contingency for the other, a fallback. We're to continue with the effort to kidnap Lincoln. Others'll work with the bomb. I have been requested to perform a darker task, but I'm not ready for that yet. People from New York have come here to coordinate the bombing. Others will come from Richmond. We'll see how it develops, and we have to be ready."

"They took Richmond," Atzerodt said, "Lee's on da run."

"That's why things will have to happen quickly."

"I read in da paper dat Stringfellow got arrested tryin' ta leave da city. But he got away from da Yankees after just two days."

"Others are ready. But Stringfellow'll be missed if he can't hook up with Mosby."

TOM HARNEY REPORTED TO COLONEL MOSBY on the northern neck on April 4th. He found things in turmoil. Mosby conferred with Sergeant Harney in front of his tent.

"You might be our last gasp," the colonel said, "I'm assigning you to Company H under Captain George Baylor. His unit will infiltrate you and your ordinance into Washington."

"We can do it, Colonel," Harney claimed earnestly. "I've found an entrance on the War Department side where we can plant explosives. Imagine this—they have a party, celebrating their great victory at Richmond. A band plays music and they all gather, with Lincoln, right over where we set off the mine. It'll work. I know it will."

"It better. Richmond fell sooner than anticipated. Lee's army's short on food and has Grant at its heels. We had hoped for an orderly withdrawal from Richmond. That is no longer possible.

"Sergeant, we're to link up with Stringfellow, who's supposed to have the explosives." Word of the spy's capture and escape had not yet reached them.

"I have the fuses and timing devices. If I'm found out I'll just say that I was bringing ordnance to you."

"Baylor will escort you. May God be with you. Stringfellow will take you to a contact in Washington."

"It's the fourth today. Everything is set for the eleventh. That gives us one week."

IN WASHINGTON, TOM CONRAD sent a message for Jesse to meet with him. Jesse trusted that Kate would not reveal him to other Confederate agents if she was true to her word that she didn't want Lincoln kidnapped. Besides, she and Surratt had departed for Montreal.

The two men met on the banks of the Potomac. As the wide waters gurgled by them, the Confederate agent confided in Jesse.

"You've certainly been a help to us. Unfortunately, our attempt to take Lincoln failed. Someone informed. They must have."

"Not necessarily, Tom. It seems that periodically a patrol goes with the president. We might just have had bad timing or someone shot off their mouth in Surrattsville."

"Whatever happened, it's over now. We have a new plan to move forward."

"What's that?"

"Within the week we need to rendezvous with Captain Baylor of Mosby's regiment. He has a special package for us we need to safely move into Washington."

"What's the package?"

"I just need your help to move it. Frankly, it's best if you don't know what it is or how it's to be used. The fewer with knowledge of the mission, the better."

"When?"

"We cross the Navy Yard Bridge on the night of April 10th. We'll need to get by the sentries. Can you get passes? I can't be seen in the city."

"I think so, how many?"

Conrad counted to himself. "Six."

"I'll do it. Where do we rendezvous?"

"The stables again, same as last time, at sunset."

"I'll be there."

THAT AFTERNOON JESSE MET with Ward Lamon in the President's House. He took a seat in Lamon's office off the hallway leading to the Oval Office.

"Something big's being planned again," Jesse revealed.

"What?"

"I don't know. We meet at a horse stable and leave for Maryland over the Navy Yard Bridge on the night of the tenth. They're going after the president again, I just know it."

"Go there. I'll have Colonel Baker and his men follow at a discreet distance. Whatever needs to be done, they'll do it."

"Mr. Lamon, I have a favor to ask."

"What's that?"

"I have another friend from Minnesota who's here. He has only one arm, but don't let that fool you. He can be very tenacious. I want him to go with Baker. For one thing, Baker and his men don't know me. Nathan Cates does. I want this for two reasons: first, self-protection from an accident by our side; and second, he can really help us."

"Done, have him report here."

COVERT OPERATIONS CONTINUED on the Confederate side. Plans had to be readied on several fronts. Benjamin Stringfellow, after his escape, sent word through an agent that he had explosives and would meet Harney at a safe house in Washington.

Baylor and his troop prepared to escort Harney through the neck and over the river to Surrattsville and on to Washington.

On April 9 Robert E. Lee surrendered to General Grant at Appomatox Court House in Virginia. Lee's path of retreat to North Carolina was blocked, and his troops' hasty departure from Richmond resulted in food supplies being left behind. Lee had no choice but to surrender his hungry and destitute Army of Northern Virginia.

Grant wrote out the surrender terms by hand. He dictated terms that reflected the words of his Union president to "let 'em down easy." The war was essentially over.

PLANS AND DESTINY WERE TUMBLING rapidly toward a conclusion. At the appointed hour on April 10th, with passes in hand, Jesse met Conrad and four other men at the stables behind the theater.

"Bad news about Lee," Conrad announced, "this really is our last hope. We have to give Johnston and his men in North Carolina some reason to hold on awhile longer. Let's go and let's do it right. Complete victory!" he shouted.

His men cried back, "Or come retribution!"

They mounted and headed to the Navy Yard Bridge.

Minutes later Colonel LaFayette Baker of the Union's Secret Service and his men furtively trailed Conrad's band. Nathan Cates rode alongside Baker.

In the northern neck of Virginia, a force of 150 under Captain Baylor had left Mosby on April 8th. They were to escort Tom Harney toward Washington for a meeting with Conrad.

Kate was at the tavern in Surrattsville. She and John Surratt had been midway to Canada when word reached them that Richmond had fallen. John had continued on to Montreal, while Kate turned back south to contemplate her future. She stood on the tavern porch and breathed in the clear, fresh spring air, escaping the smoke-tainted atmosphere of the bar.

A full moon illuminated the countryside in a soft white glow as Conrad's squad thundered past the tavern to a rendezvous point three miles to the south. Kate was startled as the six riders streamed past. One was Jesse, she was sure of it.

She sensed where they must be going. The rendezvous point at Burke's Creek was well-known among Confederate agents. She mounted her horse and headed after the riders.

Baylor's men had reached Burke's Creek and were resting in a grove of trees waiting for Conrad to arrive. Harney kept his demolition packs nearby and waited in anticipation.

Baylor urged Harney to be ready. "With Lee's surrender, everything is topsy-turvy, Tom. As soon as Conrad gets here, you need to go. Good luck to you. We don't have much going for us anymore."

"Captain, I'm ready and eager. We still might turn this around."

Within the hour, one of Baylor's scouts came to his captain with word of an impending arrival. "I put my ear to the ground and heard hoof beats. They must be coming for Harney."

In minutes Jesse and the rest of Conrad's squad rode into Burke's Creek. Baylor and Harney met the mounted men as they entered the camp.

"Captain Conrad, here's your package, the best explosives expert known to man on either side of the Mason-Dixon. Take good care of him."

"Get yourself a horse, Sergeant," Conrad ordered. "Soon as we water our horses we're heading back."

A moment later Kate appeared on horseback. Jesse dismounted and hurried to her. She slid off her saddle and into his waiting arms.

"I had to see you," she whispered.

Ecstatic as he was to see her, Jesse knew he must urge her to leave immediately. "The war's over, but it's very dangerous here, Kate. You must go! You know I don't care about the past or what sides we were on. I want to be with you forever. Please, leave. You're not safe here."

A soldier raced up to Baylor. "Captain, more horses are comin'. They're comin' fast, a lot of 'em!"

Baylor shouted, "Mount up, men! Hit the road runnin'!"

Moments later Baker's troop galloped into Burke's Creek. Shots rang out on both sides. Baylor's force tried to hold its ground at first and then slowly gave way. Nathan wheeled to a stop before Jesse and Kate.

"Stay put!" he yelled. "They'll think you're a rebel."

But Nathan was in danger, too. A Confederate soldier raised a rifle and took aim at him. Jesse spotted him in the moonlight and snapped up his own carbine. The flash from his rifle flitted across Jesse's face as the bullet from his gun splatted into the rebel's chest.

Tom Conrad's rage boiled over when he saw Jesse fire. "You're the one!" he screamed. "You're the traitor!"

Conrad trained his rifle on Jesse and prepared to pull the trigger.

Screaming "NO!" Kate protectively flung herself in front of Jesse. Conrad fired. The bullet burrowed into her chest.

Nathan raised his pistol and fired at Conrad. The bullet whizzed near the rebel captain's head as he mounted a horse and thundered away.

Jesse knelt at Kate's side. "Kate! Kate!" he cried. "Don't leave me!"

Kate's eyes flickered open. "Jesse, I love you, Jesse," she murmured faintly.

Jesse's voice choked with emotion. "And I love you, Kate."

Her lips moved as Kate tried to speak. Jesse held his ear to her mouth.

A moment later he turned to Nathan in stunned disbelief. "She's gone."

"I'm sorry, Jesse, what did she say?"

"Watch out for Booth."

After a running fight along and down road, Baker's force cut off four men and drove them into some brush. Realizing they were surrounded, the rebels surrendered. One of them was Tom Harney. The bomb threat ended with his capture.

ঙ 44 ଔ

APRIL 11, WASHINGTON

ROM A WINDOW IN JESSE'S ROOMING HOUSE on H Street, he and Nathan viewed the revelry sweeping Washington. Government buildings shone with lights in every window. Torchlight parades gaily snaked through the streets.

But Jesse couldn't connect with the jubilation. He felt stone cold inside. "This is one of the most joyous moments in our country's history, and I wish I were dead."

Nathan placed his hand on his friend's shoulder. "Jesse, I can only imagine how you feel. In scarcely over a year you've lost two women who were dear to you. But the threat to the president is not over. You need to stay vigilant."

"I know. People will be gathering soon around the White House. I'll need to be there. But Nathan, it's so very hard."

A rap sounded at the door. Jesse opened it to find Charles Chiniquy standing in the entrance.

"Father, come in, what brings you to me?"

"Worry, Mr. Miller. I'm worried."

"This is my friend Nathan," he gestured. "Sit down and tell me what's bothering you."

"I met with President Lincoln. He seemed happy at first and then slipped into a melancholy fatalism. I warned him to stay safe, and he implied that if someone wanted to kill him, they would and no one could stop it."

"It can be stopped," Jesse replied firmly. "But Lincoln needs to cooperate."

"Recently the president asked me to attend a séance with him. He wanted a man of the cloth to verify the event."

"They hold séances in the White House?" Nathan was incredulous.

"Not usually. Sometimes they do. There's a house in Georgetown where they go, Mrs. Lincoln more often. She really can't get over the death of their little boy, Willie. It's been nearly three years.

"Lincoln's a politician, he knows that he can't openly consort with spiritualists. But Mary does," Chiniquy continued. "This last time the medium was a young girl, about twenty, named Nettie Colburn. They call her a trance medium and say she can link with a spirit who can foretell events."

"I can't abide charlatans bilking distraught mourners!" Jesse snapped.

"No," Chiniquy explained, "Miss Colburn said she doesn't accept money and won't profit from a gift from God. Lincoln has visions too, you know."

"Like what?" Nathan wondered.

"The night he was first elected, he awoke and looked into a mirror. He saw two images of himself, one still young and strong, the other old and haggard. A medium explained to him that he'd be elected twice but that he would die in office."

"So, what did Nettie Colburn tell the president?" Jesse blurted.

"She reminded Mr. Lincoln that her 'friends' had foretold long before the vote that he would be re-elected. They also said that a shadow hung over him. Lincoln looked as if all was lost. I'll never forget the conversation between them. He said, 'I've received warnings from other mediums that my life was in danger, but I don't believe anyone really wants to harm me.' Miss Colburn answered by saying that the danger lay in his overconfidence in his fellow man. Lincoln sadly shook his head and tenderly held her hand. He said, 'I will live until my work is done and after that it won't matter.' Then the president asked if she would come to see him in the fall. The girl replied, 'I promise to come, if you are still here.'"

Jesse looked somber. "I agree with the girl. I wish the president were more cautious. Going into Richmond the day after it fell, standing to look over parapets in the midst of battle, why does he take such risks? Why does he want to do that?"

"He's a fatalist. He believes God will decide when his life will end and there's nothing he can do about it. There are forces beyond what we comprehend that bring danger to him," Chiniquy responded.

"I urge you," he looked at Nathan, "both of you, to be vigilant. I have long feared that the Catholic Church will involve itself in a plot against Lincoln. Political insurrection is steeped in the history of the church."

Jesse sighed. "There are many avenues to explore. But the war's nearly over. Maybe the real danger is past."

"Don't count on it, gentlemen. I repeat to you, stay vigilant."

"Reverend, the president has promised to give a speech tonight. I must be there."

"May God guide you," Chiniquy concluded as he left the room.

NATHAN AND JESSE WERE SOON NAVIGATING the crowded streets toward the White House. Amidst the cheers and impromptu singing, the two men could feel the emotion surging through the mass of people.

"It's like a great euphoria," Nathan noted.

"Or like one big drunk," Jesse rejoined.

A crowd swelled around the President's House. Cries broke out in anticipation of Lincoln's appearance. "Abe! Abe! Abe!"

AMONG THOSE IN THE THRONG were John Wilkes Booth and Lewis Powell.

Booth was consumed with bitterness. For nearly a year he had been preparing himself for the biggest role of his career. He had prepared, readied his plan, spent much of his own money, and only a change in Lincoln's plans had thwarted the actor's abduction scheme.

He glared as the French doors opened and Lincoln stepped onto the second floor balcony of the White House, his son Tad at his side. A rank amateur had taken Booth's place in the starring role that should have been his.

The crowd roared approval, expecting a victory speech to whip it into even more frenzy. But the president had other thoughts in mind. He knew that the time had finally come to bind the wounds of war and to convey a tone of reconciliation and reunification. He began with a gesture to the South.

"My friends," he shouted in his firm but slightly high-pitched voice, "'Dixie' has always been one of my favorite songs. I'd like the band to play it now."

The band immediately struck up the familiar song and the crowd erupted again with joyous enthusiasm.

Then Lincoln continued. "We meet this evening, not in sorrow, but in gladness of heart. The evacuation of Petersburg and Richmond, and the surrender of the principal insurgent army, give hope of a righteous and speedy peace whose joyous expression cannot be restrained.

"In the midst of this, however, He from whom all blessings flow must not be forgotten. A call for a national thanksgiving is being prepared, and will be duly promulgated. Nor must those whose harder part gives us the cause of rejoicing, be overlooked.

"Their honors must not be parceled out with others. I myself was near the front, and had the high pleasure of transmitting much of the good news to you, but no part of the honor, for plan or execution, is mine. To General Grant, his skillful officers and brave men, all belongs."

Lincoln continued to describe his reconstruction plans for the South and particularly Louisiana in some detail. It was a somber speech and not what the crowd expected.

Then the president addressed the status of former slaves. "It is also unsatisfactory to some that the elective franchise is not given to the colored man. I would myself prefer that it were now conferred on the very intelligent, and on those who serve our cause as soldiers."

Booth's face turned crimson with rage. He whispered harshly to Powell, "Nigger citizenship will never happen. I don't care how smart they are. While I have a breath left in my body I will fight them. I'll never stand on equal ground with coloreds. Lewis, shoot the tyrant now! In this crowd no one will notice, we can escape."

Powell looked around. "No, Mr. Booth, not here."

"Do it, I say. Now!" the actor snarled.

"No, Mr. Booth."

Booth glared. "That will be the last speech he will ever make, I swear it."

NATHAN SPOTTED THE ACTOR as Powell and Booth eased out of the crowd. "Look there, Jesse. I've seen that man around Surratt's. Who is he?"

"That's one of the most famous men in America, the man I believe Kate warned us about, the actor, John Wilkes Booth."

ᴓ45ᴔ

APRIL12, VIRGINIA BRUSH

J UDAH BENJAMIN AND ALBERT PIKE had escaped Richmond the day before it fell to Grant. Anticipating that Lee would join up with Johnston in North Carolina, the two Confederate officials and a small army escort headed south.

They had camped in the Virginia brush. A smoky campfire smoldered in front of them as the two leaders discussed the future.

"I still hold out hope," Pike proclaimed. "Grant's surrender may not be the final nail in our coffin. As long as Johnston still can maneuver his army, our last-straw attempt may mean something."

"Can it work? Be realistic, Albert. We've sent raids into Union territory from Canada. We've incited riots in New York. We've attempted to influence the elections in the North. We've procured money from the great banking houses of Europe. You started Indian wars. We tried to kidnap Lincoln, and we even plotted to blow up the White House. Nothing, absolutely nothing, has worked."

"We have one agent left with a fire still burning bright inside him. Booth. I've sent him a letter."

"Risky, isn't it?"

"Yes," Pike acknowledged, "but at this stage, who cares? I've urged him to follow through with the plan to kill Lincoln. Sanders laid it out for him in Boston. Not just Lincoln but the top leaders of the government, Johnson, Seward, even Grant. Seward's confined to his bed after a carriage accident, he's a sitting duck. If the head is cut off the snake, it'll have no direction. There will finally be the kind of chaos we've tried to obtain. The

208

Confederacy can rise out of the ashes. With Lincoln out of the way, we can bring slavery back in another form."

"Really? I don't see how, Albert. Our economy's a wreck, our railroads destroyed. How can this happen? Even if the North falls apart, we aren't ready to build again."

"Maybe not today or even tomorrow. But Judah, we can do it in time. Remember, our treasury and money from our friends is in the millions."

"It'll all be in the hands of the Yankees soon."

Pike's laugh was sinister, his massive shoulders shaking with vengeful glee. "No, it won't. I've taken care of that. I've sent details of our brothers, the Knights of the Golden Circle, to the southeast and southwest. They are to hide Confederate gold in secret places."

"How will it be marked?"

"Brother James came up with an idea. Carve Masonic symbols into stone and let them lead the way. Only those in our order above thirty-third degree will be able to find them."

Benjamin was skeptical. "Do you really trust Brother James? He's not much more than a child."

"He earned high praise from Captain Quantrell. He fought ferociously. His older brother, Frank, brought him to us. Both of them are committed to one world, just as we are. When the money's needed, the markers will lead us to it. I have the code."

Benjamin shook his head. "Albert, I admire your passion, and I pray your plan bears fruit. I can't wait. You spent much of this war in the shadows. But the Yankees are trying to hunt down people like me. It's the same with President Davis. The dogs won't stop howling until they have us. I'm leaving, Albert. I'm going to England. We have friends there, financial backers and Illuminati. I believe it's the only way I can keep my head out of a noose."

"Do what you must, Judah. I'm going to keep stirring the pot here. This isn't the end, you know. I may even head north. I firmly believe that in the next hundred or so years there will be three world wars. It will take these wars and the fear of war to forge the one world order that'll save mankind. And it all started here. We won't live to see it come to fruition, but Judah, it started with us, here, in this very uncivil but necessary war. And our brothers in the future will see that our work was not in vain."

Pike emitted another evil-sounding chuckle. "Oh, by the way . . . Booth became a Catholic after going to mass with Dr. Mudd. They'll be investigating a Catholic plot or assert that Booth acted alone. Our brotherhood and the Confederacy will never be suspected. Sanders will see to that. He's already planting evidence implicating Catholics and Andrew Johnson."

ᔍ 46 ᔆ

ENERAL GRANT ARRIVED IN WASHINGTON on April 13 and checked in at the Willard Hotel.

Booth had begun to ratchet up his plans. The day before he had visited a bar located above the lobby of Grover's Theater and talked with the bartender, an acquaintance named John Deery.

"I've heard the president will attend the theater on Friday night," he said to the barkeep. "Would you reserve the right-hand box at Grover's for me, the one next to the president's box?"

"Sure I could, Mr. Booth, but why don't you just do it yerself?"

"I want to pay for the ticket. If I try to buy one, Mr. Hess, the manager will insist on giving me the box."

"Sure thing, Mr. Booth. I'll do it for ya," Deery agreed.

Grover's was planning on commemorating the fall of Fort Sumter, which had occurred exactly four years earlier, and had invited Lincoln.

Later Booth walked by Seward's house. He imagined the interior as he looked up at the stately brick building. He already had a pretty good idea of the layout. The actor had befriended a chambermaid who worked there. A little dose of smooth Booth charm had produced the desired results. Booth knew where the injured secretary of state was convalescing.

Spotting a friend during his walk, Booth boasted, "I have the biggest thing on my hands that has ever turned up. There's a great deal of money in it."

He met with Lewis Powell later in the evening. Fireworks blazed in the sky as military bands played and crowds of revelers filled the streets once again. General Grant arrived to watch the illuminated city from Stanton's home.

Powell urged Booth, "Get rid of Atzerodt. We can find other ways to get through the northern neck or wherever we decide to go. He's a drunken bum and I don't trust 'im."

"I agree with you, Lewis. George knows way too much, and he drinks too much. I need to keep him close so I can keep track of him. Besides, I have a job in mind for him. How do you like your room in the Herndon?"

Powell smiled. "Better than I'm used to, but I figgur I can git used to it."

"Good. I'm thinking of moving Atzerodt into the Kirkwood."

"What! In that red-carpeted fancy place? George'll stand out like a sore thumb! He dresses like a bum jest off a train, Wilkes. And the vice-president lives there, ya know."

"Yes, I know, and I have my reasons for wanting George to get noticed."

At Stanton's residence, onlookers turned toward the fireworks that sent bright flashes across their faces. Grant puffed on a cigar and brushed ashes from his heavy dark beard. "The president wants my wife and me to go to the theater with him tomorrow night," the general informed Stanton.

Stanton winced as if in pain. "This is a southern town. It has many people who hate Lincoln and want to do him harm. I've urged the president not to attend. I encourage you to turn down his invitation and to tell him not to go, either."

"Doesn't he listen to you?" Grant asked.

"I'm afraid not. I've turned down many invitations myself."

"Well, my wife wants to visit our daughter in New York. I'll tell the president at the cabinet meeting tomorrow my wife and I can't come."

Stanton was encouraged by that prospect. "With luck, at that late hour the president won't be able to find anyone else, and he'll cancel his theater party."

BOOTH SPENT THE REST OF THE EVENING putting the final pieces of his puzzle into place. Herold had been sent to the nearby village of T.B., where he would spend the night with a distant cousin and arrange for fresh horses for the next night. With Powell at the Herndon and Atzerodt comfortably ensconced at the Kirkwood, Booth went to his room at the National.

He opened his trunk and put personal letters inside. He included the letter from Sam Arnold in which Arnold informed Booth that, while he and O'Laughlen had been willing to participate in a kidnapping, they wanted no part of a murder plot.

The actor gave a sweeping bow and issued a self-congratulatory smile as he closed the trunk lid with enormous satisfaction. "I told them they would regret turning on me. This shall seal it."

He had also included a letter from his brother Edwin which some could find incriminating. Booth was keenly aware that once his plan unfolded, his room would be searched, and the letter incriminating Arnold and O'Laughlen and others would be found in the trunk.

Booth slipped out of his room. He would spend the night elsewhere.

NATHAN NOW ACCOMPANIED JESSE on his surveillance assignment. Both were troubled by Kate's last words about Booth coupled with spotting the actor at Lincoln's speech the night of April eleventh.

"What does it mean?" Nathan asked.

"Mr. Lincoln loves the theater. He's seen Booth perform many times."

"I've seen Booth at Surratt's several times, too, often with men that I'd consider unsavory."

"I'll watch Lincoln. Nathan, I think you should keep an eye on Booth."

ɛɔ 47 ೮ঽ

APRIL 14, WASHINGTON

GOOD FRIDAY IN THE NATION'S CAPITOL dawned with the promise of a beautiful spring day. The sun rose in a cloudless sky and quickly warmed the city. President Abraham Lincoln felt buoyant and happy. A great burden had been lifted from him, and the realization of it was settling in. He looked forward to a more cheerful life in the days ahead.

Mary joined him for a simple breakfast of one egg and coffee. Their sons Robert, twenty-one, and Tad, twelve, joined them.

"Abraham, we're scheduled to go to Grover's tonight to see *Aladdin*. But I just saw that tonight is Laura Keene's benefit and the final performance for *Our American Cousin* at Ford's Theater. I'd rather see that."

"I hate to disappoint Grover's," the president replied. "But," he smiled, "I'd much rather not disappoint you. Ford's it is."

"We can send Tad with someone to Grover's. He'd like that play better anyway."

"I sure would!" Tad agreed.

"Let's do that, Mary." Lincoln's voice softened. "We've both been too miserable lately. In fact, let's take a carriage ride this afternoon."

"Is General Grant going to accompany us to the theater? He's been invited," Mary reminded her husband.

"I'll go to the War Department and see what I can find. Now I have a cabinet meeting and a meeting with Vice-President Johnson. Save the afternoon for me."

Their son Robert hurried over to Lincoln as he approached the door to leave. "I've been to Richmond. I brought you this." Robert jokingly handed his father a picture of Robert E. Lee.

Lincoln somberly regarded the picture. "He has a good face."

At 9:00 a.m. the president read the morning newspapers and then greeted visitors. At 10:00 a.m. John Hale, the former New Hampshire senator and now ambassador to Spain, arrived.

Hale congratulated Lincoln on the Union victory and about his expectations for Spain. The ambassador volunteered, "It'll be good to get away from here for a while."

"Why is that, Mr. Ambassador?"

"It's my daughter, Lucy, she seems to be much taken with the actor Wilkes Booth."

"John Wilkes Booth," Lincoln smiled. "A fine actor. I've enjoyed his plays."

"As have I. However, I don't want an actor for a son-in-law. They are together as we speak. He came to see her as I was leaving. I'm hoping that distance will dampen his ardor."

"It could just inflame it, you know," Lincoln laughed.

Then Lincoln called to an assistant. "Please tell Grover's that my son Tad will be attending there in my place tonight. Please secure my box at Ford's as well. My wife and I and the Grants will attend the play there tonight."

The president met with his cabinet later that morning. The seven members were there along with a guest, General Grant. The main topic on the agenda was a discussion of reconstruction issues. Grant reviewed the status of the Union victory.

Lincoln leaned back in his chair at the head of the long table. "I've had some strange dreams lately."

His old friend Joshua Speed, now the attorney general, discounted their importance. "Mr. President, you've been having strange dreams as long as I've known you, back to Illinois days."

"This is different," Lincoln said. "In my dream, I awoke and there was a death-like stillness about me. Then I heard sobs, as if a number of people were weeping. I left my bed and wandered downstairs until I arrived at the East Room. Before me was a catafalque, on which rested a corpse wrapped in funereal vestments. 'Who is dead in the White House?' I demanded of one of the soldiers. 'The president,' was the answer. 'He was killed by an assassin.' Then came a loud burst of grief from the crowd, which awoke me from my dream. I slept no more that night."

For a moment silence hung heavily in the room. Then Stanton spoke up. "It's just a dream, Mr. President, but I keep reminding you that you must be careful. I often have dreams before great events. I expect to hear from Sherman soon with some very great news. At least my thoughts run in that direction, as I suppose yours do, too."

"Mr. President," Assistant Secretary of War Charles Dana spoke up, "we have word that Jacob Thompson, the Confederate agent in Canada who organized raids into St. Albans and other places, will be traveling through Portland, Maine, tonight. What shall we do?"

"Arrest him!" Stanton thundered.

Lincoln's reply was more reasoned. "When you have an elephant by the hind leg and he's trying to run away, it's best to let him run."

Following the meeting General Grant approached Lincoln. "My wife, Julia, is very eager to visit our daughter in New York. Regretfully, I can't accept your theater invitation tonight."

"Mrs. Lincoln will be very disappointed, General, but I understand. Your family is more important. I'll find a replacement for you."

"We plan to take the evening train for New Jersey. Mr. President, should you go yourself? I don't think it's safe yet."

Lincoln smiled. "I see the God of War's hand in this."

Lincoln immediately turned to Stanton, who also declined the invitation and denied talking to Grant.

"I'll be by the War Department to find someone else," the president commented. "Next I meet with Vice-President Johnson. I don't believe Mrs. Lincoln would be happy if I invited him to the play."

When they met early that afternoon it was the first time Lincoln had exchanged any meaningful words with his vice-president since Johnson's embarrassing behavior on Inauguration Day, March 4. They spoke for twenty minutes. Lincoln again outlined his plans for reconstruction and urged that there be no retribution.

JUST AFTER NOON, LUCY HALE LEFT the hotel café where she had been meeting with Booth. She was off to spend the afternoon taking Spanish lessons from John Hay.

Jesse watched from a distance under a tree as Lincoln crossed the street to the War Department. He wondered if Nathan was having any luck with Booth. Halfway across the street, the president stopped and turned toward Jesse, smiled broadly and waved. Jesse had never seen Lincoln look so happy.

In the War Department offices Lincoln complained to Stanton of Grant's cancellation.

"Give up the theater," Stanton urged.

"I can't hide, and Mrs. Lincoln has her heart set on this."

"Well, at least have a competent guard with you."

Lincoln looked at Stanton's assistant. "Mr. Secretary, did you know that Eckert can break a poker over his arm?"

"No. Why do you ask such a question?"

"Well, I've seen him break five pokers, one after the other, over his arm, and I'm thinking he'd be the kind of man to go with me this evening. May I take him?"

"Eckert has to work late here tonight."

Lincoln turned to the assistant. "Can't you do your work tomorrow and come along with me tonight?"

Major Eckert realized that the president was goading his boss and decided not to risk the secretary of war's wrath.

"I'm sorry, sir. Mr. Stanton will not let me postpone my work."

"All right, I'll take Major Rathbone because Stanton insists upon having someone to protect me, but I'd much rather have you since I know you can break a poker over your arm."

Lincoln laughed to himself as he left the War Department. He enjoyed needling his secretary of war. He remained gleeful during the carriage ride with Mary and talked with her of travel once his term was over. The president suggested they should travel west and to the Holy Land.

His bright spirits lifted Mary's. She was often depressed since the death of their son Willie.

"My dear husband, you almost startle me by your great cheerfulness," she laughed with delight.

"Oh, by the way, I have replacements for the Grants," Lincoln shared with Mary. "They are Major Rathbone and his fiancee, Clara Harris. We'll pick them up along the way to the theater."

A one-armed soldier spotted the Lincolns as they approached. He called out, "I would almost give up my other hand if I could shake the hand of Abraham Lincoln." After telling his driver to stop the carriage, the president reached toward the soldier and said, "You shall do that and it shall cost you nothing."

The Lincolns then returned to the White House, where Lincoln greeted a few more visitors and then ate a light supper before preparing for the theater.

Booth had a very active day. Nathan watched him leave the National Hotel and head for Ford's Theater. Booth stopped in front of the theater to speak with stagehands.

"You've got some mail," Tom Raybold told him.

"Good, I travel so much it's good to have a permanent address here."

The crew man handed him a bundled stack of envelopes. Booth began to rifle through them.

"Big night here tonight," Henry Ford, the manager of the theater, said as he approached the small group.

"How so?" Booth wondered.

"The president and General Grant along with their wives will be here. Good Friday is usually not a good day. Maybe this will pick things up. *Our American Cousin* is a stale, old comedy. But it should do some business tonight. It'll be a whale of an attraction."

Booth suppressed the glee that wanted to sweep across his face. Lincoln at Ford's and not Grover's, and Grant, too. It couldn't be better!

Booth left the others and sat down on the stone steps leading into Ford's. He began opening his mail and smiled as he read two letters from admiring women. Then he opened an envelope with no return address. It was from Albert Pike. His final instructions had arrived.

For nearly half an hour, Booth sat on the steps deep in thought. This was the perfect play for him to perform the task before him. He knew *Our American Cousin* inside and out. His brother-in-law, Asia's husband, had produced it in Richmond when John was a stock actor.

Booth entered the theater and watched the actors rehearse the play he knew so well. He looked over the familiar layout of the theater. Then he casually strolled to the aisle door leading to the president's box and opened it.

The short passageway had two doors on one side, both leading to the boxes. He observed an empty chair in the passageway. The guard would be sitting there. Booth expected he'd have to kill him, too.

Booth had spotted a stray nail outside the theater and had picked it up with the idea that it may come in handy. Now he rapped the nail through the door. Then he wrenched the bit of metal back and forth until he could pull it out, leaving a peep hole. He stood outside the passageway in the dress circle until he heard the line he was waiting for, the laugh line that would be his signal to act, to act one last time.

He sat down and wrote out a few pages of explanation for what he intended to do. Booth addressed this note to the *National Intelligencer* and left Ford's to mail the letter. On the street he saw an old friend and fellow actor, John Matthews.

"John, my friend," he called. "I've got a letter here I'd like delivered to the *National Intelligencer* tomorrow. Would you do that for me? I want them to have it tomorrow, not today, and I'll be out of town."

"Certainly, Wilkes," Matthews answered. "I'd be glad to deliver it."

It was 2:00 when Booth reached Mary Surratt's Boarding House.

"Any news about John?" he asked.

"He's still up in Canada, as far as I know," Mary answered.

"I need you to deliver a package and a message for me. I can't risk the words being written down and discovered. Remember this for John Lloyd: 'I am coming tonight. Have the rifles and other weapons ready.' The package holds binoculars that I will need."

"How do I get there? It's four hours away."

"Ask Weichmann," Booth suggested. "He's a boarder and a good friend of your son's."

After Booth departed, Mary Surratt approached Lou Weichmann. "I find it necessary to go into the country to see about a debt owed me by John Nothey. Would you have any objections to driving me down?"

Weichmann agreed and sent a boy to find a horse and buggy for the trip.

Next, Booth went to the Herndon House and told Powell to be ready. They would move tonight. He continued on to the Kirkwood, where he found Atzerodt in the bar. Messy and drinking heavily, George was grossly conspicuous in the upscale hotel.

"Do you have the passes?" Booth asked.

"Not yet, I can't git ta Johnson."

"We need the passes to cross the Navy Yard Bridge tonight. I *must* have them."

"Well, I can't git 'em."

"Davy will be by later. Stay here, George, and no more drinking." The actor smiled at the bartender and flipped him a coin. "Here, my good man. George here has some important business to do later tonight. No more alcohol for him, please."

The bartender was most agreeable. "Whatever you say, Mr. Booth."

Next, Booth asked the desk clerk to take a message for the vice-president. He wrote: "Don't wish to disturb you. Are you at home? John Wilkes Booth."

NATHAN WATCHED AS BOOTH left the hotel and sauntered confidently into the bright, sunny day.

DAVY HEROLD WAS AT NAYLOR'S STABLES, haggling over a roan horse with the manager of the stables, John Fletcher.

"I tell ya, boy, that mare over there might be small, but she'll do ya good."

"I want the roan." Davy was adamant.

"Look," Fletcher countered, "that's my best horse and I don't even know you."

"Do ya know John Wilkes Booth?"

"The actor? Of course I do, why?"

"Because this horse's for him, and he wants a saddle with English steel stirrups and a double-rein bridle."

"Oh, all right, but it's gonna cost ya more, and I want ya back here with the horse by 9:00 at the latest."

"No problem, here." Davy placed coins in Fletcher's hand. "That should take care of it."

BOOTH WAS INVOLVED IN THE SAME ACTIVITY. He went to another livery stable and rented a small mare. He mounted up and made a grand show, tipping his hat to ladies and waving at people along the way to make sure he was noticed. It was time to ride around Ford's Theater to plan the escape route.

Booth intended to return to the stable later and take a bay horse that looked strong to him. His masquerade would cause others later on to describe Booth's mount incorrectly.

A carriage passed. Booth swore to himself that Grant was one of the passengers. They were heading directly for the railroad station. Booth galloped down the street and passed the carriage. He stared intently at the people inside, then wheeled around and trotted by them again, his eyes focused on Grant and his family.

JULIA GRANT, SEEING BOOTH'S CLOSE ATTENTION, turned to her husband. "What a strange man. Have we seen him before?"

"This morning," the general answered, "at breakfast, at the Willard. He was at a table nearby with a young woman. But I don't know who he is."

"I'm glad we'll be on a train soon. He bothers me."

Grant patted his wife's hand. "Yes, we'll soon be in New York, he won't bother you there."

BOOTH WAS IRRITATED. *It's Grant. He's leaving. Lincoln better not cancel!* He continued down the street and met Herold riding toward him. Davy brought his horse around to ride alongside Booth.

"Well, Davy, things are coming together."

"Do we have the passes?"

"That's a snag. Atzerodt failed us. I need you to get to Johnson and get the passes. Tell him they're for me and you. He knows me. Remind him of our escapade in Nashville if he needs prodding. One other thing. We seem to be one man short. Grant's leaving the city. I need to send someone after him. It can't be Atzerodt, and I need you and Powell here. In a couple of days we would have John Surratt here, but he's still in Montreal."

"You have Jim Donaldson," Davy suggested. "He met with us at Surratt's, and he's supposed to meet with us tonight at the Herndon."

"Hmm, I had other plans for him. But Davy, you're right. I'll meet with him before our Herndon meeting and send him after Grant. Now, go get the passes."

∽ 48 ∾

ST. JOSEPH, MINNESOTA, WAS A SMALL, sleepy prairie village. Its claim to fame was a nearby Roman Catholic monastery. Near the center of town was a combination tavern and hotel owned by John Linneman.

Reverend Francis Conwell and a friend, Horace Bennet, were en route to St. Cloud, twelve miles distant. They stopped to spend the night in St. Joseph. Black-robed priests were leaving the hotel as Conwell and Bennet entered Linneman's establishment. The proprietor stood behind the bar. Reverend Conwell noticed at once that his countenance seemed to be a mixture of agitation and excitement.

"What's wrong, sir?" Conwell wondered.

"Have you heard?" asked Linneman.

"Heard what?"

"About President Lincoln and Secretary Seward. They's both been assassinated!"

"What?" Conwell was incredulous.

"Where did you hear that?" Bennet demanded.

"Those priests from the monastery . . . they told me."

"When did this happen?" Conwell wanted to know.

"Today, I guess."

Bennet stared in wonder. "Where's the nearest telegraph?"

"Anoka, forty miles from here."

"Forty miles?" Conwell's brow furrowed. "Wait a minute. How did word get here so fast? This doesn't add up."

223

"Them priests," Linneman explained, "they go from here to Washington and priests from Washington come here. It's back and forth with them all the time. They must o' heard something."

"Well, I don't believe it," Conwell decided. "All you have is rumor and hearsay."

"I don't know," the tavern owner countered, "I've heard talk about priests staying at a hotel in Washington and hearing things about people wantin' to get Lincoln."

Unconvinced, Conwell turned to Bennet. "The pope sent a letter to President Davis condemning Lincoln as a bloodthirsty tyrant. He accused Lincoln of outraging the God of heaven and earth. Chiniquy told me of the letter when I saw him in Washington. Could there be some connection?"

"I don't see how, Reverend. I really don't."

Two days later, in St. Cloud, Conwell was handed a telegram as he prepared to enter a church. It announced that Abraham Lincoln had been shot on April 14 at approximately 10:30 p.m. Washington time. This was the first such notice of any kind to reach that part of Minnesota, except for St. Joseph.

Conwell gazed heavenward and said a quick prayer. "Dear God, we knew about the assassination in St. Joseph four hours before it happened."

ఏ 49 ಏ

EVENING, APRIL 14, WASHINGTON

SHORTLY BEFORE 6:00 P.M. BOOTH shared a conversation and a drink with Ed Spangler, one of the stagehands at Ford's Theater. Then he met Davy Herold and asked, "Did you get the passes?"

"In my pocket." Davy patted them.

"Any trouble with Johnson?"

"None. I found him outside the Kirkwood."

"What about Ella Starr? Did you give her my message? Did she accept?"

"Yes to both questions. Ella will do her part."

"Tell Atzerodt and Powell to meet with us at the Herndon at 8:00 p.m."

Booth left Herold and went to his room at the National. Opening a closet door to reveal a floor-length mirror, he carefully prepared himself for his sinister role. This would be the greatest costume change of his life.

Booth wrapped himself in black clothes. He pulled on calf-length boots and sparkling new spurs. He checked his trunk and made sure the letters incriminating Arnold, O'Laughlen and his brother Edwin were easy to find. Atzerodt was to be his patsy, and Herold was taking care of him.

Booth took a derringer pistol from his pocket. It was a single shot. He carefully loaded it with a .44 caliber ball. He wouldn't need more than one shot. Then he strapped a long-bladed knife to his belt as a backup, slipped his appointment book and a compass into his pocket and departed.

At the Kirkwood, Davy found George Atzerodt in his room and told him that Booth had called for a meeting. Then Davy furtively completed another task his superior had demanded: he abandoned his coat, knife, and pistol in George's room. Inside the coat pocket were Booth's bank book and a map of Virginia. These would once again link Atzerodt to Booth.

Oblivious to Davy's parting gifts, George clumsily locked the door and took the key with him. They went to find Booth.

Nathan found Jesse outside of the White House. Just as he got there, he saw Abraham and Mary Lincoln board the carriage for the ride to Ford's. They would pick up Major Rathbone and Miss Harris along the way.

"Stop them," Nathan cried, "something's up! I know it!"

"What's happening?" Jesse demanded.

"I don't know. It has to do with Booth. I know Lincoln's in danger!"

"I need more than that. Lamon won't stop the president on a whim."

"Then we've got to follow. Come on, Jesse, his life may be at stake!"

The pair hurried behind the carriage as it rolled down the street toward Ford's Theater.

At 8:00 p.m. Booth and his conspirators gathered in a room at the Herndon House. Powell, Atzerodt, and Herold sat on chairs while Booth stood before them as if on stage. His eyes blazed with passion as he spoke directly to the three men.

"This is it! This is the night we've been waiting for. This is the night Lincoln pays for the sins he's bestowed upon our country! Lewis, I've gone over the details of Seward's house with you. As close to 10:15 as possible I want you to enter his room and kill him."

"How do I get in?"

"Our pharmacist clerk Davy here came up with a marvelous idea. You'll say that a doctor, Seward's own Dr. Verdi, sent you with medicine and that you must deliver it in person to make sure it's properly administered. Davy has procured actual medicine. Here." He gave a small pouch to Powell. "It's his special mixture."

"George, you stay at the Kirkwood. You know where the vice-president stays. You'll kill Andrew Johnson."

Atzerodt paled in shock. "Mr. Booth, I didn't sign on fer this. I'm a boat man. I was jest gonna bring you and the president 'cross the river once you took 'im. I din't sign up to murder no one."

Booth's eyes blazed hot sparks of anger. "You coward! I'll shoot you on the spot."

"Shoot me if you wanna. I won't be killin' nobody. I'm goin' home."

"It's too late for you to back out. You could quit us right now, but the government will connect you to us and hang you anyway."

"I'm not killin' nobody," Atzerodt stubbornly repeated.

"All right. Davy, you kill Johnson."

Herold nodded.

"George," Booth continued, "there's one thing you must do tonight. Get your horse and meet us at the Navy Yard Bridge at 10:15. We need you to guide us to the proper escape route in Maryland. I'll meet you there after I've killed Lincoln."

The four parted company. Atzerodt immediately hit the bars of Washington to drink away the memory of the horrible night to come. As each of the men left for his appointed duties, a horrible realization struck Herold. His knife and pistol were in Atzerodt's room. George was gone and had the key. Davy couldn't get at his weapons.

Herold knew that Johnson was in his room. Ella Starr had been sent to entertain him. But Davy had no weapon to complete his mission. He hurried after Powell. On the train bound for New York, Jim Donaldson fingered the pistol in his pocket as he gazed through the door at the end of a railway car. It was Grant's compartment.

$\mathcal{SO}$ 50 $\mathcal{CR}$

LATE NIGHT, APRIL 14, 1865, WASHINGTON

NATHAN AND JESSE STUDIED THE ACTIVITIES outside Ford's Theatre as an assortment of people paraded along the sidewalk. The two had seen Lincoln and his party enter. Strains of "Hail to the Chief" and crowd applause reached their ears shortly afterward.

Booth was seen entering Ford's and then leaving for a tavern next door. Jesse and Nathan trailed him into the bar. The actor sat alone at a table and drank a whiskey. Other patrons of the tavern greeted the familiar actor.

One man, tipsy from drinking, needled Booth. "You'll never be half the actor your father was," he sneered.

Booth smiled gratuitously at him. "Come to Ford's. You'll see some fine acting there tonight." Then he exited the bar and walked back toward the theater. This time he mounted his horse and rode behind to the rear entrance of Ford's. He dismounted and called for Ed Spangler, the stagehand he had been drinking with earlier.

"Ned," he said, "hold this mare for about ten or fifteen minutes for me."

Occupied with other business, Spangler called out to a boy nicknamed "Johnny Peanuts." "Hold Mr. Booth's horse," Spangler ordered.

"Ned, I'm s'posed to guard the backstage door."

"Don't worry, Johnny, I'll take the blame if anything goes wrong."

"Okay, gimme the reins."

The mare was agitated and stomped her hooves, clacking on the stone surface. Johnny attempted to calm the animal by walking her around the alley. The backstage door was now open and unattended.

A single lamplight cast a faint glow that shaded into the blackness of an otherwise dark alley.

Jesse and Nathan came around the corner of Ford's as Booth walked through the back door.

"He's up to no good. He's been meeting with a strange assortment of people all day." Nathan was emphatic.

"Let's head into Ford's," Jesse urged. "He's after Lincoln. I can smell it."

A threatening voice cut like ice from the darkness. "Hold where you are, gentlemen."

Jesse and Nathan whirled around. Faint light silhouetted a large, block-shaped man. A tall, slender man stood beside him, with two more lurking behind them.

"Captain," the large man said, "I think these men are attempting to change history and to upset our plans for tonight."

"That would be unfortunate," the slender man replied as a pistol click broke the stillness of the night.

"No," the larger man ordered. "Hold fire. We can't shoot 'em here. The sound would alert others." He turned back to Jesse and Nathan. "You two, I know you've got pistols. Drop them."

Each man dropped a pistol that clattered to the street.

"Now come here, and it better be slow or we will shoot."

Nathan and Jesse edged toward the others.

Recognition flashed across Nathan's face. "Pike, it's you isn't it?"

"Yes, my one-armed former subordinate. It's your commander."

"You know damn well you're not my commander."

"Yes, I believe we lost you in Little Crow's camp, didn't we?"

"I never should have been with you in the first place."

Pike's tone was gruff and sinister. "But, Captain Thomas—or is it Cates—we do meet again, and you are once again engaged in an activity that puts our efforts in peril. Captain Stringfellow and I can't allow that. Now, keep walking down into the street. We'll be right behind you and we'll tell you where to go. You've got four pistols on you. Keep that in mind. Now, get walking."

Jesse and Nathan stepped into the street, which was softly illuminated by lamplight, with the four men right on their heels.

Jesse whispered, "We've gotta make a move. They might get us but we've got no chance otherwise."

Nathan nodded.

Jesse whispered again, "Follow my lead."

A crowd of revelers, typical of the nightly celebrations that released emotions in Washington like a national sigh of relief, rolled toward the two men and their adversaries. Several began firing pistols into the air and shouted Union slogans.

Pike, sensing his plan was on the verge of being foiled, barked to his men, "Get them now! They'll get away!"

The two captives sought escape among the revelers. They were followed by Pike's three men, guns drawn. Jesse grabbed a drunken man and twisted a pistol from his hand. Nathan slammed his fist into another man's face and snared his pistol as it tumbled.

Finding an opening, one of Pike's men squeezed a shot at Nathan. The bullet ripped into his left shoulder. Jesse retaliated by snapping a shot in return and dropping the assailant.

Nathan gripped his shoulder, and crimson blood trickled between his fingers. He alerted the crowd, "It's rebs! They wanna get at the president! The big one said to kill Lincoln!"

The throng of Yankees immediately directed hostile attention toward Pike, Stringfellow, and the remaining gunmen. All three of the armed Confederates leveled their weapons at the advancing mob.

"We're not rebs!" Pike yelled. "But take one more step and we'll shoot!"

The crowd stopped as Jesse and Nathan broke from them and ran up the street.

Pike gave his men orders in a low voice. "We can't risk a battle on the street. Shoot over their heads. These cowards will break and run."

The three slipped their aim above the crowd.

Pike yelled, "Now! Shoot!"

Flames spit from the pistol barrels as bullets whizzed over the heads of those before them. The realities of death and danger sobered the revelers as they came to realize that discretion was the better part of valor. They broke and ran.

AT ABOUT THE SAME TIME JESSE AND NATHAN were escaping from Pike, Lewis Powell was reaching Seward's residence. It was 10:00 p.m. Davy Herold had joined Powell after he realized he couldn't get his weapons from Atzerodt's locked room because the boat man had disappeared with the key.

Davy knew that Powell was unfamiliar with the streets of Washington and could use help. As Powell knocked on the door of Seward's stately brick home, Davy held the bay horse Booth had loaned to the assassin. It had been Herold's idea for Lewis to pose as a pharmacist's assistant. In carrying out Booth's plan, Powell would do the acting this night.

Powell carried a vial of "medicine" to the door. It was Davy Herold's special potion, a fast-acting poison. William Bell, the Seward's black servant, answered the door.

"It's late," Bell complained. "What you want here at this hour?"

"I've got medicine for the secretary."

"From who?"

"His doctor, Verdi."

"Give it to me. I'll take it to him."

Powell shoved past. "I've gotta give it to him personally, make sure it's given correctly."

He continued into the house and up the stairs leading to Seward's room. Everything was just as Booth had said it would be. Then Frederick Seward, the secretary's son, blocked him at the top of the stairs.

"Who are you and what do you think you're doing?" the young man demanded.

"Pharmacist's assistant. I'm here to give medicine to Mr. Seward. Dr. Verdi sent me."

"My father's sleeping. I'll not wake him for this. Give me the medicine."

"No," Powell challenged. "Dr. Verdi said I had to give it to him."

The bedroom door opened and Fanny, Frederick's sister, peeked out. "What's wrong?" she asked. "Please be quiet. Father's almost asleep."

"Look," Powell countered, "he's still awake. Let me in now."

Young Seward's suspicions flared. "Either give the medicine to me or take it back to Verdi. You're not going into my father's room. Bell," he motioned to the servant who had followed Powell up the stairs, "escort this man out of here."

Bell started down the stairs and Powell began to follow. Then, as Frederick turned to go back to his room, Lewis leaped back up the stairs with pistol drawn. Young Seward turned and was stunned to see the revolver pointed at his head.

Powell squeezed the trigger. The gun misfired. Rather than trying to fire again, he slammed the pistol barrel over Seward's head. The young man crumpled unconscious to the floor, his skull smashed.

Fanny opened the door to see about the commotion in the hallway. Powell shoved her aside, burst into the room, and spied his quarry in the bed.

A carriage accident had seriously injured Seward. Metal braces bound his body. Powell wasn't deterred by this vulnerable state. He leveled his pistol at Seward's head and pulled the trigger.

It didn't fire. Powell examined his weapon. The blow to Frederick's skull had been so severe that the steel ramrod had broken, jamming the pistol's cylinder. Powell tossed the gun aside and drew his knife.

Seward's eyes gaped in wide terror as he saw the blade of the knife descending. He twisted sideways, but the knife caught the side of his cheek and ripped the skin to his jawbone.

A nurse, George Robinson, rose from a chair and grabbed Powell from behind. The powerful assassin spun around and slashed Robinson twice with his knife, then delivered a crippling punch to his face that dropped the nurse to the floor.

As blood gushed from a gaping wound on the side of Seward's face, Powell plunged his knife into him twice more. One blow was so severe that it broke the man's jaw. Powell sought a killing blow to the neck's jugular vein, but the thick metal brace across Seward's neck covered the vein and the blade could not penetrate it.

Fanny erupted into blood-curdling shrieks. "Murderer! Murderer! Help! Oh, God! Help!"

Robinson struggled to his feet, his chest soaked with blood, and again tried to wrest Powell away from Seward. Augustus, Seward's other son, rushed into the room and joined the nurse in dragging Powell toward the hallway. Lewis ripped his knife over the younger Seward's head, slicing half of his scalp. The three tumbled to the floor struggling through legs, fists and blood.

Bell, the servant, raced out into the street screaming at the top of his lungs, "Murder! Murder!"

Herold, hearing the cries and tumult, decided to save himself and left Powell still struggling in the house. He galloped down the street toward the Navy Yard Bridge.

The powerful Powell finally shook off the other two men and raced down the stairs, shouting, "I'm mad! I'm mad!" A State Department messenger was entering the house as Powell reached the doorway.

The unarmed messenger confronted the wild-eyed assassin and turned in panic. Powell jabbed his knife into the man's back. He found his horse where Herold had left it tied. He worked to regain control of his emotions before mounting the animal.

Bell raced after him, pointing and yelling, "Murderer! Murderer!"

Powell frantically dug his spurs into his horse and galloped down the street.

51

NIGHT, APRIL 14, WASHINGTON

ESSE PULLED NATHAN ONTO A SIDE STREET and away from the lights as the crowd rushed by. He balled up a handkerchief from his pocket and pressed it firmly against his friend's bloody shoulder.

"Hold it here. Are you all right?"

"It hurts. Had worse. Go get those bastards before they get Lincoln. Found a pistol on the street. I'll be okay. Get to Lincoln. Hurry!"

"I hate to leave you, but you're right. Sit back in the shadows and keep your pistol ready. I'll get back here with help as soon as I can."

Jesse raced down the street toward Ford's. He constantly swiveled his head from side to side on the lookout for Pike. He dashed through the main entrance of the theater and bounded up the audience steps to the president's box. The sharp pop of a revolver echoed through the hall.

Fearing the worst, Jesse tried to wrench open the door to the president's box. It was jammed, absolutely wouldn't budge. He heard a loud thump, followed by a shout, "Sic Semper Tyrannis!" "Death to all tyrants!"

Then he saw Booth struggling across the stage. A sick feeling washed over Jesse like a cold rain. Booth regained his balance and charged toward Harry Hawk, the only actor on the stage. Hawk turned and rushed off in panic.

Ed Spangler was supposed to extinguish the stage lights, but actress Jennie Gourlay was standing in front of the control box with orchestra leader William Withers. They blocked Spangler from his assignment.

Tall, gangly Colonel Joe Stewart climbed up onto the stage and charged after Booth. Withers and Gourlay moved to a backstage passage-

234

way. Attempting to get out of the way, they unintentionally barricaded Booth's path. The actor roughly shoved Gourlay to the side and menacingly turned his knife on Withers.

Withers's escape efforts were futile, but he was protected by his thick coat. Booth's knife sliced through the fabric and left Withers trembling in terror but physically unscathed.

The actor bolted through the unguarded back door and into the alley. There he grabbed the reins of his horse from Johnny Peanuts and galloped away. Colonel Stewart reached the door just in time to see Booth race past.

Jesse had found it fruitless to try to force himself through the crowd to get at Booth. He was trapped in stunned pandemonium. Screams and cries of anguish resonated as the audience realized what had happened.

Doctors and guards broke through the box door and reached the stricken president. Lincoln was still alive but just barely. Within minutes he was carried across the street to the Peterson House and placed on a bed in an upstairs room.

In a bar near Ford's, John Matthews heard the commotion outside. "What's happened?" he wondered.

"Lincoln got shot! Looks like Booth, the actor, did it."

Matthews delved into his pocket and took out the letter for the newspaper that Booth had given him earlier that day. He opened it, read it, then held it above a candle flame on the bar table. He watched as the letter disintegrated into ashes.

∞ 52 ∞

LATE NIGHT, APRIL 14, 1865, NAVY YARD BRIDGE

AVY HEROLD COULDN'T WAIT for Powell or Booth. The commotion at Seward's led him to fear that the plot was falling apart. Booth had told him that in the event things went awry, they should meet on the far side of the Navy Yard Bridge.

Trotting his horse toward the bridge, Davy checked for a vital slip of paper in his vest pocket. Yes, the pass to cross was still there. For months there had been a strict order that no one was to pass over the Navy Yard Bridge after 9:00 p.m. However, bearing a note signed by Vice-President Johnson would secure easy passage. *Having friends in high places sure works for Booth*, Davy reflected.

His path brought him along Naylor's Stable, where he had rented his horse. Stable foreman John Fletcher was bedding down other returned horses when he spotted Herold riding past. Fletcher immediately recognized his prize horse.

"Hey, you," he hollered, "get back here! You're late returning my horse!"

Herold dug his spurs into the roan's side and the animal bolted into a gallop.

It took Fletcher several minutes to saddle a horse and give pursuit. Meanwhile, Herold thundered past the rendezvous point with Atzerodt. He had no time to stop, even if the boatman was there. At the bridge a sentry demanded to see a pass. Herold produced the crumbled slip of paper.

The sentry scrutinized it closely. "I'll let you cross, but remember you can't come back 'til tomorrow morning."

"No problem with that, I've got a place to stay."

"Pass." The sentry waved him by.

A short time later Fletcher wrenched his horse to a halt at the bridge and demanded, "I'm after a man with an English saddle and metal stirrups on a roan horse. Did he come by a few minutes ago?"

"Yeah," the sentry answered, "he went across."

"He stole my horse, let me cross to get him!"

The sentry considered for a moment and replied, "I'll let you cross, but you can't come back over until morning."

Fletcher regarded the man in disgust. "I'll let the police handle it. I'm not going to stumble around all night looking for him in the dark."

NATHAN, WEAK FROM LOSS OF BLOOD, sprawled in the shadows of the alleyway, his back against the brick wall of the passageway's dead end. He was concealed in the pitch black, away from the dim light offered at the street end.

He tensed when a covered carriage rolled into the alley and its driver struggled to turn it around to face the main street. Then he heard the *clip clop* of trotting hooves as a lone horseman entered the alley.

A man swung from the carriage and shook hands with the horseman. Their hushed conversation carried to Nathan.

"Mission successful, Captain Boyd."

"Wilkes, you did it? Really?"

"I put a bullet in his head from a foot away. He's gone."

"Has the plan changed?"

"No, Atzerodt should be waiting for you just this side of the bridge to guide you. When you cross, take the Surrattsville road. Davy Herold will meet you."

"Does he know I'm switching places with you?"

"No, and as long as you stay in shadows tonight, he won't know the difference. You've acted, you've been a stand-in for me on stage, Herold won't figure it out until morning. By then it'll be too late.

"If he objects or if he ever threatens to expose that you're not me, tell him this. I've planted evidence that his mother and sisters were intimately involved in Lincoln's assassination. If he betrays the plan, my agent will reveal evidence incriminating his family. They'll face horrible punishment for those hungry to avenge the president."

"But your hair is black. Mine's auburn."

"A small detail. You're of my size and physique, you have a mustache, you even have a tattoo on your arm with your initials, J.B.—but for you it means James Boyd—just as I do."

"What will you do, Wilkes?"

"Disappear. You'll have the glory. I'll have the satisfaction of committing a great service for my people. Herold and Atzerodt will lead you to safety in Virginia. I have some items that should help you to pass as me. Here are my notebook, pictures of various women in my life and here," he handed over a wadded-up bundle, "the 5,000 dollars I promised you for this mission."

"Do you have the money you need?" Boyd wondered.

Booth smirked. "I've been paid well for my services. There are Knights who look over me. Ironically, I would've done it for nothing."

"What of the others?"

"Much money went to many people in this conspiracy. At least a hundred were involved in one way or another. They didn't all get paid. Now, take my horse and hurry to the bridge. Weapons are at Surrattsville and you'll find safe houses along the way. Oh, one more thing." Booth dug into a pocket, "Here's the pass to get you over the bridge. It's signed by Andrew Johnson. You should have no difficulty getting across. Good luck to you."

"And to you, Wilkes. God bless you."

Boyd noticed Booth limped as he turned to climb into the carriage.

"Are you hurt, Wilkes?"

"I injured my ankle in my jump to the stage floor. I'll be fine."

BOYD MOUNTED BOOTH'S HORSE and trotted into the street. The escaping assassin climbed into the carriage, rolled into the street and headed in the opposite direction.

Nathan watched in stunned silence. He wished he could have shot both men, but he knew that, in his weakened condition, he couldn't hold his heavy revolver to fire it accurately. He struggled to his feet, needing to do something to stop the men, but he fainted from the exertion and loss of blood and fell back onto the alleyway.

Meanwhile, Jesse, dismayed and heartbroken over the shooting of the president, watched as Lincoln was carried into the rooming house across the street. Much as he wanted to stay and listen for news about the president's condition, he knew without question that he must tend to his stricken friend. A horseman rapidly approached as Jesse headed back to Nathan. It was Boyd, but Jesse thought nothing of it, for many people were hurrying toward the Peterson House.

When he reached his friend's side, Nathan was passed out on the ground. Jesse shook him gently. "Nathan, Nathan, come back to me. Nathan!"

His friend's eyes fluttered open. "I'm all right, just weak."

"I'll get you to a doctor. The president, he's . . ."

Recollection flooded Nathan's mind like a raging river. "I know, Jesse. He's been killed. Booth. He did it. He came into this alley. You won't believe . . . what I heard." His voice weak and halting, Nathan gasped to Jesse what had transpired in the alley.

"I'll get you help," Jesse said. "This is all so horrible. Lincoln isn't dead yet, but I fear it's just a matter of time. I've got to get to Stanton and Lamon but first I'll get you to a doctor."

AS THEY SPOKE, BOYD RODE FRANTICALLY toward the Navy Yard Bridge. He paused at the rendezvous point with Atzerodt but the boat man was nowhere to be seen. He advanced at a trot toward the bridge and the sentry guard.

"Hold!" the sentry commanded. "No passage without a pass after nine."

Boyd handed over the pass. The sentry checked it in mild surprise.

"Two passes in the same night signed by Johnson. Some people got contacts. What's yer name?"

"Booth," Boyd answered.

The sentry examined the pass more closely and motioned Boyd over the bridge.

Upon reaching the opposite side of the Potomac, Boyd took the Surrattsville road. He was soon met by Davy Herold, who had no idea that the man in the darkness was not John Wilkes Booth. The two continued toward the tavern and the cache of weapons.

❧ 53 ❧

MORNING, APRIL 15, 1865, WASHINGTON

RESIDENT LINCOLN WAS CARRIED to an upstairs bedroom in the Peterson House. At six-foot-four, he didn't fit in the bed and had to be stretched out diagonally. Cabinet officers and other government officials rushed to be at his side. Mary Lincoln became extremely distraught and had to be removed to a sitting room.

Doctors hovered over Lincoln but soon realized they were on a death watch. It would only be a matter of hours before he expired. Leonard Farwell, former governor of Wisconsin, was among the theatergoers at Ford's that night. He considered himself a personal friend of the vice-president and rushed to the Kirkwood to alert Johnson.

Once at the door of Johnson's room, Farwell rapped sharply several times and shouted Johnson's name. Shortly the door swung open. The vice-president stood before him in his bed clothes.

Farwell's peripheral vision glimpsed a figure disappearing into the sitting room and the door shutting. Was it a woman? He couldn't be sure. Farwell locked and bolted the door as he rapidly explained what had happened.

"You need a hotel guard here now! I told the clerk as much before I came up here. Stanton's sending men as well. Stay here with the door locked until government men get here. Open the door for no one."

Farwell left. Soon Major O'Beirne arrived with a guard detail. Johnson was taken to the Peterson House. He refused to go by buggy and insisted that he walk the three and one-half blocks. In the Peterson House he conferred with Stanton in a room adjacent to the death vigil.

Stanton's long chin beard quivered with emotion. "He'll die soon. If it happens while you're here you'll take the oath immediately. Otherwise we'll summon you from the Kirkwood."

"Do they know who did this?" Johnson inquired.

"Eyewitnesses say it was actor John Wilkes Booth."

Johnson's face blanched a pasty white. "I signed two passes for him this afternoon."

"I know you did, but no one else can find out. The sentry has been taken care of."

"I . . . I couldn't know," Johnson claimed defensively, "I knew Booth from Nashville. We were friends. He asked for the passes as a favor. Lincoln himself gave passes. How could I know?"

"I don't suspect you in this," Stanton said crisply, "but there are those who might, and that would be a disaster. It'll be hard enough to recover from this. Mrs. Lincoln herself would lead the charge against you. She hates you, you know."

Johnson nodded.

"This must be our secret," Stanton said in a low voice. "We must never, ever repeat it. The preservation of the union and our republic is at stake."

"I owe you much for this." Johnson's voice was trembling. "It must be kept a great secret."

"It must and it will, Mr. Vice-President. I've taken charge of the manhunt. We closed the routes leaving Washington, but we know Booth went over the Navy Yard Bridge. We had a mix up and, strangely, word didn't reach them to close the bridge until after Booth had crossed. That's when we found out about Booth and the passes. Baker and his men are now heading into Maryland after them. Now, go back to your room. Mrs. Lincoln doesn't want you around. We'll tell you when it's over."

AROUND 2:00 A.M. JESSE FINALLY WAS admitted to the sitting room to see Stanton.

"I really don't have time to see you," the tired and beleaguered secretary of war snapped. "If Lamon hadn't requested this, I wouldn't have. Now tell me what you have to say."

Nathan's story from his alley encounter with Booth tumbled from Jesse's lips. Stanton listened in amazement, then spoke decisively. "Lieutenant Buchanen, you and Mr. Cates will never speak of this to anyone. Our national security depends on it. Besides, no one would ever believe it. We'll catch Boyd, Booth, or whoever, you can be sure of that. If everyone thinks that Boyd is Booth, so be it. I certainly want Booth to pay for what he did. But more important, the people of the United States must be convinced that the man who killed our beloved President Lincoln has paid for his crime."

Jesse nodded.

"Let me assure you he will pay. The people will believe the results of my investigation and of the eventually successful manhunt after Booth. Anything else will be thought of as a fairy tale. I assure you of this. For the good of the country the people must believe that John Wilkes Booth is dead. It is my fervent hope we get the right Booth, but if we don't, we will and must have *a* Booth. Do you understand?"

"Yes, sir, I do. Nathan and I shall keep quiet."

Jesse left the Peterson House in a daze of conflicting thoughts and emotions. He might become part of the greatest lie in American history. It was a lie to preserve the Union.

———

AT 7:22 ON THE MORNING OF APRIL 15, President Abraham Lincoln died. Edwin Stanton proclaimed at his bedside, "Now he belongs to the ages."

ഇ 54 cs

EPILOGUE

ESSE WAITED UNTIL WORD OF THE PRESIDENT'S death was announced and then went to the hospital where he had left Nathan. His friend was somewhat groggy but seemed stronger.

"He's dead, isn't he?" Nathan asked.

"Yes, he's gone."

"Are they after Booth and Boyd?"

"Nathan, I've talked with Stanton. What we know can never be told."

Jesse continued to explain the conversation he had had with Secretary Stanton.

Nathan thought deeply and then responded, "It'll be a terrible shame if Booth gets away and Boyd pays for his crime. But if you knew more about me, Jesse, and what I've been through, you'd understand why I can't bring attention to myself. It would be bad for me and for Emily. The secret is safe with me."

"What will you do next?"

"I'll go back to Crow Creek and Emily. Then I'll wait and see what life has in store. How about you?"

"Back to Minnesota. I think my getting out of the way will make Stanton happy. Thank you, my friend. We've had great adventures together."

Nathan gazed weakly at his friend. "I wish this one had ended better."

IN THE SOUTHWEST PART OF THE NATION, two soldiers finished fitting a stone with strange markings into a niche on the side of a hill.

"We got it done. I just hope folks can find it when it's needed," a man called to his leader looking on from horseback.

"I'm keeping a log. When the Confederacy rises again, they can find the money they need. It's here and in the other spots along the way where we hid it."

"Who keeps track of this?"

Jesse James smiled and folded the log book into his pocket. "My brother Knights will know."

NATHAN DID GO BACK TO CROW CREEK and Emily. Eventually he received a call to join his uncle, Union General George Thomas, in California.

Boyd and Herold continued into Maryland. Boyd's horse slipped and fell, breaking Boyd's leg. Still, they found their weapons at the tavern in Surrattsville and took them. Then the two journeyed to the home of Dr. Samuel Mudd, who treated Boyd's leg. He identified the man as Booth.

After a twelve-day manhunt through Maryland and Virginia, Herold and Boyd were cornered in a barn at Garrett's farm on April 26th. Herold surrendered. A soldier named Boston Corbett fatally shot Boyd in the barn, which was now in flames. Booth's appointment book and pictures of women were found on Boyd's body.

Stanton spread out a web of investigators to snare conspirators. Booth's bank book, a knife and pistol were found in Booth's coat in Atzerodt's room at the Kirkwood. It led them to arrest the boat man.

When Booth's room at the National was searched, they found his trunk with incriminating letters from Arnold and O'Laughlen. Both were arrested.

The investigation led them to the Surratt Boarding House where they had been told the plot was hatched. Mrs. Surratt was being arrested as Lewis Powell, lost in Washington, turned up. He was carrying a pickaxe and announced he was there to dig a gutter for Mrs. Surratt. When Mary Surratt would not support his story, he was arrested as well.

The stagehand, Ed Spangler, also took up residence in the Old Prison in Washington.

On July 7th, Herold, Powell, Atzerodt, and Mary Surratt were hanged simultaneously for conspiring to kill Abraham Lincoln. In his final interview Powell proclaimed, "You ain't got near half of us."

Dr. Samuel Mudd, Sam Arnold, Ed Spangler and Michael O'Laughlen were found guilty of conspiracy and sent to life imprisonment in the Dry Tortugas at Fort Jefferson. After a yellow fever epidemic during which Mudd was credited with saving many lives at the prison, Mudd, Arnold and Spangler were pardoned in 1869. O'Laughlen had died in prison in 1867.

John Surratt escaped through Canada to Italy where he became a member of the Vatican guards. He eventually was captured and brought to trial in 1867. He was found not guilty and later lectured about the assassination.

Benjamin Stringfellow traveled through a series of northern safe houses to safety in Canada.

Benjamin Judah escaped to England where he lived the rest of his life as an attorney.

Jefferson Davis was captured on May 10th, 1865, and charged with treason. After serving nearly a year in jail awaiting trail, he was freed and never tried.

Henry Rathbone and Clara Harris were married in 1867. In 1883 Rathbone shot and then stabbed his wife with a knife. He was committed to an insane asylum where he died.

Robert Lincoln had a long career in public service. He was present at the assassinations of Presidents Garfield and McKinley.

Edwin McMasters Stanton died in 1869, just after having been appointed an associate justice of the Supreme Court. Many of the mysteries surrounding the assassination died with him.

Andrew Johnson joined up with southern allies and fought the Republicans' more harsh reconstruction plan. He was impeached for trying to remove Stanton as secretary of war. He survived removal from office by one vote. To her dying day, Mrs. Lincoln believed that Johnson was somehow involved in the murder of her husband. Pike eventually saw Johnson become a thirty-three-degree Mason.

Charles Chiniquy left the Roman Catholic church. He wrote a book entitled Fifty Years In the Church of Rome in which he claimed the church had killed Lincoln. Through his work and the efforts of others, suspicion and prejudice against Catholics for involvement in Lincoln's assassination rose to high levels.

Solomon Foot became a postmaster in Stearns County, Minnesota.

James Atkinson returned to Forest City, Minnesota, after fighting Confederates in the South.

Alfred Sully participated in various campaigns against Indian people, including the Nez Perce War in the mid 1870s. He was assigned to command at Fort Vancouver in Washington Territory where he died in 1879. A descendent from his Indian marriage is the author, Vine DeLoria.

Inkpaduta was at Little Big Horn with Sitting Bull when Custer met the end predicted for him by Sully many years earlier.

Jesse Buchanen went back to Minnesota.

SOURCES

Henry Hasting Sibley, Divided Heart, Rhoda R. Gilman, 2004, Minnesota Historical Society Press, St. Paul, Minnesota.

No Tears for the General, the Life of Alfred Sully 1821-1879, Langdon Sully, 1974, Western Biography Series, American West Publishing Company, Palo Alto, California.

Diary of James Atkinson, 1864, scout for Alfred Sully.

Fifty Years in the Church of Rome, Pastor Charles Chiniquy.

A Threat to the Republic, The Secret of the Lincoln Assassination that Preserved the Union, Jerrod Madonna, 2006.

Manhunt, James L. Swanson, 2006, Harper-Collins Publishing, New York, New York.

We Saw Lincoln Shot, Timothy S. Good, 1995, University of Mississippi Press, Jackson, Mississippi.

The Lincoln Murder Conspiracies, William Hanchett, 1986, University of Illinois Press, Urbana and Chicago, Illinois.

Come Retribution, William A. Tidwell, with James O. Hall and David Winfred Gaddy, 1988, University Press of Mississippi, Jackson, Mississippi.

Excerpt from: *The Escape and Suicide of John Wilkes Booth*, by Finis Langdon Bates, 1907.